Praise for

'A splendid series . . . with a backdrop of the city so vivid you can almost smell it' *Sunday Telegraph*

'Commissario Brunetti, most charismatic current Euro-cop, uncovers deadly ants' nests of corruption. Highly accomplished' *Guardian*

'An excellent sense of location, strong characterization and a murky but believable plot' *Independent*

'An evocative peep into the dark underworld of the beauteous city' *Time Out*

'The series has become one of the adornments of current detective fiction . . . Written with cool lucidity. Ms Leon has created a gem of a book' *Scotsman*

'Donna Leon's novels pinpoint the charm as well as the corruption of the city . . . very spooky'

Mail on Sunday

'Exactly the right cop for the right city. Long may he walk, or wade, through it'

Sarah Dunant, *Sunday Times*

ACQUA ALTA

Donna Leon has lived in Venice for many years and previously lived in Switzerland, Saudi Arabia, Iran and China, where she worked as a teacher. Her previous novels featuring Commissario Brunetti have all been highly acclaimed; including *Friends in High Places*, which won the CWA Silver Dagger Award.

Also in Donna Leon's Brunetti series

Donna Leon

ACQUA ALTA

PAN BOOKS

First published 1996 by Macmillan

This edition published 2012 by Pan Books
an imprint of Pan Macmillan, a division of Macmillan Publishers Limited
Pan Macmillan, 20 New Wharf Road, London N1 9RR
Basingstoke and Oxford
Associated companies throughout the world
www.panmacmillan.com

ISBN 978-1-4472-0165-6

Visit **www.panmacmillan.com** to read more about all our books
and to buy them. You will also find features, author interviews and
news of any author events, and you can sign up for e-newsletters
so that you're always first to hear about our new releases.

For Guy Santa Lucia

Dalla sua pace la mia dipende,
quel che a lei piace vita mi rende,
quel che le incresce morte mi dà.
S'ella sospira, sospiro anch'io,
è mia quell'ira, quel pianto è mio
e non ho bene s'ella non l'ha.

My peace depends upon hers:
what pleases her gives me life,
that which pains her gives me death.
If she sighs, I will sigh as well,
her anger and her sorrows are mine
and I have no joy unless she shares it.

Mozart, *Don Giovanni*

Chapter One

DOMESTIC TRANQUILLITY prevailed. Flavia Petrelli, the reigning diva of La Scala, stood in the warm kitchen and chopped onions. In separate heaps in front of her lay a pile of plum tomatoes, two cloves of garlic chopped into fine slices, and two plump-bottomed aubergines. She stood at the marble counter, bent over the vegetables, and she sang, filling the room with the golden tones of her soprano voice. Occasionally, she pushed at a lock of dark hair with the back of her wrist, but it was no sooner anchored behind her ear than it sprang loose and fell across her cheek.

At the other end of the vast room that took up much of the top floor of the fourteenth-century Venetian *palazzo*, its owner and Flavia's lover, Brett Lynch, sprawled across a beige sofa, bare feet propped against the far arm, head resting on the other, following the score of *I Puritani*, the music of which blared out, neighbours be damned, from two tall speakers resting on mahogany pedestals. Music swelled up to fill the room, and the singing

Elvira prepared to go mad – for the second time. Eerily, two Elviras sang in the room: the first the one Flavia had recorded in London five months before and who now sang from the speakers; the second was the voice of the woman chopping the onions.

Occasionally, as she sang in perfect union with her own recorded voice, Flavia broke off to ask, 'Ouf, whoever said I had a middle register?' or 'Is that a B flat the violins are supposed to be playing?' After each interruption, her voice returned to the music, her hands to the chopping. To her left, a large frying-pan sat on a low flame, a pool of olive oil waiting for the first vegetables.

From four floors below, the doorbell rang. 'I'll get it,' Brett said, placing the score face down on the floor and standing. 'Probably the Jehovah's Witnesses. They come on Sundays.' Flavia nodded, brushed a strand of dark hair from her face with the back of her hand, and returned her attention to the onions and to Elvira's delirium, in the midst of which she continued to sing.

Barefoot, glad of the warmth of the apartment on this late January afternoon, Brett walked across the beamed floor and out into the entrance hall, picked up the speakerphone that hung beside the front door, and asked, '*Chi è?*'

A man's voice answered, speaking Italian, 'We're from the museum. With papers from Dottor Semenzato.'

2

Strange that the director of the museum at the Doge's Palace would send papers, especially on a Sunday, but perhaps he had been alarmed by the letter Brett had sent him from China – though he certainly hadn't sounded that way earlier in the week – and wanted something read before the appointment he had grudgingly given for Tuesday morning.

'Bring them up, if you don't mind. Top floor.' Brett replaced the phone and pressed the button that opened the door four floors down, then walked to the door and called to Flavia across the weeping violins, 'Someone from the museum. Papers.'

Flavia nodded, picked up the first of the aubergines and sliced it in half, then, without missing a beat, returned to the serious business of losing her mind for love.

Brett went back towards the front door, paused to bend down and turn over the corner of a carpet, then opened the door to the apartment. Footsteps approached from below, and two men came into sight, pausing at the bottom of the final ramp of steps. 'There are only sixteen more,' Brett said, smiling down at them in welcome, then, suddenly aware of the frigid air of the stairwell that edged in, covered one bare foot with the other.

They stood on the steps below and looked up towards the open door. The first one carried a large manila envelope. They paused for a moment before beginning the final flight and Brett smiled again, calling down encouragement: '*Forza.*'

The first one, short and fair-haired, smiled back and started up the last flight of steps. His companion, taller and darker, took a deep breath, then came up behind him. When the first man got to the door, he paused and waited for the other to join him.

'Dottoressa Lynch?' the blond one asked, pronouncing her last name in the Italian fashion.

'Yes,' she answered, stepping back from the door to allow them to enter.

Politely, both of them muttered, '*Permesso,*' as they stepped into the apartment. The first one, whose light hair was cut very close to his head and who had attractive dark eyes, held out the envelope. 'These are the papers, Dottoressa.' As he handed them to her, he said, 'Dottor Semenzato asked that you look at them immediately.' Very soft, very polite. The tall one smiled and turned away, his attention distracted by a mirror that hung to the left of the door.

She bent her head and began to open the flap of the envelope, which was held together with red sealing wax. The blond man stepped a bit closer to her, as if to take the envelope from her and help her open it, but suddenly he moved past her and grabbed her from behind by both arms, his grip fierce and tight.

The envelope fell, bounced off her bare feet,

and landed between her and the second man. He brushed it aside with his foot, as if careful of its contents, and stepped up close in front of her. As he moved, the other one tightened his grip on her arms. The tall one brought his face down from his considerable height and said, voice low and very deep, 'You don't want to keep that appointment with Dottor Semenzato.'

She felt anger before she felt fear, and she spoke out of the first. 'Let me go. And get out of here.' She twisted sharply in an attempt to pull herself free of the man's grip, but he tightened his hands, pinning her arms to her sides.

Behind her, the music soared up and Flavia's double voice filled the room. So perfectly did she sing the passage that no one could tell there were two voices, not one, that sang of pain and love and loss. Brett turned her face towards the music, but then by a conscious act of will stopped the motion and asked, turning back to the man in front of her, 'Who are you? What do you want?'

His voice changed as did his face, both growing ugly. 'Don't ask questions, bitch.'

Again, she tried to twist herself free, but it was impossible. Bracing her weight on one foot, she kicked backward with the other, but her bare heel had no effect on the man who held her.

From behind her, she heard the one who held her say, 'All right. Do it.'

She was turning her head to look at him when

the first blow came, catching her in the centre of the stomach. The sudden, explosive pain pulled her forward with such force that she almost broke free from the man who held her, but he pulled her back and jerked her upright. The one in front of her hit her again, this time catching her below the left breast, and her response was the same, an involuntary motion that pulled her body forward to protect itself from this awful pain.

Then quickly, so quickly that she lost count of how many times he did it, he began to punch at her body, catching her repeatedly on the breast and ribs.

Behind her, Flavia's voices sang now of the blissful future she looked forward to, so soon to be Arturo's bride, and then he hit her on the side of the head. Her right ear buzzed, and then she could hear the music only with the left.

She was conscious of just one thing: she couldn't make any noise. She couldn't scream, cry out, moan. The soprano voices blended behind her, exultant with joy, and her lip split open under the man's fist.

The one behind her released her right arm. There was no longer any need to restrain her, but he kept one hand on her arm to hold her upright and pulled her around until she was facing him. 'Don't keep your meeting with Dottor Semenzato,' he said, voice still very low and polite.

But she was gone from him, no longer listening

to what he said, dimly conscious of the music and the pain, and the dark fear that these men might kill her.

Her head hung and she saw only their feet. She sensed the taller one make a sudden motion towards her, and she felt warmth on her legs and face. She had lost control of her body and smelled the sharp stench of her own urine. Tasting blood, she saw it drip on to the floor and splash on to their shoes. She hung between them, thinking only that she couldn't make a sound and wishing only that they would let her drop, let her roll herself up into a ball to reduce the pain that came at her from all over her body. And all the while this was happening, the double voice of Flavia Petrelli filled the room with the sounds of joy, soaring up over the voices of the chorus and the tenor, her sweet lover.

With greater effort than she had applied to anything in her life, Brett raised her head and looked into the eyes of the tall one, who now stood directly in front of her. He smiled back at her with a smile so intimate that she might have seen it on a lover's face. Slowly, he reached out and cupped her left breast in his hand, squeezing it gently, and he whispered, 'Want some more, *cara*? It's better with a man.'

Her reaction was entirely involuntary. Her fist caught his face and glanced off without doing any harm, but the sudden motion pulled her free of the hand of the other one. She fell back against the wall and was conscious, in a disembodied way, of its solidity under her back.

She felt herself sinking down, felt her sweater being pulled up by the heavy grain of the brick wall behind her. Slowly, slowly, as in a freeze-frame film, she sank down against the wall, its rough face scratching at her flesh as gravity pulled at her entire body.

Things grew very confused. She heard Flavia's voice singing the *cabaletta*, but then she heard Flavia's other voice, no longer singing, scream in fury, 'Who are you? What are you doing?'

'Don't stop singing, Flavia,' she tried to say, but she couldn't remember how to say it. She sank to the floor, head tilted towards the entry to the living room, where she saw the real Flavia outlined against the light that streamed in from the other room, heard the same outline of glorious music that splashed in with her, and she saw the large chopping knife in Flavia's hand.

'No, Flavia,' she whispered, but no one heard her.

Flavia launched herself across the space that separated her from the two men. As surprised as she, they had no time to react, and the knife slashed across the upraised forearm of the shorter one. He howled in pain and pulled the arm to him, covering the wound with his other hand. Blood surged up through the fabric of his jacket.

Another freeze frame. Then the taller man started towards the still-open door. Flavia pulled the knife back level with her hip and took two steps towards him. The wounded one kicked at her with his left foot, catching her on the side of the knee. She fell but landed kneeling, knife still pulled back beside her.

Whatever communication passed between the two men was entirely silent, but at the same instant they both broke towards the door. The tall one paused long enough to snatch at the envelope, but the kneeling Flavia lashed out at his hand with the knife, and he backed away, leaving it on the floor. Flavia pushed herself to her feet and ran down a few steps after them but stopped and went back into the apartment, kicking the door closed behind her.

She knelt beside the supine form of the other woman. 'Brett, Brett,' she called, looking down at her. The bottom half of her face was streaked with blood that streamed from her nose and lip and from a patch of broken skin that ran across the left side of her forehead. She lay with one knee bent under her, her sweater bunched up under her chin, breasts exposed. 'Brett,' Flavia said again and for a moment believed that this utterly motionless woman was dead. She pushed that idea away immediately and placed her hand against the side of Brett's throat.

As slowly as dawn on a heavy winter morning,

one eye opened, then the other, though, beginning to swell, it could open only halfway.

'*Stai bene?*' Flavia asked.

The only answer she heard was a low moan. But it was an answer.

'I'm going to call for help. Don't worry, *cara*. They'll be here soon.'

She ran into the other room and reached for the telephone. For a second, she didn't recognize what it was that prevented her from picking up the phone, but then she saw the bloody knife, her hand white-knuckled around the handle. She dropped it to the floor and grabbed the receiver. With stiff fingers, she jabbed out 113. After ten rings, a woman's voice answered and asked her what she wanted.

'This is an emergency. I need an ambulance. In Cannaregio.'

Bored, the voice asked the exact address.

'Cannaregio 6134.'

'I'm sorry, signora. It's Sunday and we have only one ambulance. I'll have to put your name on the list.'

Flavia's voice rose. 'There's a woman here who's hurt. Someone tried to kill her. She has to get to the hospital.'

The voice took on a tone of wearied patience. 'I've explained to you, signora. We have only one ambulance, and there are two calls for it to make first. As soon as it's free, we'll send it to you.'

When she had no response from Flavia, the voice asked, 'Signora, are you still there? If you give me the address again, I'll put your name on the list. Signora? Signora?' In response to Flavia's silence, the woman at the other end broke the connection, leaving Flavia with the receiver in her hand, wishing she still had the knife.

Hand trembling, Flavia replaced the receiver and went back into the hall. Brett remained where she had left her but had somehow managed to turn over on to her side and lay still, holding one arm across her chest, moaning.

Flavia knelt beside her. 'Brett, I have to get a doctor.'

Flavia heard a muffled noise, and Brett's hand came slowly towards her own. Her fingers barely made contact with Flavia's arm, then fell to the floor. 'Cold,' was the only thing she said.

Flavia got to her feet and went into the bedroom. She ripped the covers from the bed and dragged them back into the foyer, where she spread them over the motionless form on the floor. She opened the door to the apartment, not bothering to check through the spyhole to see if the two men had returned. Leaving the door open behind her, she ran down two flights of stairs and pounded heavily on the door of the apartment below.

After a few moments, the door was opened by a middle-aged man, tall and balding, who held a cigarette in one hand and a book in the other.

'Luca,' Flavia gasped, fighting the impulse to scream as this went on and on and no one came to help her lover, 'Brett's hurt. She's got to have a doctor.' Suddenly her voice cracked and she was sobbing. 'Please, Luca, please, get a doctor.' She grabbed at his arm, no longer capable of speech.

Without a word, he stepped back into his apartment and grabbed his keys from a table beside the door. He dropped the book on the floor, pulled the door closed behind him, and disappeared down the steps before Flavia could say anything else.

Flavia went up the steps two at a time and back into the apartment. She looked down and saw that a small pool of blood now spread out under Brett's face, a strand of her hair floating on the surface. Years ago, she had read or been told that people in shock should be kept awake, that it was dangerous for them to go to sleep. So she knelt again beside her friend and called her name. By now, one eye was swollen shut, but at the sound of her name, the American opened the other just a slit and looked at Flavia without giving any sign that she recognized her.

'Luca went. The doctor will be here in a minute.'

Slowly, the eye seemed to go out of focus, then pulled itself back to look at her. Flavia crouched lower. She wiped Brett's hair back from her face, feeling the blood trail across her fingers. 'It's going to be all right. They'll be back in a minute, and you'll be all right. Everything's going to be all right, darling. Don't worry.'

The eye closed, opened, drifted into long focus, then came back. 'Hurt,' she whispered.

'It's all right, Brett. It's going to be all right.'

'Hurt.'

Flavia knelt by her friend, gazing into the one eye, willing it to stay open and in focus, and she continued to mutter things that, in future, she never remembered having said. Some time later, she began to weep, but she was not aware of this.

She saw Brett's hand, half hidden by the covers, and she grabbed at it, held it softly, as though it were made of the same down as the covers around it. 'It's going to be all right, Brett.'

Suddenly, from below, she heard the sound of footsteps and raised voices. For an instant, it occurred to her that this might be the two men, come back to finish whatever it was they had come to do. She got to her feet and went to the door, hoping to be able to close it in time, but when she looked, she saw Luca's face and, behind him, a man in a white jacket with a black bag in his hand.

'Thank God,' she said and was surprised to find that she meant it. Behind her, the music stopped. Elvira was at last reunited with her Arturo, and the opera was at an end.

13

Chapter Two

FLAVIA STEPPED back from the door to allow the two men to enter. 'What is it? What happened?' Luca asked, looking down at the heap of covers on the floor and what they covered. '*Dio mio,*' he said involuntarily and bent towards Brett, but Flavia stopped him with an out-thrust arm and pulled him aside, allowing room for the doctor to approach the fallen woman.

He bent down over her, reached out his hand, and felt for the pulse at her neck. Feeling it, slow but strong, he pulled back the covers to see how badly she was hurt. Her sweater was bunched in a blood-streaked tangle under her throat, exposing her ribs and torso. Her skin was red and broken in places and beginning to turn livid and dark.

'Signora, can you hear me?' the doctor asked.

Brett made a noise; words were too difficult now.

'Signora, I'm going to move you. Just a little, so I can see what's happened.' He gestured to Flavia, who knelt down on the other side of the motionless woman. 'Hold her shoulders. I have to straighten out her legs.' He reached down and took her left leg by the calf, stretching it out, then did the same with the right. Slowly he turned her on to her back, and Flavia lowered her shoulder to the floor. All of this flickered through to Brett as a new wave of pain, and she moaned.

Turning back to Flavia, the doctor said, 'Get me a pair of scissors.' Obedient, Flavia went back into the kitchen and took a pair of scissors from a large flowered ceramic pot on the counter. As she stood there, she felt the heat radiating up from the pan of olive oil, still on the burner, hissing and sizzling at her. She snapped off the flame and went quickly back to the doctor.

He took the scissors and cut through the bloody sweater, then pulled it back from her body. The man who had beaten her had worn a heavy ring on the fourth finger of his right hand, and it had left signs of itself behind, small circular impressions that stood out in greater darkness from the livid flesh around them.

The doctor bent over her again and said, 'Signora, please open your eyes.'

Brett struggled to obey, but she could get only one of them to open. The doctor took a small flashlight from his bag and pointed the light into her pupil. It contracted and she involuntarily closed her eye.

'Good, good,' the doctor said. 'Now I'd like you to move your head a bit, just a little.'

Though it cost her a great deal, Brett managed to do it.

'And now your mouth. Can you open that?'

When she tried that, she gasped with the pain of it, a sound that pushed Flavia up against the other wall.

'Now I'm going to touch your ribs, signora. Tell me when it hurts.' Gently, he prodded at her ribs. Twice, she moaned.

He took a packet of surgical gauze from his bag and ripped it open. He dampened it from a bottle of antiseptic and slowly began to clean the blood from her face. As soon as he wiped it away, more seeped from her nostril and from the gaping seam in her lower lip. He signalled to Flavia, who knelt again beside him. 'Here, keep this on her lip, and don't let her move.' He handed the bloody gauze to Flavia, who did as she was told.

'Where's the phone?' the doctor asked.

Nodding her head, Flavia indicated the living room. The doctor disappeared through the door, and Flavia could hear him dialling and then speaking to someone at the hospital, ordering a stretcher. Why hadn't she thought of that? The house was so close to the hospital they had no need of an ambulance.

Luca hovered over her, finally contenting himself with bending down and pulling the covers back over Brett.

The doctor came back and stooped down beside Flavia. 'They'll be here soon.' He looked down at Brett. 'I can't give you anything for pain until we've taken X-rays. Is there much pain?'

To Brett, there was nothing else but pain.

The doctor saw that she was shivering and asked, 'Are there more blankets?' Hearing that, Luca went into the bedroom and came back with a quilt, which he and the doctor placed on top of her, though it seemed to do no good. The world had become cold, and she knew only cold and growing pain.

The doctor stood and turned to Flavia. 'What happened?'

'I don't know. I was in the kitchen. I came out, and she was on the floor, like that, and there were two men.'

'Who were they?' Luca asked.

'I don't know. There was a tall one and a short one.'

'What happened?'

'I went for them.'

The men exchanged a glance. 'How?' Luca asked.

'I had a knife. I was in the kitchen, cooking, and when I came out, I still had the knife, and when I saw them, I didn't think, I just went at them. They ran down the steps.' She shook her head, uninterested in all of this. 'How is she? What have they done?'

Before he answered, the doctor moved a few steps away from Brett, though she was far removed from hearing or understanding his words. 'There are some broken ribs, and some bad cuts. And I think her jaw might be broken.'

'*Oh, Gesù*,' Flavia said, clapping her hand to her mouth.

'But there are no signs of concussion. She responds to light, and she understands what I say to her. But we have to take X-rays.'

Even as he spoke, they heard voices from below. Flavia knelt beside Brett. 'They're coming now, *cara*. It's going to be all right.' All she could think of to do was place her hand on the covers over Brett's shoulder and leave it there, hoping that its warmth would sink down to the woman below. 'It's going to be all right.'

Two white-jacketed men appeared at the door, and Luca waved them into the apartment. They had left their stretcher four flights below, near the front door, as it was always necessary to do in Venice, and carried with them instead the wicker chair they used to navigate the sick down the narrow, winding staircases of the city.

Entering, they glanced down at the blood-covered face of the woman lying on the floor as though they were accustomed to seeing things like this every day, as perhaps they were. Luca removed himself into the living room, and the doctor warned them to be especially careful when they picked her up.

Through all of this, Brett felt nothing but the strong embrace of pain. It came at her from all over her body, from her chest that tightened and made each breath an agony, from the very bones that made up her face, and from her back, which burned. At times, she could feel separate pieces of the pain, but then it all melted together and flowed across her, blending into itself and blotting out anything that wasn't pain. Later, she was to remember only three things: the doctor's hand on her jaw, a touch that turned itself into a white flash of light to her brain; Flavia's hand on her shoulder, the only warmth in this sea of cold; and the moment when the men lifted her from the ground, when she screamed and fainted.

Hours later, when she woke, the pain was still there, but something kept it at arm's length. She knew that, if she were to move, even so little as a millimetre, it would come back and be even worse, so she lay perfectly motionless, feeling into each separate part of her body to see where the worst of the pain was lurking, but before she could command her mind to begin, she was overpowered by sleep.

Later, she woke again and, this time, with great caution sent her mind exploring to various parts of her body. The pain was still being held far away from her, and it no longer seemed that motion would be so dangerous. She brought her mind to her eyes and tried to determine what lay beyond them, light or darkness. She couldn't tell, so she let her mind roam on, down across her face, where pain lurked, then to her back, which throbbed warmly, and then to her hands. One was cold, the other warm. She lay motionless for what seemed hours and considered this: how could one hand be cold and the other warm? She lay still for eternity and let her mind consider that puzzle.

One warm and one cold. She determined that she would move them to see if that made a difference, and, an age later, she began. She tried to pull them into fists and managed to move them only slightly. But it was enough – the warm one found itself embraced by increased warmth and the gentlest of pressures from above and below. She heard a voice, one that she knew to be familiar but couldn't recognize. Why was that voice speaking Italian? Or was it Chinese? She understood what it said, but she couldn't remember what language it was. She moved her hand again. How pleasant that answering warmth had been. She tried it again, and she heard the answering voice, felt the warmth. Oh, how magical that was. There was speech that she understood, and warmth, and a part of her body that was free of pain. Comforted by this, she slept again.

Finally she was conscious and realized why one

hand was warm and one cold. 'Flavia,' she said, barely making a noise.

The pressure on her hand increased. And the warmth. 'I'm here,' Flavia said, voice very close to her.

Without knowing how she knew it, Brett knew that she couldn't turn her head to speak to or look at her friend. She tried to smile, tried to say something, but some force held her mouth shut and prevented her from opening it. She tried to scream out or cry for help, but the invisible force held her mouth shut and prevented her.

'Don't try to talk, Brett,' Flavia said, increasing the pressure on her hand. 'Don't move your mouth. It's wired. One of the bones in your jaw is cracked. Please don't try to talk. It's all right. You'll be all right.'

It was very difficult to understand all those words. But the weight of Flavia's hand was enough, the sound of her voice sufficient to calm her.

When she woke, she was fully conscious. It was still something of an effort to open her eye, but she could do it, though the other wouldn't open. She sighed in relief that cunning was no longer necessary to outwit her body. She looked around and saw Flavia asleep, hunched down in her chair, mouth agape and head tilted back. Her arms hung slack on either side of her chair, leaving her completely abandoned to sleep.

As she watched Flavia, Brett again scouted her

own body. She might be able to move her arms and legs, though it would be painful, in a generalized, unspecified way. She seemed to be lying on her side, and her back ached, a dull, fiery pain. At last, knowing that this was the worst, she tried to open her mouth and felt the terrible inner pressure against her teeth. Wired shut, but she could move her lips. The worst was that her tongue was trapped in her mouth. At the realization, she felt real panic. What if she coughed? Choked? She pushed that thought away violently. If she was this lucid, then she was all right. She saw no tubes running from her bed, knew nothing was in traction. So this was as bad as it was going to be, and this was bearable. Just. But bearable.

Suddenly, joltingly, she was conscious of thirst. Her mouth burned with it, throat aching. 'Flavia,' she said, voice soft, barely audible, even to herself. Flavia's eyes opened and she stared about herself in near-panic, the way she always did when she woke suddenly. After a moment, she leaned forward in her chair and brought her face close to Brett's.

'Flavia, I'm thirsty,' she whispered.

'And good morning to you, too,' Flavia answered, laughing out loud in relief, and Brett knew then that she was going to be all right.

Turning, Flavia picked up a glass of water from the table behind her. She bent the plastic straw and set it between Brett's lips, careful to place it on the left side, away from the swollen cut that pulled her mouth down. 'I've even got it filled with ice, the way you like it,' she said, holding the straw steady in the glass while Brett tried to sip from it. Her dry lips were sealed closed, but finally she managed to pry one corner open, and blessed cold, blessed wet water spilled across her teeth and down her throat.

After she had taken only a few swallows, Flavia pulled the glass away, saying, 'Not so much. Wait for a bit, and then you can have more.'

'I feel doped,' Brett said.

'You are, *cara*. A nurse comes in every few hours and gives you an injection.'

'What time is it?'

Flavia looked down at her watch. 'Quarter to eight.'

The number had no meaning at all. 'Morning or night?'

'Morning.'

'What day?'

Flavia smiled and answered, 'Tuesday.'

'In the morning?'

'Yes.'

'Why are you here?'

'Where else do you expect me to be?'

'Milan. You have to sing tonight.'

'That's why they have understudies, Brett,' Flavia said dismissively. 'To sing when the principal singers get sick.'

'But you aren't sick,' Brett said, made dull by pain and drugs.

'Don't let the general manager of La Scala hear you say that, or I'll make you pay the fine for me.' It was difficult for Flavia to keep her voice light, but she tried.

'But you never cancel.'

'Well, I did, and that's the end of it. You Anglo-Saxons are so serious about work,' Flavia said, voice now artificially light. 'Do you want some more water?'

Brett nodded and immediately regretted the motion. She lay still for a few moments and closed her eyes, waiting for the wave of nausea and dizziness to pass. When she opened her eyes, she saw Flavia leaning over her with the cup. Again, she tasted the blessed coolness, closed her eyes, and drifted away for a while. Suddenly, she asked, 'What happened?'

Alarmed, Flavia asked, 'Don't you remember?'

Brett closed her eyes for a moment. 'Yes, I remember. I was afraid they'd kill you.' Her head rang with the dull resonance created by her wired teeth.

Flavia laughed at this, consistent in her bravado. 'No chance of that. It must have been all those Toscas I've sung. I just went at them with the knife, and I got one of them right across the arm.' She waved her arm in the air in front of her, repeating the gesture and smiling at the memory,

Brett was sure, of the knife cutting into him. 'I wish I'd killed him,' Flavia said in an absolutely conversational voice, and Brett believed her.

'Then what?'

'They ran. Then I went downstairs and got Luca, and he went for the doctor, and we brought you here.' As Flavia watched, Brett's eyes drifted closed, and she slept for a few minutes, lips open, steel wires grotesquely visible.

Suddenly, her eye snapped open and she looked around the room as if surprised to find herself there. She saw Flavia and grew calm.

'Why did they do it?' Flavia asked, voicing the question that had been with her for two days.

A long time passed before Brett answered. 'Semenzato.'

'At the museum?'

'Yes.'

'What? What did they say?'

'I don't understand.' If she had been capable of shaking her head without pain, Brett would have done it. 'Makes no sense.' Her voice was garbled by the heavy trap that held her teeth together. She said Semenzato's name again and closed her eyes for a long time. When she opened them, she asked, 'What's wrong with me?'

Flavia was ready for this question and answered it briefly. 'Two ribs are broken. And your jaw is cracked.'

'What else?'

'That's the worst. Your back is badly scraped.'
She saw Brett's confusion and explained. 'You fell
against the wall and dragged your back down the
bricks when you fell. And your face is very, very
blue,' Flavia concluded, trying to make light of it.
'The contrast makes your eyes stand out, but I
don't think I like the total effect.'

'How bad is it?' Brett asked, not liking the
joking tone.

'Oh, not so bad,' Flavia said, obviously lying.
Brett gave a long one-eyed look that forced Flavia
to amend things. 'You have to keep the ribs band-
aged, and you'll be very stiff for a week or so. He
said there'll be no permanent damage.' Because it
was the only good news she had, she completed
the doctor's report. 'They'll take the wires out in
a few days. It's just a hairline crack. And your teeth
are all right.' When she saw how little encouragement Brett took from this, she added, 'And your
nose.' Still no smile. 'There won't be any scars on
your face: once the swelling goes away, you'll be
fine.' Flavia said nothing about the scars that would
remain on Brett's back, nor did she say anything
about how long it would take for the swelling and
bruising to disappear from her face.

Suddenly Brett realized how tired this brief conversation had made her, and she felt new waves of
sleep pulling at her body. 'Go home for a while,
Flavia. I'll sleep and then . . .' Her voice trailed
away before she could finish, and she was asleep.

Flavia pushed herself back into her chair and studied the damaged face that lay sideways on the bed in front of her. The bruises that spread across the forehead and the cheeks had gone almost black during the last day and a half, and one eye was still swollen shut. Brett's lower lip was swollen up and around the vertical split that left it gaping wide.

Flavia had been forcibly kept out of the emergency room while the doctors worked on Brett, cleaning her back and taping her ribs. Nor had she been there to watch them thread the thin wires between her teeth, binding her jaws together. She had been left to pace the long corridors of the hospital, joining her fear with that of the other visitors and patients who walked, crowded into the bar, caught what little light filtered into the open courtyard. She had paced for an hour, begging three cigarettes from different people, the first she had smoked in more than ten years.

Since late Sunday afternoon, she had been at the side of Brett's bed, waiting for her to wake up, and had gone back to the apartment just once, the day before, and then only to shower and make a few phone calls, inventing the phantom illness that was to keep her from singing at La Scala that evening. Her nerves were pulled tight by too little sleep, too much coffee, the renewed craving for a cigarette, and the oily slick of fear that clings to the skin of all those who spend too long a time inside a hospital.

27

She looked across at her lover and wished again that she had killed the man who did this. Flavia Petrelli had no comprehension of regret, but there was very little she didn't understand about revenge.

Chapter Three

BEHIND HER, a door opened, but Flavia didn't turn her head to see who it was. Another nurse. Hardly a doctor: they were in rare supply here. After a few moments, she heard a man's voice ask, 'Signora Petrelli?'

She turned, wondering who it was and how they had found her here. Just inside the door stood a man, tallish and heavily built, who looked vaguely familiar but whom she couldn't place. One of the ward doctors? Worse, a reporter? He stood by the door, seeming to wait to be invited into the room and closer to Brett.

'Good morning, signora,' he said, not moving from the door. 'I'm Guido Brunetti. We met a few years ago.'

It was that policeman, the one who had investigated the Wellauer affair at La Fenice. He had been not unintelligent, she recalled, and Brett, for reasons Flavia had never been able to fathom, had found him *simpatico*.

'Good morning, Dottor Brunetti,' Flavia

answered formally, keeping her voice low. She stood, gave a look at Brett to see that she was still sleeping, and went over to where he stood. She extended her hand and he took it, shaking it briefly.

'Did they assign you to this?' she asked. As soon as she spoke, she realized how aggressive her question was and regretted it.

He ignored the tone and answered the question. 'No, signora, I recognized Dottoressa Lynch's name on the report of the assault, so I came to see how she was.' Even before Flavia could remark on his slowness, he explained, 'The case was given to someone else; I didn't see the report until this morning.' He looked over towards the sleeping woman, letting his glance ask the question.

'Better,' Flavia said. She stepped back and gestured for him to come closer to the bed. Brunetti walked across the room and stopped just behind Flavia's chair. He set his briefcase on the floor, rested both hands on the back of the chair, and looked down at the face of the beaten woman. Finally, he asked, 'What happened?' He had read the report and the transcripts of the account Flavia had given, but he wanted to hear her version of it.

Flavia resisted the impulse to tell him that this was precisely what he was supposed to be finding out; instead, she explained, keeping her voice low, 'Two men came to the apartment on Sunday. They said they were from the museum and had some papers for Brett. She answered the door. After she had been out in the hall with them a long time, I went to see what was keeping her, and I found her on the floor.' As she spoke, he nodded; all of this was in the report she had given to two different policemen.

'When I went out, I had a knife in my hand. I'd been chopping vegetables, and I simply forgot I had it. When I saw what they were doing, I didn't think. I cut one of them. Very badly, on the arm. They ran out of the apartment.'

'Robbery?' he asked.

She shrugged. 'It's possible. But why would they have done that?' she asked, waving her hand towards Brett.

He nodded again and muttered. 'Right, right.' He backed away and returned to stand near her, then asked in a normal voice, 'Is there much of value in the apartment?'

'Yes, I think so. Carpets, paintings, ceramics.'

'So it could have been a robbery?' he asked, and it sounded to Flavia as if he were trying to convince himself.

'They said they were from the director of the museum. How did they know to say that?' she asked. Robbery made no sense to her, and it made less sense each time she looked at Brett's face. If this policeman didn't understand that, he understood nothing.

'How badly is she hurt?' he asked, not answering

her question. 'I haven't had time to speak to the doctors.'

'Broken ribs and a cracked bone in her jaw, but there's no sign of concussion.'

'Have you spoken to her?'

'Yes.' Her brusque reply reminded him that there had been no great sympathy between them the last time they met.

'I'm sorry this happened.' He said it like a man, not a public official.

Flavia nodded in cursory acknowledgement but said nothing.

'Is she going to be all right?' The question, phrased like that, honoured her intimate knowledge of Brett, acknowledged her ability to, as it were, touch her spiritual pulse and see how much damage it would do her to have been treated like this.

Flavia was confused by her desire to thank him for asking the question and, with it, acknowledging her position in Brett's life. 'Yes, she'll be all right.' And then, more practically, 'What about the police? Have you found anything?'

'No, I'm afraid not,' Brunetti said. 'The descriptions you gave of the two men don't correspond to anyone we know here. We've checked the hospitals, here and in Mestre, but no one was admitted with a knife wound. We're checking the envelope for fingerprints.' He did not tell her that the blood covering one side of it made that difficult to do, nor did he tell her that the envelope had proved to be empty.

Behind him, Brett shifted on the bed, sighed, and then was quiet.

'Signora Petrelli,' he began, then paused, searching for the right words. 'I'd like to sit with her for a while, if you don't mind.'

Flavia caught herself wondering why she was so flattered by his casual acceptance of what she and Brett were to each other, then surprised herself even more by realizing that she had no clear idea of what that was. Spurred by those thoughts, she pulled a chair from behind the door and placed it next to the one she had been sitting on.

'*Grazie*,' he said. He sat, leaned back in the chair, and crossed his arms. She had the impression that he was prepared to sit there all day, if necessary.

He made no further attempt to speak to her, sat quietly and waited for whatever would happen. She took her place on the chair next to him, surprised by how little need she felt to make conversation with him or be socially correct. She sat. Ten minutes passed. Gradually, her head fell back against the top of the chair and she drifted off to sleep, then yanked awake when her head fell forward. She glanced at her watch. Eleven thirty. He had been there an hour.

'Has she been awake?' she asked him.

'Yes, but only for a few minutes. She didn't say anything.'

33

'Did she see you?'

'Yes.'

'Did she know who you are?'

'Yes, I think so.'

'Good.'

After a long pause, he said, 'Signora, would you like to go home for a while? Perhaps get something to eat? I'll stay here. She's seen me with you, so she won't be afraid if she wakes up and I'm here.'

Hours ago, Flavia had felt gnawing hunger; now all sign of it had disappeared. But the combination of fatigue and dirt lingered with her, and at the thought of a shower, clean towels, clean hair, clean clothes, she almost gasped with yearning. Brett was asleep, and who safer to leave her with than a policeman? The idea grew too strong. 'Yes,' she said, getting to her feet. 'I won't be long. If she wakes up, please tell her where I've gone.'

'Certainly,' he said, standing as Flavia gathered her bag and took her coat from behind the door. At the door, she turned in farewell and gave him the first real smile she had ever given him, then left the room, careful to close the door quietly after her.

When Signorina Elettra had handed him the robbery report that morning, he had barely glanced at it, especially when he saw that it was being handled by the uniformed branch. When she saw him place it to the side of his desk, Signorina Elettra had said, 'You might want to take a look at that, Dottore,' before going back down to her office.

The address had meant nothing to him, but addresses were relatively meaningless in a city with only six separate mailing addresses. The name had jumped up from the page: Brett Lynch. He had no idea she was back from China, had forgotten about her in the years that had elapsed since their last meeting. It was the memory of that meeting and all that preceded it that had brought him to the hospital.

The beautiful young woman he had met some years ago was unrecognizable, could easily have changed places with any of the scores of battered and beaten women he had seen during his years with the police. Looking at her, he drew up a list of the men he knew to be capable of this sort of violence towards a woman – not one they knew, but one they met in the commission of a crime. It turned out to be a very short list: one of them was in jail in Trieste, and the other was in Sicily or believed to be. The list of those who would do it to women they knew was much longer, and some of them were in Venice, but he doubted that any of those men would know her or, if they did, would have cause to do this.

Robbery? Signora Petrelli had told the two policemen who interviewed her that the two men who had come to the apartment had no idea that anyone else was there, so the beating made no sense. If they had come to rob Brett's apartment, they could have tied her up or locked her in a room and then taken whatever they wanted at their leisure. None of the thieves he knew in Venice would have done something like this. If not a robbery, then what?

Because she didn't open her eyes, her voice, when she spoke, surprised him. '*Mi dai da bere?*'

Startled, he moved closer to her.

'Water,' she asked.

On the table beside the bed he saw a plastic carafe and a cup with a plastic straw. He filled the cup and held the straw to her lips until she had drunk all the water. Behind her lips, he saw the cage of wires that bound her jaws together. That accounted for the slurred speech, that and the drugs.

Her right eye opened, a brighter blue than the flesh around it. 'Thank you, Commissario.' The single eye blinked, stayed open. 'Strange place to meet again.' Because of the wires, her voice sounded as if it issued from a badly tuned radio.

'Yes,' he agreed, smiling at the absurdity of her remark, at its banal formality.

'Flavia?' she asked.

'She's gone home for a moment. She'll be back soon.'

Brett moved her head on her pillow, and he

heard the sudden intake of breath. After a moment, she asked, 'Why are you here?'

'I saw your name on the crime report, so I came to see how you were.'

There was the faintest motion of her lip, a smile, perhaps, cut off by pain. 'Not very good.'

Silence stretched out between them. Finally, he asked, though he had told himself he wouldn't, 'Do you remember what happened?'

She made a noise of assent and then began to explain. 'They had papers from Dottor Semenzato, at the museum.' He nodded, familiar with both the name and the man. 'I let them in. Then this . . .' Her voice trailed off, then she said, 'Started this.'

'Did they say anything?'

Her eye closed and she lay silent for a long time. He couldn't tell if she was trying to remember or deciding whether to tell him. So long a time passed that he began to think she had gone back to sleep. But finally she said, 'Told me not to go to meeting.'

'What meeting?'

'With Semenzato.' So it hadn't been a robbery. He said nothing. This was not the time to push her, not now.

Voice growing thicker and slower, she explained. 'This morning, at the museum. Ceramics in the China exhibition.' There was a long pause and she fought to keep her eye open. 'They knew about me and Flavia.' After that, her breathing slowed and he realized she was asleep again.

He sat, watching her, and tried to make some sense out of what she had said. Semenzato was the director of the museum at the Doge's Palace. Until the reopening of the restored Palazzo Grassi, it had been the most famous museum in Venice, Semenzato the most important museum director. Perhaps he still was. After all, the Doge's Palace had mounted the Titian show; all Palazzo Grassi had presented in recent years was Andy Warhol and the Celts, both shows the product of the 'new' Venice and hence more the outcome of media hype than of serious artistic study.

It was Semenzato, Brunetti recalled, who had helped arrange, about five years ago, the exhibition of Chinese art, and it was Brett Lynch who had served as intermediary between the city administration and the Chinese government. He had seen the show long before he met her, and he could still remember some of the exhibits: the life-size terracotta statues of soldiers, a bronze chariot, and a full suit of decorative mail, constructed from thousands of interlocking pieces of jade. There had been paintings as well, but he had found them boring: weeping willows, men with beards, and the same old flimsy bridges. The statue of the soldier, however, had stunned him, and he remembered standing motionless in front of it, studying the face and reading in it fidelity, courage and honour, signs of a common humanity that had spanned two millennia and half the world.

Brunetti had met Semenzato on various occasions and had found him an intelligent, charming man, with the patina of graceful manners that men in public positions acquire with the passing of years. Venetian, of an old family, Semenzato was one of several brothers, all of whom had to do with antiquities, art, or the trade in those things.

Because Brett had arranged the show, it made sense that she would see Semenzato when she was back in Venice. What made no sense at all was that someone would try to prevent that meeting and would go to such brutal lengths to do so.

A nurse with a pile of sheets in her arms came into the room without knocking and asked him to leave while she bathed the patient and changed the linen. Obviously, Signora Petrelli had been at work on the hospital staff, seeing that the little envelopes, *bustarelle*, were delivered into the proper hands. In the absence of those 'gifts', even the most basic services wouldn't be performed for patients in this hospital, and even in their presence, it often fell to the family to feed and bathe the patient.

He left the room and stood at a window in the corridor, gazing down into the central courtyard that was part of the original fifteenth-century monastery. Opposite him he saw the new pavilion that had been built and opened with such public shouts of glory – nuclear medicine, most advanced technologies to be had in all of Italy, most famous doctors, a new age in health care for the exorbitantly taxed citizens of Venice. No expense had been spared; the building emerged an architectural wonder, its high marble arches giving a modern-day reflection of the graceful arches that stood out in Campo SS. Giovanni e Paolo and led the way into the main hospital.

The opening ceremony had been held, there had been speeches and the press had come, but the building had never been used. No drains. No sewers. And no responsibility. Was it the architect who had forgotten to put them in the original blueprints, or the builders who had failed to put them where they were meant to go? The only thing that was certain was that responsibility fell on no one and that the drains would have to be added to the already finished building, at enormous expense.

Brunetti's reading of the event was that it had been planned like this from the very moment of inception, planned so that the builder would get not only the original contract to construct the new pavilion but the work, later, to destroy much of what had been built in order to install the forgotten drains.

Did one laugh or cry? The building had been left unprotected after the opening that was not an opening, and vandals had already broken in and damaged some of the equipment, so now the hospital paid for guards to patrol the empty corridors, and patients who needed the treatments and procedures it was supposed to provide were sent to other hospitals, or told to wait, or told to go to private clinics. He could no longer remember how many billion lire had been spent. And nurses had to be bribed to change the sheets.

Suddenly, Flavia Petrelli appeared at the far end of the courtyard, and he watched her progress, all but imperial, across its open space. No one recognized her, but every man she passed noticed her. She had changed into a long purple dress which swirled from side to side as she walked. Over her shoulder she had draped a fur, nothing so prosaic as mink. As he watched her cross the courtyard, he was reminded of a passage he had read, years ago, that described a woman's entrance into a hotel. So secure was she in her wealth and position that she had shrugged her mink from her shoulders without looking, certain that there would be a servant there to catch it. Flavia Petrelli had no need to read about such things in a book: she had that same absolute certainty about her place in the world.

He watched as she passed into one of the arched stairwells that led to the upper floors. She took the steps, he noticed, two at a time, a haste which was entirely at odds with both the dress and the fur.

Seconds later, she appeared at the top of the steps, and her face grew tense when she saw him outside the room. 'What's the matter?' she asked, walking quickly towards him.

'Nothing. A nurse came in.'

She entered the room without bothering to knock. Minutes later, the nurse emerged, carrying an armful of bedding and an enamel pan. He waited a few minutes more, then knocked on the door and was told to enter.

When he came into the room, he saw that the head of the bed had been raised minimally, and Brett was lying up, head cushioned by pillows. Flavia stood beside her and held the cup to her lips, while she drank through a straw. The effect of her face was less shocking now, either because he had had time to grow accustomed to it or because he could see that parts of it were unbruised.

He stooped down and picked up his briefcase from where he had left it and approached the bed. Brett took one hand out from under the covers and slid it across the bed towards him. He covered it briefly with his own. 'Thank you,' she said.

'I'll come back tomorrow, if I may.'

'Please. I can't explain now, but I will.'

Flavia began to object but cut herself off short. She gave Brunetti a smile that began as a professional one but surprised both of them by becoming entirely natural. 'Thank you for coming,' she said, surprising both of them again with the sincerity of her voice.

'Until tomorrow, then,' he said, giving Brett's hand a squeeze. Flavia remained at the bedside while he let himself out of the room. He took the steps she had used and turned left at the bottom, into the covered portico that ran alongside the open courtyard. An old woman wrapped in an army overcoat sat in a wheelchair at the side of the corridor, knitting. At her feet three cats fought over the body of a mouse.

Chapter Four

AS HE WALKED back towards the Questura, Brunetti found himself troubled by what he had seen and heard. She would heal, he realized; her body would become well and return to what it had been before. Signora Petrelli believed she would be all right, but his experience told him that the effects of violence such as this would linger, perhaps for years, if only as a real and sudden fear that would come on her unexpectedly. Well, perhaps he was wrong and Americans were tougher than Italians, and perhaps she would emerge the same person, but he couldn't stifle his concern for her.

When he entered the Questura, one of the uniformed officers approached him. 'Dottor Patta is looking for you, sir,' he said, keeping his voice low and neutral. It seemed that everyone in the place kept their voices low and neutral when they spoke of the Vice-Questore.

Brunetti thanked him and proceeded towards the steps at the back of the building, the quickest way to his office. The intercom was ringing as he entered. He set his briefcase down on top of the desk and picked up the receiver.

'Brunetti?' Patta asked, quite unnecessarily, even before Brunetti could say his name. 'Is that you?'

'Yes, sir,' he answered, flicking through the papers that had accumulated on his desk in the hours he had been gone.

'I've been trying to get you on the phone all morning, Brunetti. We've got to make a decision about the Stresa conference. Come down to my office right now,' he ordered, then tempered it with a very grudging, 'would you?'

'Yes, sir. Immediately.' Brunetti hung up, leafed through the rest of the papers, opening one letter and reading it through twice. He walked over to stand by the window and again read through the report of the attack at Brett's house, then left and went down to Patta's office.

Signorina Elettra was not at her desk, but a low bowl overflowing with yellow freesias filled the room with a scent almost as sweet as her presence.

He knocked and waited to be told to enter. A muffled sound told him to do so. Patta was posed in the frame created by one of the large windows in his office, gazing across at the eternally scaffolded façade of the church of San Lorenzo. What little light came in managed to glimmer from the radiant points on Patta's body: the tips of his shoes, the gold chain that ran across the front of his vest, and the tiny ruby that flickered dully in his tie-pin. He glanced at Brunetti and crossed the room to his desk. As he did, Brunetti was struck by how much his progress across the room strove to imitate Flavia Petrelli's through the hospital. The contrast lay in her complete indifference to the effect she might be making; to Patta, that was the purpose of his every motion. The Vice-Questore took his place behind the desk and gestured to Brunetti to take a chair in front of him.

'Where have you been all morning?' Patta asked without preamble.

'I went to speak to the victim of an attempted robbery,' Brunetti explained. He kept his remarks as vague and, he hoped, as meaningless as possible.

'That's why we have men in uniform.'

Brunetti made no response.

Turning his attention to the business at hand, Patta asked, 'What about the Stresa conference? Which of us is going to attend?'

Two weeks before, Brunetti had received an invitation to a conference being organized by Interpol, to be held at the resort town of Stresa on Lago Maggiore. Because it would allow him to renew friendships and contacts with police officers from the various members of the Interpol network and because the programme offered training in the latest computer techniques for the storage and retrieval of information, Brunetti wanted to attend. Patta, who knew Stresa to be one of the most fashionable resorts in Italy, possessed of a climate that invited escape from the damp chill of a late Venetian winter, had suggested that it might be better were he to go instead. But as the invitation was specifically directed to Brunetti and bore a handwritten note to him from the organizer of the conference, Patta had found it hard to convince Brunetti to renounce his right to go. With great reluctance, Patta drew the line just short of ordering him not to attend.

Brunetti crossed his legs and pulled his notebook from his pocket. As always, the pages were blank of anything that pertained to police business, but Patta, as always, failed to realize this. 'Let me check the dates,' Brunetti said, flicking through the pages. 'The sixteenth, isn't it? Until the twentieth?' His pause was dramatic, orchestrated to Patta's mounting impatience. 'I'm not sure any longer that I'm free that week.'

'What dates did you say?' Patta asked, flipping his desk calendar forward a few weeks. 'Sixteenth to the twentieth?' His pause was even more dramatic than Brunetti's had been. 'Well, if you can't do it, I might be able to go. I'd have to reschedule a meeting with the Minister of the Interior, but I think I might be able to do so.'

'That might be better, sir. Are you sure you can allow the time?'

Patta's glance was illegible. 'Yes.'

'Well, that's settled, then,' Brunetti said with false heartiness.

It must have been something in his tone, or perhaps in his alacrity, that triggered alarm bells in Patta. 'Where were you this morning?'

'I told you, sir, speaking to the victim of a reported robbery attempt.'

'What victim?' Patta asked, voice heavy with suspicion.

'A foreigner who lives here.'

'What foreigner?'

'Dottoressa Lynch,' Brunetti answered and watched Patta's face register the name. For a moment, his face was blank, but then his eyes narrowed as he pulled up the memory of who she was. As Brunetti watched, he registered the precise moment when Patta remembered not only who, but what, she was.

'The lesbian,' he muttered, showing what he thought of her with the contempt with which he pronounced the word. 'What happened to her?'

'She was attacked in her home.'

'Who did it? Some butch dyke she picked up in a bar?' When he saw the effect his words had on Brunetti, he moderated his tone and asked, 'What happened?'

'She was attacked by two men,' Brunetti explained, and added, 'neither of whom appeared to be a "butch dyke". She's in hospital.'

Patta struggled to prevent himself from remarking on this and instead asked, 'Is this why you're too busy to attend the conference?'

'The conference isn't until next month, sir. I've got a number of cases current.'

Patta snorted to express his disbelief then suddenly asked, 'What did they take?'

'Apparently nothing.'

'Why? If it was a robbery?'

'Someone stopped them. And I don't know that it was a robbery.'

Patta ignored the second part of what Brunetti said and jumped on the first. 'Who stopped them, that singer?' he asked, suggesting that Flavia Petrelli sang on street corners for coins rather than at La Scala for a fortune.

When Brunetti didn't rise to this, Patta continued, 'Of course it was robbery. She's got a fortune in that place.' Brunetti was surprised, not by the raw envy in Patta's voice, which seemed his normal response to wealth, but by the fact that he had any idea of what was in Brett's apartment.

'Perhaps,' Brunetti said.

'There's no perhaps about it,' Patta insisted. 'If it was two men, it was robbery.' Did women, Brunetti prevented himself from asking, busy themselves naturally with other crimes? Patta looked directly at him. 'That means it belongs to the robbery squad. Leave it to them. This isn't a social club here, Commissario. We're not in business to help your friends when they get into trouble, especially not your lesbian friends,' he said in a tone that conjured up scores of them, as if Brunetti were a latter-day St Ursula, eleven thousand young women following in his train, all virgin and all lesbian.

Brunetti had had years to accustom himself to the fundamental irrationality of much of what his superior said, but there were times when Patta still managed to amaze him with the breadth and passion of some of his wilder pronouncements. And anger him. 'Will that be all, sir?' he asked.

'Yes, that will be all. Remember, this is a robbery, and it's to be handled—' He broke off at the sound of the telephone. Irritated by the noise, Patta grabbed the receiver and shouted into the mouthpiece, 'I told you not to put through any calls.' Brunetti waited to see him slam the phone down but, instead, Patta pulled it closer to his ear, and Brunetti saw shock register.

'Yes, yes, I'm certainly here,' Patta said. 'Put him through.'

Patta sat a little bit higher in his chair and ran one hand through his hair, as if he expected the caller to look through the receiver and see him. He smiled, smiled again, and waited for the voice at the other end. Brunetti heard the far-off rumble of a man's voice, and then Patta answered, 'Good morning, sir. Yes, yes, very well, thank you. And you?'

An answer of some sort filtered through to Brunetti. As he watched, Patta reached for the pen that lay at the side of his desk, forgetting the Mont

Blanc Meisterstück in his jacket pocket. He grabbed at a piece of paper and pulled it in front of him. 'Yes, yes, sir. I've heard about it. In fact, I was just discussing it now.' He paused and more words floated to him over the phone, arriving at Brunetti as no more than a dim murmur.

'Yes, sir. I know. It's terrible. I was shocked to hear of it.' Another pause to wait for the voice to say something else. His eyes flashed to Brunetti and then as quickly away. 'Yes, sir. One of my men has already spoken to her.' There was a sharp eruption of words from the other end. 'No, sir, of course not. It's someone who knows her. I told him, specifically, not to disturb her, merely to see how she was and to speak to her doctors. Of course, sir. I realize that, sir.'

Patta picked up the pen by its point and tapped it rhythmically on the desk. He listened. 'Of course, of course, I'll assign as many men as necessary, sir. We know of her generosity to the city.'

He shot another look at Brunetti, then glanced down at the tapping pen, forcing himself to lay it flat on the desk.

He listened for a long time, staring at the pen. Once or twice, he tried to speak, but the distant voice cut him off. Finally, hand clenched on the phone, he managed to say, 'As soon as possible. I'll keep you informed myself. Yes, sir. Of course, sir. Yes.' He didn't have time to say goodbye; the voice at the other end was gone.

He put the phone down gently and looked at Brunetti. 'That, as I suppose you realize, was the mayor. I don't know how he found out about this, but he did.' He made it clear that he suspected Brunetti of having called and left an anonymous message in the mayor's office.

'It seems the Dottoressa,' he began, pronouncing the word in a tone that called into question the quality of instruction of both Harvard and Yale, the schools from which Dottoressa Lynch had taken her degrees, 'is a friend of his, and,' he added, after a pregnant pause, 'a benefactor of the city. So the mayor wants this looked into and settled as quickly as possible.'

Brunetti remained silent, knowing how dangerous it would be for him to make any sort of suggestion at this point. He glanced down at the paper on Patta's desk then up at his superior's face.

'What are you working on now?' Patta asked, which, Brunetti realized, meant that he was to be given the investigation.

'Nothing that can't wait.'

'Then I want you to look into this.'

'Yes, sir,' he said, hoping that Patta wouldn't suggest any specific steps.

Too late. 'Go over to her apartment. See what you can find out. Talk to her neighbours.'

'Yes, sir,' Brunetti said and stood, hoping to cut him off.

'Keep me up to date on this, Brunetti.'

'Yes, sir.'

'I want this settled quickly, Brunetti. She's a friend of the mayor's.' And, Brunetti knew, any friend of the mayor's was a friend of Patta's.

Chapter Five

BACK IN HIS office, he called down and asked Vianello to come up. After a few minutes, the sergeant came in and lowered himself heavily into the chair in front of Brunetti's desk. He took a small notebook from his uniform pocket and gave Brunetti an inquisitive glance.

'What do you know about gorillas, Vianello?'

Vianello considered the question for a moment and then asked, unnecessarily, 'The kind in the zoo or the kind that get paid to hurt people?'

'The kind that get paid.'

Vianello paused for a moment, running through lists he appeared to keep filed in his mind. 'I don't think there are any here in the city, sir. But in Mestre there are four or five of them, mostly Southerners.' He paused for a moment, flipping through more lists. 'I've heard that there are a few in Padua and some who work in Treviso and Pordenone, but they're provincials. The real ones are the boys in Mestre. Trouble with them here?'

Because the uniformed branch had done the

initial investigation and conducted the interviews with Flavia, Brunetti knew Vianello had to be aware of the attack. 'I spoke to Dottoressa Lynch this morning. The men who attacked her told her not to attend a meeting with Dottor Semenzato.'

'At the museum?' Vianello asked.

'Yes.'

Vianello considered this for a moment. 'Then it wasn't a robbery?'

'No, it would seem not. Someone stopped them.'

'Signora Petrelli?' Vianello asked.

The Swiss bank secret wouldn't last a day in Venice. 'Yes. She drove them off. But it didn't seem they were interested in taking anything.'

'Short-sighted on their part. It would be a good place to rob.'

At this, Brunetti broke down. 'How do you know that, Vianello?'

'My sister-in-law's next-door neighbour is her maid. Goes in three times a week to clean, keeps an eye on the place for her when she's in China. She's talked about what's in there, says it must be worth a fortune.'

'Not the best thing to be saying about a place that's left empty so much, is it?' Brunetti asked, voice stern.

'That's just what I told her, sir.'

'I hope she listened.'

'I do, too.'

His indirect reprimand having failed to work, Brunetti returned to the gorillas. 'Check the hospitals again to see if the one she wounded has been in. It sounds like she cut him badly. What about the prints on that envelope?'

Vianello looked up from his notebook. 'I've sent copies to Rome and asked them to let us know what they have.' Both of them knew how long that could take.

'Try Interpol, as well.'

Vianello nodded and added the suggestion to his notes. 'What about Semenzato?' Vianello asked. 'What was the meeting about?'

'I don't know. Ceramics, I think, but she was too drugged to explain anything clearly. Do you know anything about him?'

'No more than anyone in the city does, sir. He's been at the museum for about seven years. Married, wife from Messina, I think. Somewhere in Sicily. No children. Good family, and his reputation at the museum is good.'

Brunetti didn't bother to ask Vianello how he came by this information, no longer surprised by the archive of personal information the sergeant had accumulated during his years with the police. Instead, he said, 'See what you can find out about him. Where he worked before he came here and why he left, where he studied.'

'You going to talk to him, sir?'

Brunetti considered this for a moment. 'No. If

whoever sent them wanted to scare her away from him, then I want them to believe they succeeded. But I want to see what there is to find out about him. And see what you can learn about those men in Mestre.'

'Yes, sir,' Vianello answered, making note of this. 'You ask her about their accent?'

Brunetti had already thought of this, but there had been too little time with Brett. Her Italian was perfect, so their accents would have given her an idea of what part of the country they came from. 'I'll ask her tomorrow.'

'In the meantime, I'll look into gorillas in Mestre,' Vianello said. With a grunt, he got out of the chair and left the office.

Brunetti pushed back his chair, pulled the bottom drawer of his desk open with his toe, and rested his crossed feet on it. He slouched down in his chair and latched his fingers behind his head, then turned and looked out of the window. From this angle, the façade of San Lorenzo wasn't visible, but he could see a patch of cloudy, late-winter sky, a monotony that might induce thought.

She had said something about the ceramics in the show, and that could only mean the show she had helped arrange four or five years ago, the first time in recent years that museum-goers in the West had been allowed to see the marvels currently being excavated in China. And he had thought her to be in China still.

He had been surprised to see her name on the crime report that morning, shocked to see her bruised face in the hospital. How long had she been back? How long was she intending to stay? And what had brought her back to Venice? Flavia Petrelli would be able to answer some of those questions; Flavia Petrelli might herself be the answer to one of them. But those questions could wait; for the moment, he was more interested in Dottor Semenzato.

He let his chair drop forward with a bang, reached for the phone, and dialled a number from memory.

'*Pronto*,' said the familiar deep voice.

'*Ciao*, Lele,' Brunetti responded. 'Why aren't you out painting?'

'*Ciao, Guido, come stai?*' Then, without waiting for an answer, he explained. 'Not enough light today. I went out to the Zattere this morning, but I came back without doing anything. The light's flat, dead. So I came back here to fix lunch for Claudia.'

'How is she?'

'Fine, fine. And Paola?'

'Good, so are the kids. Look, Lele, I'd like to talk to you. Can you spare me some time this afternoon?'

'Talk talk or police talk?'

'Police talk, I'm afraid. Or I think it is.'

'I'll be at the gallery after three if you want

to come over then. Until about five.' From the background, Brunetti heard a hissing sound, a muttered, '*Puttana Eva*,' and then Lele said, 'Guido, I've got to go. The pasta's boiling over.' Brunetti barely had time to say goodbye before the phone went dead.

If anyone would know about Semenzato's reputation, it was Lele. Gabriele Cossato, painter, antiquarian, lover of beauty, was as much a part of Venice, it seemed, as were the four Moors, poised in eternal confabulation to the right of the basilica of San Marco. For as far back as Brunetti could remember, there had been Lele, and Lele had been a painter. When Brunetti remembered his childhood, he recalled Lele, a friend of his father, and he remembered the stories, told then even to him, for he was a boy and so was expected to understand, about Lele's women, that endless succession of *donne, signore, ragazze*, with whom Lele would appear at the Brunettis' table. The women were all gone now, forgotten in his love for his wife of many years, but his passion for the beauty of the city remained, that and his limitless familiarity with the art world and all it encompassed: antiquarians and dealers, museums and galleries.

He decided to go home for lunch and then go to see Lele directly from there. But then he remembered that it was Tuesday, which meant that Paola would be having lunch with the members of her department at the university, and that in its turn meant that the children would eat with their grandparents, leaving him to cook and eat a meal alone. To avoid that, he went to a local trattoria and spent the meal thinking about what could be so important about a discussion between an archaeologist and a museum director that it had to be prevented with such violence.

A little after three, he crossed the Accademia Bridge and cut left towards Campo San Vio and, beyond it, Lele's gallery. The artist was there when he arrived, perched on a ladder, a torch in one hand, a pair of electrical clippers in the other, reaching into a spaghetti-like mass of electrical wires housed behind a wooden panel above the door to the back room of the gallery. Brunetti was so accustomed to seeing Lele in his three-piece pin-striped suits that, even though the painter was perched at the top of the ladder, his position seemed not at all incongruous. Looking down, Lele greeted him, '*Ciao*, Guido. Just a minute while I join these together.' So saying, he laid the torch on the top of the ladder, peeled back the plastic covering of one wire, twisted the exposed part around a second wire, then took a thick roll of black tape from his back pocket and bound the two together. With the point of the clippers, he poked the wire back among the others that ran parallel to it. Then, looking down at Brunetti, he said, 'Guido, go into the storeroom and throw the switch for the current.'

Obedient, he went into the large storeroom on the right and stood for a moment at the door, waiting for his eyes to adjust to the deeper darkness.

'Just on the left,' Lele called.

Turning, he saw the large electrical panel attached to the wall. He pulled the main circuit breaker down, and the storeroom was suddenly flooded with light. He waited again, this time for his eyes to adjust to the brightness, then went back into the main room of the gallery.

Lele was already down from the ladder, the panel closed above him. 'Hold the door,' he said and walked towards Brunetti, carrying his ladder. He quickly stored it in the back room and emerged, brushing dust from his hands.

'*Pantegana*,' he explained, giving the Venetian name for rat, a word which, though it named them clearly – rat – still managed to make them, in the naming, somehow charming and domestic. 'They come and eat the covering on the wires.'

'Can't you poison them?' Brunetti asked.

'Bah,' Lele snorted. 'They prefer the poison to the plastic. They thrive on it. I can't even keep paintings in the storeroom any more; they come in and eat the canvas. Or the wood.'

Brunetti looked automatically at the paintings hanging on the walls of the gallery, vividly coloured scenes of the city, alive with light and filled with Lele's energy.

'No, they're safe. They're too high up. But some day I expect to come in and find the little bastards have moved the ladder in the night and climbed up to eat them all.' The fact that Lele laughed when he said this made him sound no less serious about it. He dropped the clippers and tape into a drawer and turned to Brunetti. 'All right, what is this talk that might be police talk?'

'Semenzato, at the museum, and the Chinese exhibition held there a few years ago,' Brunetti explained.

Lele grunted in acknowledgement of the request and moved across the room to stand under a wrought-iron candelabrum attached to the wall. He reached up and bent one of the leaf-shaped prongs a bit to the left, stepped back to examine it, then leaned forward to bend it a tiny bit more. Satisfied, he went back to Brunetti.

'He's been at the museum for about eight years, Semenzato, and he's managed to organize a number of international shows. That means he's got good connections with museums or their directors in foreign countries, knows a lot of people in lots of places.'

'Anything else?' Brunetti asked, voice neutral.

'He's a good administrator. He's hired a number of excellent people and brought them to Venice. There are two restorers he all but stole from the Courtauld, and he's done a lot to change the way the exhibitions are publicized.'

'Yes, I've noticed that.' At times, Brunetti felt that Venice had been turned into a whore forced to choose between different johns: first the city was offered the face from a Phoenician glass earring, saw the poster reproduced a thousand times, then that was quickly replaced with a portrait by Titian, which in turn was driven out by Andy Warhol, himself then quickly banished by a Celtic silver deer as the museums covered every available surface in the city and vied endlessly for the attention and box office receipts of the passing tourists. What would come next, he wondered, Leonardo T-shirts? No, they already had them in Florence. He'd seen enough posters for art shows to last a lifetime in hell.

'Do you know him?' Brunetti asked, wondering if that was the reason for Lele's uncharacteristic objectivity.

'Oh, we've met a few times.'

'Where?'

'The museum has called me in a few times to ask about majolica pieces they were offered, if I thought they were genuine or not.'

'And you met him then?'

'Yes.'

'What did you think of him personally?'

'He seemed a very pleasant, competent man.'

Brunetti had had enough. 'Come on, Lele, this is unofficial. It's me, Guido, asking you, not Commissario Brunetti. I want to know what you think of him.'

Lele looked down at the surface of the desk that stood beside him, moved a ceramic bowl a few millimetres to the left, glanced up at Brunetti, and said, 'I think his eyes are for sale.'

'What?' asked Brunetti, not understanding at all.

'Like Berenson. You know, you become an expert on something, and then people come to you and ask you if a piece is genuine or not. And because you've spent years or perhaps even your entire life studying something, learning about a painter or a sculptor, they believe you when you say a piece is genuine. Or that it's not.'

Brunetti nodded. Italy was full of experts; some of them even knew what they were talking about. 'Why Berenson?'

'It seems he sold his eyes. Gallery owners or private collectors would ask him to authenticate certain pieces, and sometimes he'd say that they were genuine, but later they'd turn out not to be.' Brunetti started to ask a question, but Lele cut him off. 'No, don't even ask if it could have been an honest mistake. There's proof that he was paid, especially by Duveen, that he got a share of the take. Duveen had a lot of rich American clients; you know the type. They can't be bothered learning about art, probably don't even like it much, but they want to be known to have it, to own it. So Duveen matched their desire and their money with Berenson's reputation and expertise, and everyone was happy; the Americans with their paintings, all with clear attributions; Duveen with the profits from the sales; and Berenson with both his reputation and his cut of the take.'

Brunetti paused a moment before he asked, 'And Semenzato does the same?'

'I'm not sure. But of the last four pieces they brought me in to take a look at, two were imitations.' He thought for a moment, then added, grudgingly, 'Good imitations, but still imitations.'

'How did you know?'

Lele looked at him as though Brunetti had asked him how he knew a particular flower was a rose and not an iris. 'I looked at them,' he said simply.

'Did you convince them?'

Lele weighed for a moment whether to be offended by the question or not, but then he remembered that Brunetti was, after all, only a policeman. 'The curators decided not to acquire the pieces.'

'Who had decided, originally, to buy them?' But he knew the answer.

'Semenzato.'

'And who was offering to sell them?'

'We were never told. Semenzato said it was a private sale, that he had been contacted by a private dealer who wanted to sell the pieces, two plates that were supposed to be Florentine, fourteenth century, and two Venetian. Those two were genuine.'

'All from the same source?'

'I think so.'

'Could they have been stolen?' Brunetti asked.

Lele considered this for a while before he answered. 'Perhaps. But major pieces like that, if they're genuine, people know about them. There's a record of sales, and people who know majolica have a pretty good idea of who owns the best pieces and when they're sold. But that's not an issue with the Florentine pieces. They were fakes.'

'What was Semenzato's reaction when you said they were?'

'Oh, he said that he was very glad I'd discovered it and saved the museum from an embarrassing acquisition. That's what he called it, "an embarrassing acquisition", as though it was perfectly all right for the dealer to try to sell pieces that were frauds.'

'Did you say any of this to him?' Brunetti asked.

Lele shrugged, a gesture that summed up centuries, perhaps millennia, of survival. 'I didn't have the feeling that he wanted to hear anything like that.'

'And what happened?'

'He said he'd return them to the dealer and tell him that the museum wasn't interested in those two pieces.'

'And the others?'

'The museum went ahead and bought them.'

'From the same dealer?'

'Yes, I think so.'

'Did you ask who it was?'

That question earned Brunetti another of those looks. 'You can't ask that,' Lele explained.

Brunetti had known Lele all his life, so he asked, 'Did the curators tell you who he was?'

Lele laughed in open delight at having his high-minded pose so easily shattered. 'I asked one of them, but they had no idea. Semenzato never mentioned the name.'

'How did he know the seller wouldn't try to sell the ones you didn't buy again, to another museum or to a private collector?'

Lele smiled his crooked smile, one side of his mouth turning down, the other up, a smile Brunetti had always thought best expressed the Italian character, never quite sure of gloom or glee and always ready to switch from one to the other. 'I saw no point in mentioning it to him.'

'Why?'

'He's always struck me as the kind of man who doesn't like to be questioned or given advice.'

'But you were called in to look at the plates.'

Again, that grin. 'By the curators. That's why I said he didn't like to be given advice. He didn't like it that I said they weren't genuine. He was gracious and he thanked me for my help, said the museum was grateful. But he still didn't like it.'

'Interesting, isn't it?' Brunetti asked.

'Very,' Lele agreed, 'especially from a man whose job is to protect the integrity of the museum's collection. And,' he added, 'to see that fakes don't remain on the market.' He moved in front of Brunetti and crossed the room to straighten a painting hanging on the far wall.

'Is there anything else I should know about him?' Brunetti asked.

Facing away from Brunetti, looking at his own painting, Lele replied, 'I think there's probably a lot more you should know about him.'

'Such as?' he asked.

Lele came back towards him and studied the picture from the greater distance. He seemed pleased with whatever correction he had made. 'Nothing specific. His reputation is very high in the city, and he has a lot of friends in high places.'

'Then what do you mean?'

'Guido, ours is a small world,' Lele began and then stopped.

'Do you mean Venice or those of you who work with antiques?'

'Both, but especially us. There are only about five or ten of us in the city who really count: my brother, Bortoluzzi, Ravanello. And most of what we do is done by suggestions and hints so subtle that no one else would understand what was happening.' He saw that Brunetti didn't understand this, so he tried to explain. 'Last week, someone showed me a polychrome Madonna with the

68

Christ Child lying asleep in her lap. She was perfect fifteenth century. Tuscan. Perhaps even the end of the fourteenth century. But the dealer who showed it to me picked up the baby – they were carved in separate pieces – and pointed to a place on the back of the statue, just below the shoulder, where the faintest of patches could be seen.' He waited for Brunetti's response.

When that didn't come, he continued. 'That meant it was an angel, not a Christ Child. The patch covered the place where the wings had been, where they had been taken out, who knows when, and covered up so that it would look like a Christ Child.'

'Why?'

'Because there have always been more angels than Christs. So the removal of the wings . . .' Lele's voice trailed off.

'Gave him a promotion?' Brunetti asked, understanding.

Lele's shout of laughter filled the gallery. 'Yes, that's it. He was promoted to Christ, and the promotion meant he'd earn a lot more money when he was sold.'

'But the dealer showed you?'

'That's what I'm getting at, Guido. He told me by not telling me, just by showing me that tiny patch, and he would have done the same with any one of us.'

'But not a casual client?' Brunetti suggested.

'Perhaps not,' Lele agreed. 'The patch was so well done, and the paint covered it so perfectly, that very few people would have noticed it. Or if they had noticed it, would not have known what it meant.'

'Would you have?'

Lele nodded quickly. 'Eventually, yes, I would have noticed it, if I had taken it home and lived with it.'

'But not the casual buyer?'

'No, probably not.'

'Then why did he show you?'

'Because he thought I might still like to buy the piece. And because it's important to us to know that, at least among ourselves, we won't lie or cheat or try to pass something off as what we know it isn't.'

'Is there a moral in all of this, Lele?' Brunetti asked with a smile. Since his childhood, there had often been a lesson hidden in what Lele had told him.

'I'm not sure if it's a moral, Guido, but Semenzato is not a member of the club. He isn't one of us.'

'And who made that decision, he or you?'

'I don't think anyone ever really decided it. And I've certainly never heard anything about him directly.' Lele, a man of images and not of words, looked out of the wide gallery window and studied the patterns of light on the canal beyond. 'It's more a question that he was never assumed to be one of us than that he was consciously excluded.'

'Who else knows this?'

'You're the first person I've told about the majolica. And I'm not sure that anyone can be said to "know" this, at least not at any level he'd be aware of. It's just something that we all understand.'

'About him?'

With a laugh, Lele said, 'About most of the antique dealers in the country, if you want the truth.' Then, more soberly, he added, 'And, yes, about him, too.'

'Not the best recommendation for the director of one of the leading museums in Italy, is it?' Brunetti asked. 'It would make a person reluctant to buy a polychrome Madonna from him.'

With another loud burst of laughter, Lele said, 'You should meet some of the others. I wouldn't buy a plastic hairbrush from most of them.' Both laughed at that for a moment, but then Lele asked, serious now, 'Why are you interested in him?'

Part of Brunetti's sworn trust as an officer of the law was never to reveal police information to anyone unauthorized to hear it. 'Someone doesn't want him to talk about the China exhibition, the one held here five years ago.'

'Um?' Lele murmured, asking for more information.

'The person who arranged the show had an

71

appointment to see him, but she was beaten, badly beaten, and told not to keep it.'

'Dottoressa Lynch?' Lele asked.

Brunetti nodded.

'Have you spoken to Semenzato?' Lele asked.

'No. I don't want to call any attention to him. Let whoever did this believe the warning worked.'

Lele nodded and rubbed his hand lightly across his lips, something he always did when trying to work out a problem.

'Could you ask around, Lele? See if there's any talk about him?'

'What kind of talk?'

'I don't know. Debts, perhaps. Women. Whether you can get an idea of who that dealer was, or any other people he might know who are involved in . . .' He trailed off, not sure what to name it.

'He's bound to know everyone in the trade.'

'I know that. But I want to know whether he's involved with anything illegal.' When Lele didn't answer, Brunetti said, 'I'm not even sure what that means, and I'm not sure you can find it out.'

'I can find out anything,' Lele said dispassionately; it was a statement of fact, not a boast. He said nothing for a moment, hand still rubbing lightly back and forth on his compressed lips. Finally, he took his hand down and said, 'All right. I know a few people I can ask, but I'll need a day or two. One of the men I need to talk to is in

Burma. I'll call you by the end of the week. Is that all right?'

'It's fine, Lele. I don't know how to thank you.'

The painter dismissed this with a wave of his hand. 'Don't thank me until I find out something.'

'If there is anything,' Brunetti added, as if to disarm the antipathy he had sensed in Lele towards the museum director.

'Oh, there's always something.'

Chapter Six

WHEN HE LEFT Lele's gallery, he turned left and ducked into the underpass that led out to the Zattere, the long, open *fondamenta* that ran alongside the canal of the Giudecca. Across the water he saw the church of the Zittelle and then, further along, that of the Redentore, their domes soaring up above them. A strong wind came in from the east, stirring up whitecaps that knocked and bounced the vaporetti around like toys in a tub. Even at this distance, he could hear the thundering reverberation as one of them crashed against its mooring, saw it buck and tear at the rope that held it to the dock. He pulled up his collar and let the wind push him forward, keeping to the right, close against the buildings, to avoid the spray that spewed up from the embankment. Il Cucciolo, the waterside bar where he and Paola had spent so many hours during the first weeks after their meeting, was open, but the vast wooden deck in front of it, built out over the water, was completely empty, stripped of tables, chairs and umbrellas. To Brunetti, the first real sign of spring was the day when those tables and chairs appeared after their winter's hibernation. Today, the thought made him shiver. The bar was open, but he avoided it, for the waiters were the rudest in the city, their arrogant slowness tolerable only in exchange for idle hours in the sun.

A hundred metres along, past the church of the Gesuati, he pulled open the glass door and slipped into the welcoming warmth of Nico's bar. He stamped his feet a few times, unbuttoned his coat, and approached the counter. He ordered a grog and watched the waiter hold a glass under the spigot of the espresso machine and shoot it full of steam that quickly condensed to boiling water. Rum, a slice of lemon, a generous dash of something from a bottle, and then the barman placed it in front of him. Three sugars, and Brunetti had found salvation. He stirred the drink slowly, cheered by the aromatic steam that rose up softly from it. Like most drinks, it didn't taste as good as it smelled, but Brunetti had grown so accustomed to this truth that he was no longer disappointed by it.

The door opened again, and a rush of icy wind blew two young girls in before it. They wore ski parkas lined with fur that burst out and surrounded their glowing faces, thick boots, leather gloves, and woollen slacks. From the look of them, they were American, or possibly German; if they were rich enough, it was often hard to tell.

75

'Oh, Kimberly, are you sure this is the place?' the first one said in English, sweeping the place with her emerald eyes.

'It said so in the book, Alison. Nico's is, like, famous.' (She pronounced 'Nico' to rhyme with 'sicko', a word Brunetti had picked up at his last Interpol convention.) 'It's famous for *gelato*.'

It took a moment for the possibility of what might be about to happen to register on Brunetti. The instant it did, he sipped quickly at his grog, which was still so hot it burned his tongue. Patient, he took his spoon and began vigorously to stir the drink, moving it up high on the sides of the glass in hopes that this would somehow force it to cool more rapidly.

'Oh there it is, I bet, under those round lid things,' the first one said, coming to stand next to Brunetti and peering over the bar, down at where Nico's famous *gelato*, production severely cut back in acknowledgement of the season, did indeed lie under those round lid things. 'What flavour do you want?'

'Do you think they'd have Heath Bar?'

'Nah, not in Italy.'

'Yeah, I guess not. I guess we're gonna have to stick to, like, basics.'

The barman approached, smiling in acknowledgement of their beauty and radiant good health, to make no mention of their courage. '*Sì?*' he asked, smiling.

'Do you have any *gelato*?' one of them asked, pronouncing the last word loudly, if not correctly.

Without a pause, apparently accustomed to this, the barman smiled again and reached behind him to pull two cones from a tall pile on the counter.

'What flavour?' he asked in passable English.

'What flavours have you got?'

'*Vaniglia, cioccolato, fragola, fior di latte, e tiramisù.*'

The girls looked at each other in great perplexity. 'I guess we better stick with vanilla and chocolate, huh?' one asked. Brunetti could no longer distinguish between them, so similar was the bored nasality of their voices.

'Yeah, I guess.'

The first one turned to the barman and said, '*Due* vanilla and chocolatto, please.'

In a moment, the deed was done, the cones made and handed across the counter. Brunetti found the only consolation he could in taking a long drink of his grog, holding the half-full glass under his nose for a long time after he had swallowed.

The girls had to remove their gloves to take the cones, then one of them had to hold both cones while the other dug into her pockets for four thousand lire. The barman handed them napkins, possibly in the hope that this would keep them inside while they ate the ice cream, but the girls were not to be stopped. They took the napkins and wrapped them carefully around the base of the cones, pushed open the door, and disappeared into the increasing gloom of the afternoon. The bar filled with the sad boom of another boat as it crashed against the wharf.

The barman glanced at Brunetti. Brunetti met his eyes. Neither said a word. Brunetti finished the grog, paid, and left.

It was fully dark now, and Brunetti found himself eager to be at home, out of this cold, and away from the wind that still sliced across the open space along the waterside. He crossed in front of the French consulate, then cut back alongside the Giustiniani Hospital, a dumping ground for the old, and headed towards home. Because he walked quickly, it took him only ten minutes to get there. The entrance hall smelled damp, but the pavement was still dry. The sirens for *acqua alta* had sounded at three that morning, waking them all, but the tide had turned before the waters had seeped up through the chinks in the pavement. The full moon was only a few days away, and it had been raining heavily up north in Friuli, so there was a chance that the night would bring the first real flooding of the year.

At the top of the stairs, inside his home, he found what he wanted: warmth, the scent of a fresh-peeled tangerine, and the certainty that Paola and the children were at home. He hung his coat on one of the pegs beside the door and went into the living room. There he found Chiara, propped on her elbows at the table, holding a book open with one hand and stuffing peeled sections of tangerine into her mouth with the other. She looked up as he came in, smiled broadly, and held out a section of tangerine to him. '*Ciao, Papà.*'

He came across the room, glad of the warmth, suddenly aware of how cold his feet were. He stood beside her and bent down far enough to allow her to pop a section of tangerine into his mouth. Then another, and another. While he chewed, she finished the peeled sections that lay on a dish beside her.

'*Papà*, you hold the match,' she said, reaching across the table and handing him a book of matches. Obedient, he peeled one off and lit it, holding the flame towards her. From the pile on the table beside her, she selected a piece of tangerine peel and bent it until the two inner sides touched. As she did, a fine mist of oil shot out from the cracking skin and flared up in a blazing rocket of coloured flames. '*Che bella*,' Chiara said, eyes wide with delight that never seemed to diminish, no matter how many times they did this.

'Are there any more?' he asked.

'No, *Papà*, that was the last one.' He shrugged but not before a look of real sorrow flashed across her face. 'I'm sorry I ate them all, *Papà*. There are some oranges. Do you want me to peel you one?'

'No, angel, that's all right. I'll wait till dinner.'

He leaned to the right and tried to look into the kitchen. 'Where's *Mamma*?'

'Oh, she's in her study,' Chiara said, turning back to her book. 'And she's in a really bad mood, so I don't know when we're going to eat.'

'How do you know she's in a bad mood?' he asked.

She looked straight up at him and rolled her eyes. 'Oh, *Papà*, don't be silly. You know what she's like when she's in one of her moods. Told Raffi she couldn't help him with his homework, and she yelled at me because I didn't take the rubbish downstairs this morning.' She propped her chin on both fists and looked down at her book. 'I hate it when she's like that.'

'Well, she's been having a lot of trouble at the university, Chiara.'

She turned a page. 'Oh, you always stick up for her. But she's no fun when she's like that.'

'I'll go and talk to her. Maybe that will help.' Both of them knew the unlikelihood of this but, the optimists of the family, they smiled to each other at the possibility.

She slumped back down over her book, Brunetti bent and kissed the top of her head and switched on the overhead light as he left the room. At the end of the corridor, he stopped in front of the door to Paola's study. Talking to her seldom helped, but listening to her sometimes did. He knocked.

'*Avanti*,' she called out, and he pushed back the

door. The first thing he noticed, even before he saw Paola standing at the glass door that led to the terrace, was the chaos on her desk. Papers, books, magazines spilled across its surface; some open, some closed, some used to mark pages in others. Only the self-deceived or the vision-impaired would ever call Paola either neat or orderly, but this mess was pushed out way beyond even her very tolerant limits. She turned from the door and noticed the way he stared at her desk. 'I've been looking for something,' she explained.

'The person who killed Edwin Drood?' he asked, referring to an article she had spent three months writing the previous year. 'I thought you found him.'

'Don't joke, Guido,' she said, in that voice she used when humour was as welcome as the old boyfriend of the bride. 'I've spent most of the afternoon trying to hunt down a quotation.'

'What do you need it for?'

'A class. I want to begin with the quotation, and I need to tell them where it comes from, so I've got to locate the source.'

'Who is it?'

'The Master,' she said, in English, and Brunetti watched her go all misty-eyed, the way she always did when she talked about Henry James. Did it make sense, he wondered, to be jealous? Jealous of a man who, it seemed to him from what Paola had said about him, not only couldn't decide what his nationality was, but couldn't seem to decide what sex he was, either?

For twenty years, this had gone on. The Master had gone on their honeymoon with them, was in the hospital when both of their children were born, seemed to tag along on every holiday they had ever taken. Stout, phlegmatic, possessed of a prose style that proved impenetrable to Brunetti, no matter how many times he tried to read him in either English or Italian, Henry James appeared to be the other man in Paola's life.

'What's the quotation?'

'He said it in response to someone who asked him, late in his life, what he had learned by all his experience.'

Brunetti knew what he was meant to do. He did it. 'What did he say?'

' "Be kind and then be kind and then be kind," ' she said in English.

The temptation proved too strong for Brunetti. 'With or without commas?'

She shot him a grim look. Obviously not the day for jokes, especially about the Master. In an attempt to worm out from under the weight of that look, he said, 'Seems a strange quotation to begin a literature class.'

She weighed whether to take his remark about the commas as still standing or to address herself to his next. Luckily, for he did want to eat dinner that night, she picked up the second. 'We begin with Whitman and Dickinson tomorrow, and I'm hoping that the quotation will serve to pacify a few of the more horrible students in the class.'

'*Il piccolo marchesino?*' he asked, slighting, with the use of the diminutive, Vittorio, heir apparent to Marchese Francesco Bruscoli. Vittorio, it seemed, had been persuaded to terminate his attendance at the universities of Bologna, Padua and Ferrara, and had, six months ago, ended up at Cà Foscari, attempting to take a degree in English, not because he had any interest in or enthusiasm for literature – indeed, for anything that resembled the written word – but simply because the English nannies who had raised him had made him fluent in that language.

'He's such a dirty-minded little pig,' Paola said vehemently. 'Really vicious.'

'What's he done now?'

'Oh, Guido, it's not what he does. It's what he says, and the way he says it. Communists, abortion, gays. Any of those subjects just has to come up and he's all over them, like slime, talking about how glorious it is that Communism's been defeated in Europe, that abortion is a sin against God, and gays—' She waved a hand towards the window, as if asking the roofs to understand. 'My God, he thinks they should all be rounded up and put in concentration camps, and anyone with AIDS should be sequestered. There are times when I

83

want to hit him,' she said, with another wave of her hand but ending, she realized, weakly.

'How do these subjects come up in a literature class, Paola?'

'They rarely do,' she admitted. 'But I hear about him from some of the other professors.' She turned to Brunetti and asked, 'You don't know him, do you?'

'No, but I know his father.'

'What's he like?'

'Pretty much the same. Charming, rich, hand-some. And utterly vicious.'

'That's what's so dangerous about him. He's handsome and very rich, and many of the students would kill to be seen with a *marchese*, regardless of what a little shit he is. So they ape him and repeat his opinions.'

'But why are you so bothered about him now?'

'Because tomorrow I begin with Whitman and Dickinson, I told you.'

Brunetti knew they were poets; had read the first and not liked him, found Dickinson difficult but, when he understood, wonderful. He shook his head from side to side, asking for an explanation.

'Whitman was gay, and Dickinson probably was, too.'

'And that sort of thing is not on *il marchesino*'s list of acceptable behaviour?'

'To say the very least,' replied Paola. 'That's why I want to begin with that quotation.'

'You think something like that will make any difference?'

'No, probably not,' she admitted, sitting down in her chair and beginning to straighten out some of the mess on her desk.

Brunetti sat in the armchair against the wall and stretched his feet out in front of him. Paola continued closing books and placing magazines on neat piles. 'I had a taste of the same today,' he said.

She stopped what she was doing and looked across at him. 'What do you mean?'

'Someone who didn't like gays.' He paused and then added, 'Patta.'

Paola closed her eyes for second, then asked, 'What was it?'

'Do you remember Dottoressa Lynch?'

'The American? The one who's in China?'

'Yes to the first, and no to the second. She's back here. I saw her today, in the hospital.'

'What's the matter?' Paola asked with real concern, hands grown suddenly still over her books.

'Someone beat her. Well, two men, really. They went to her place on Sunday, said they had come on business, and when she let them in, they beat her.'

'How badly is she hurt?'

'Not as badly as she could have been, thank God.'

'What does that mean, Guido?'

'She's got a cracked jaw, and a few broken ribs, and some bad scrapes.'

'If you think that's not bad, I tremble to think of what would be,' Paola said, then asked, 'Who did it? Why?'

'It might have something to do with the museum, but it might have something to do with what my American colleagues insist on calling her "lifestyle".'

'You mean that she's a lesbian?'

'Yes.'

'But that's insane.'

'Agreed. But none the less true.'

'Is it starting here?' Clearly, rhetorical. 'I thought that sort of thing happened only in America.'

'Progress, my dear.'

'But what makes you say that's the reason?'

'She said that the men knew about her and Signora Petrelli.'

Paola could never resist a set-up. 'Before she went back to China a few years ago, you would have had trouble finding anyone in Venice who didn't know about her and Signora Petrelli.'

More literal-minded, Brunetti protested, 'That's an exaggeration.'

'Well, perhaps. But there was certainly talk at the time,' Paola insisted.

Having corrected Paola once, Brunetti was content to leave it. Besides, he was growing hungrier, and he wanted his dinner.

'Why wasn't it in the papers?' she suddenly asked.

'It happened on Sunday. I didn't find out about it until this morning and then only because someone noticed her name on the report. It had been given to the uniformed branch and was being treated as routine.'

'Routine?' she repeated in astonishment. 'Guido, things like that don't happen here.'

Brunetti chose not to repeat his remark about progress, and Paola, realizing he was going to offer no explanation, turned back to the desk. 'I can't spend any more time looking for it. I'll have to think of something else.'

'Why don't you lie?' Brunetti suggested casually.

Paola snapped her head up to look at him and asked, 'What do you mean, lie?'

It seemed clear enough to him. 'Just think of a place in one of the books where it might have been and tell them that's where it is.'

'But what if they've read the book?'

'He wrote a lot of letters, didn't he?' Brunetti knew full well that he had: the letters had gone to Paris with them two years ago.

'And if they ask what letter?'

He refused to answer so stupid a question.

'To Edith Wharton, 26 July 1906,' she supplied immediately, putting into her voice the tone of absolute certainty that Brunetti recognized as always sustaining her in her most outrageous inventions.

'Sounds good to me,' he said and smiled.

'Me, too.' She closed the last book, looked at her watch, then up at him. 'It's almost seven. Gianni had some beautiful lamb chops today. Come and have a glass of wine and talk to me while I cook them.'

Dante, Brunetti recalled, punished the Evil Counsellors by enclosing them within enormous tongues of flame, where they were to twist and burn for eternity. There had been, he remembered, no mention of lamb chops.

Chapter Seven

WHEN THE STORY finally appeared the following day, it carried the headline 'Attempted Robbery in Cannaregio' and gave the briefest of accounts. Brett was described as an expert on Chinese art who had returned to Venice to seek funding from the Italian government for the excavations in Xian, where she co-ordinated the work of Chinese and Western archaeologists. There was a brief description of the two men, who had been foiled in their attempt by an unidentified '*amica*' who happened to be in the apartment with Dottoressa Lynch at the time. When he read it, Brunetti wondered at the identity of the '*amico*' who had suppressed the use of Flavia's name. It might well have been anyone, from the mayor of Venice to the director of La Scala, attempting to protect his chosen prima donna from the possibility of harmful publicity.

When he got to work, he stopped in Signorina Elettra's office on the way up to his own. The freesias were gone today, replaced by a luminous spray of calla lilies. She looked up when he came in and said immediately, without even bothering to say good morning, 'Sergeant Vianello asked me to tell you that there was nothing in Mestre. He said he spoke to some people there, but no one knew anything about the attack. And,' she continued, looking down at a paper on her desk, 'no one has been admitted to any of the hospitals in the area with a cut on his arm.' Before he could ask, she said, 'And nothing from Rome yet about the fingerprints.'

Faced with dead ends on every side, Brunetti decided it was time to see what else there was to be learned about Semenzato. 'You used to work at Banca d'Italia, didn't you, signorina?'

'Yes, sir, I did.'

'And you still have friends there?'

'And in other banks.' Not one to hide her light, Signorina Elettra.

'Do you think you could spin a web of gossamer with your computer and see what you can find out about Francesco Semenzato? Bank accounts, stock holdings, investments of any sort.'

Her response was a smile so broad as to leave Brunetti wondering at the exact velocity with which news travelled at the Questura.

'Of course, Dottore. Nothing easier. And would you like me to check on the wife, as well? I believe she's Sicilian.'

'Yes, the wife as well.'

Even before he could ask, she volunteered.

'They've been having trouble with their phone lines, so it might take me until tomorrow afternoon.'

'Are you at liberty to reveal your source, signorina?'

'Someone who has to wait until the director of the bank's computer system goes home,' was all she revealed.

'Very well,' Brunetti said, content with her explanation. 'I'd like you to check it with Interpol in Geneva, as well. You can contact—'

She cut him short, but she smiled as she did it. 'I know the address, sir, and I think I know whom to contact.'

'Heinegger?' Brunetti asked, naming the captain in charge of the office of financial investigation.

'Yes, Heinegger,' she answered and repeated his address and fax number.

'How did you learn that so quickly, signorina?' he asked, honestly surprised.

'I dealt with him often in my last job,' she replied blandly.

Though he was a policeman, the connection between Banca d'Italia and Interpol was one he didn't want to ask about just then. 'So you know what to do,' was all he could think of to say.

'I'll bring you Heinegger's reply as soon as it comes in,' she said, turning to her computer.

'Yes, thank you. Good morning, signorina.' He turned and left the office, but not before taking another look at the flowers, framed against the open window behind them.

The rain of the last few days had stopped, taking with it the immediate threat of *acqua alta* and bringing, instead, crystalline skies, so there was no chance of catching Lele at home: he would be somewhere in the city, painting. Brunetti decided to go to the hospital and continue his questioning of Brett, for he still had no clear idea of the reasons that had brought her back halfway across the world.

When he entered the hospital room, he thought for a moment that Signorina Elettra had been at work here as well, for masses of flowers exploded from every available flat surface. Roses, iris, lilies and orchids flooded the room with their mingled sweetness, and the wastepaper basket overflowed with crumpled wrapping paper from Fantin and Biancat, the two florists where Venetians were most likely to go. He noticed that Americans, or at least foreigners, had also sent flowers: no Italian would have sent a sick person those immense bouquets of chrysanthemums, flowers used exclusively for funerals and for the tombs of the departed. He realized that it made him uncomfortable to be in a hospital room with them but dismissed the sensation as the worst sort of superstition.

Both women were, as he had either expected or hoped, in the room, Brett propped up against the raised back of the bed, head cushioned between two pillows, and Flavia sitting in a chair at her side. Spread out on the surface of the bed between them were a number of coloured sketches of women in long, elaborate gowns. Each wore a diadem that surrounded her head in a jewelled sunburst. Brett glanced up from the drawings when he came in, and her lips moved minimally; the smile was all in her eyes. Flavia, after a moment, and at a reduced temperature, did the same.

'Good morning,' he said to both of them and glanced down at the pictures. The wave-patterned border at the hem of two of the dresses made them look oriental. But, instead of the usual dragons, the dresses were patterned with abstract splashes that hurled violent colours at one another and yet managed to create harmony, not dissonance.

'What are those?' he asked with real curiosity and, as soon as he spoke, realized he should have been asking Brett how she was.

Flavia answered him. 'Sketches for the new *Turandot* at La Scala.'

'Then you are going to sing it?' he asked. The press had been buzzing with this for weeks, even though the opening night was almost a full year away. The soprano whose name had been 'hinted at' as the one 'rumoured to be' the 'possible choice' – this was the way things were expressed at La Scala – had said she was interested in the possibility and would consider it, which clearly meant she wasn't, and wouldn't. Flavia Petrelli, who had never sung the role, was named as the next possibility, and she had issued, just two weeks ago, a statement to the press saying she refused absolutely even to consider the idea, as close to a formal acceptance as a soprano could be expected to come.

'You should know better than to try to solve the riddles of *Turandot*,' Flavia said, voice falsely light, letting him know he had seen something he was not to have seen. She leaned forward and gathered the drawings together. Quickly translated, both messages meant he was to say nothing about this.

'How are you?' he finally asked Brett.

Though her jaws were no longer wired together, Brett's smile was still faintly idiotic, lips separate from one another and pulling up at the corners. 'Better. I can go home in a day.'

'Two,' Flavia corrected.

'A day or two,' Brett amended. Seeing him standing there, still in his coat, she said, 'Excuse me. Please sit down.' She pointed to a chair that stood behind Flavia. He picked it up and placed it beside the bed, folded his coat over the back and sat.

'Do you feel like talking about what happened?' he asked, encompassing both of them in the question.

Puzzled, Brett asked, 'But we talked about this before, didn't we?'

Brunetti nodded and asked, 'What did they say to you? Exactly. Can you remember?'

'Exactly?' she repeated, confused.

'Did they say enough to let you know where they came from?' Brunetti prompted.

'I see,' Brett said. She closed her eyes and put herself momentarily back in the hall of her apartment, remembered the men, their faces and voices. 'Sicilian. At least the one who hit me was. I'm less sure about the other. He said very little.' She looked at Brunetti. 'What difference does it make?'

'It might help us identify them.'

'I certainly hope so,' Flavia broke in, giving no clues whether she spoke in reproach or hope.

'Did either of you recognize any of the photos?' he asked, though he was sure the officer who had brought over the photos of men who matched the descriptions the two women had given would have told him if they had.

Flavia shook her head, and Brett said, 'No.'

'You said they warned you not to go to a meeting with Dottor Semenzato. Then you said something about ceramics from the China exhibition. Do you mean the one that was here, at the Doge's Palace?'

'Yes.'

'I remember,' Brunetti said. 'You organized it, didn't you?' he asked.

She forgot and nodded, then rested her head back on the pillows and waited a moment for the world to stop spinning. When it did, she said, 'Some pieces came from our dig, in Xian. The Chinese chose me as liaison. I know people.' Even though the wires were gone, she still moved her jaw gingerly; a deep buzz still underlay everything she said and filled her ears with its constant whine.

Flavia interrupted and explained for her. 'The show opened first in New York and then went to London. Brett went to the New York opening and then back to close it down for shipment to London. But she had to go back to China before the London opening. Something happened at the dig.' Turning to Brett, she asked, 'What was it, *cara*?'

'Treasure.'

That, apparently, was enough to remind Flavia. 'They'd just opened up the passage into the burial chamber, so they called Brett in London and told her she had to go back to oversee the excavation of the tomb.'

'Who was in charge of the opening here?'

This time, Brett answered. 'I was, I got back from China three days before it closed in London. And then I came here with it to set it up.' She closed her eyes then, and Brunetti thought she was tired with the talking, but she opened them immediately and continued. 'I left before the exhibition closed, so they sent the pieces back to China.'

'They?' Brunetti asked.

Brett glanced across at Flavia before she answered, then said, 'Dottor Semenzato was here, and my assistant came from China to close the show and send everything back.'

'You weren't in charge?' he asked.

Again, she looked at Flavia before answering. 'No, I couldn't be here. I didn't see the pieces again until this winter.'

'Four years later?' Brunetti asked.

'Yes,' she said and waved her hand as if that would help explain. 'The shipment got held up on the way back to China and then in Beijing. Red tape. It ended up in a customs warehouse in Shanghai for two years. The pieces from Xian didn't get back until two months ago.' Brunetti watched her consider her words, searching for a way to explain. 'They weren't the same. Copies. Not the soldier or the jade shroud: they were the originals. But the ceramics, I knew it, but I couldn't prove it until I tested them, and I couldn't do that in China.'

He had learned enough from Lele's offended glance not to ask her how she knew they were false. She just knew, and that was that. Prevented from asking a qualitative question, he could still ask a quantitative one. 'How many pieces were fake?'

'Three. Maybe four or five. And that's only from the dig in Xian where I am.'

'What about other pieces from the show?' he asked.

'I don't know. That's not the sort of question you can ask in China.'

Through all of this, Flavia sat quietly, turning her head back and forth as they spoke. Her lack of surprise told him that she already knew about this.

'What have you done?' Brunetti asked.

'So far, nothing.'

Given the fact that this conversation was taking place in a hospital room and she was speaking through swollen lips, this seemed, to Brunetti, something of an understatement. 'Who did you tell about it?'

'Only Semenzato. I wrote to him from China, three months ago, and told him some of the pieces sent back were copies. I asked to see him.'

'And what did he say?'

'Nothing. He didn't answer my letter. I waited three weeks, then I tried to call him, but that's not easy, from China. So I came here to talk to him.'

Just like that? You can't get through on the phone, so you jump on a plane and fly halfway around the world to talk to someone?

As if she had read his thoughts, she answered. 'It's my reputation. I'm responsible for those pieces.'

Flavia broke in here. 'The pieces could have been switched when they got back to China. It didn't have to happen here. And you're hardly responsible for what happened when they got there.' There was real animosity in Flavia's voice. Brunetti found it interesting that she sounded jealous, of all things, of a country.

Her tone wasn't lost on Brett, who answered sharply, 'It doesn't matter where it happened; it happened.'

To divert them both and remembering what Lele had said about 'knowing' that something was genuine or false, Brunetti the policeman asked, 'Do you have proof?'

'Yes,' Brett began, voice more slurred than it had been when he arrived.

Hearing that, Flavia interrupted them both and turned to Brunetti. 'I think that's enough, Dottor Brunetti.'

He looked across at Brett, and he was forced to agree. The bruises on her face seemed darker now than when he had come in, and she had sunk lower on the pillows. She smiled and closed her eyes.

He didn't insist. 'I'm sorry, signora,' he said to Flavia. 'But it can't wait.'

'At least until she's home,' Flavia said.

He glanced at Brett, to see what she thought of this, but she was asleep, head turned to one side, mouth slack and open. 'Tomorrow?'

Flavia hesitated, then gave him a reluctant 'Yes'.

He stood and took his coat from the chair. Flavia came as far as the door with him. 'She's not just worried about her reputation, you know,' she said. 'I don't understand it, but she needs to see that these pieces get back to China,' she added, shaking her head in apparent confusion.

Because Flavia Petrelli was one of the best singing actresses of her day, Brunetti knew it was impossible to tell when the actress spoke and when the woman, but this sounded like the second. Assuming that it was, he answered, 'I know that. I think it's one of the reasons I want to find out about this.'

'And the other reasons?' she asked suspiciously.

'I won't work any better if I'm doing it out of personal motives, signora,' he said, signalling the end of their brief personal truce. He pulled on his coat and let himself out of the room. Flavia stood for a moment staring across at Brett, then returned to her seat beside the bed and picked up the pile of costume drawings.

Chapter Eight

LEAVING THE hospital, Brunetti noticed that the sky had darkened, and a sharp wind had risen, sweeping across the city from the south. The air was heavy and damp, presaging rain, and that meant they might be awakened in the night by the shrill blast of the sirens. He hated *acqua alta* with the passion that all Venetians felt for it, felt an anticipatory rage at the gaping tourists who would cluster together on the raised wooden boards, giggling, pointing, snapping pictures and blocking decent people who just wanted to get to work or do their shopping so they could get inside where it was dry and be rid of the bother, the mess, the constant irritation that the unstoppable waters brought to the city. Already calculating, he realized that the water would affect him only on the way to and from work, when he had to pass through Campo San Bartolomeo at the foot of the Rialto Bridge. Luckily, the area around the Questura was high enough to be free of all but the worst flooding.

He pulled up the collar of his coat, wishing he had thought to wear a scarf that morning, and hunched his head down, propelled from behind by the wind. As he crossed behind the statue of Colleoni, the first fat drops splattered on the pavement in front of him. The only advantage of the wind was that it drove the rain at a sharp diagonal, keeping one side of the narrow *calle* dry, protected by the roofs. Those wiser than he had thought to bring umbrellas and walked protected by them, ignoring anyone who had to dodge around or under them.

By the time he got to the Questura, the shoulders of his coat were wet through and his shoes soaked. In his office, he removed his coat and put it on a hanger, then hung it on the curtain rod that ran in front of the window above the radiator. Anyone looking into the room from across the canal would see, perhaps, a man who had hanged himself in his own office. If they worked in the Questura, their first impulse would no doubt be to count the floors, looking to see if it was Patta's window.

Brunetti found a single sheet of paper on his desk, a report from Interpol in Geneva saying that they had no information about and no record of Francesco Semenzato. Below that neatly typed message, however, there was a brief handwritten note: 'Rumours here, nothing definite. I'll ask around.' And below that was a scrawled signature he recognized as belonging to Piet Heinegger.

His phone rang late that afternoon. It was Lele, saying that he had managed to get in touch with a few friends of his, including the one in Burma. No one had been willing to say anything about Semenzato directly, but Lele had learned that the museum director was believed to be involved in the antiques business. No, not as a buyer but as a seller. One of the men he had spoken to said he had heard that Semenzato had invested in an antique shop, but he knew no more than that, not where it was or who the official owner might be.

'Sounds like that would create a conflict of interest,' Brunetti said, 'buying from his partner with the museum's money.'

'He wouldn't be the only one,' Lele muttered, but Brunetti let the remark lie. 'There's another thing,' the artist added.

'What?'

'When I mentioned stolen art works, one of them said he'd heard rumours about an important collector in Venice.'

'Semenzato?'

'No,' Lele answered. 'I didn't ask, but the word is out that I'm curious about him, so I'm sure my friend would have told me if it was Semenzato.'

'Did he say who it was?'

'No. He didn't know. But the rumour is that it's a gentleman from the South.' Lele said this as if he believed it impossible for any gentleman to come from the South.

'But no name?'

'No, Guido. But I'll keep asking around.'

'Thanks. I appreciate this, Lele. I couldn't do this myself.'

'No, you couldn't,' Lele said evenly. Then, not even bothering to brush off Brunetti's thanks, Lele said, 'I'll call you if I hear anything else,' and hung up.

Believing that he had done enough for the afternoon and not wanting to be trapped on this side of the city by the arrival of *acqua alta*, Brunetti went home early and had two quiet hours to himself before Paola got back from the university. When she got home, soaked by the increasing intensity of the rain, she said that she had used the quotation, given the spurious attribution, but still the dreaded *marchese* had managed to spoil it, suggesting that a writer such as James, who was supposed to have such a good reputation, certainly could have avoided such simple-minded redundancies. Brunetti listened as she explained, surprised at how much he had come, over the last months, to dislike this young man he had never met. Food and wine tempered Paola's mood, as they always did, and when Raffi volunteered to do the dishes, she radiated contentment and well-being.

They were in bed by ten, she deeply asleep over a particularly infelicitous example of student writing and he deeply engrossed in a new translation of Suetonius. He had just reached the passage describing those little boys swimming in Tiberius' pool at Capri when the phone rang.

'*Pronto*,' he answered, hoping it wouldn't be police business but knowing that, at ten to eleven, it probably was.

'Commissario, this is Monico.' Sergeant Monico, Brunetti recalled, was in charge of the night shift that week.

'What is it, Monico?'

'I think we've got a murder, sir.'

'Where?'

'Palazzo Ducale.'

'Who is it?' he asked, though he knew.

'The director, sir.'

'Semenzato?'

'Yes, sir.'

'What happened?'

'It looks like a break-in. The cleaning woman found him about ten minutes ago and went screaming down to the guards. They went back up to the office and saw him, and they called us.'

'What have you done?' He dropped the book on to the floor at the side of the bed and began looking around the room to see where he had left his clothes.

'We called Vice-Questore Patta, but his wife said he wasn't there, and she has no idea of how to get in touch with him.' Either of which, Brunetti

105

reflected, could be a lie. 'So I decided to call you, sir.'

'Did they tell you what happened, the guards?'

'Yes, sir. The man I spoke to said there was a lot of blood, and it looked like he'd been hit on the head.'

'Was he dead when the cleaning lady found him?'

'I think so, sir. The guards said he was dead when they got there.'

'All right,' Brunetti said, flipping back the covers. 'I'll go over there now. Send whoever's there – who is it tonight?'

'Vianello, sir. He was here on night shift with me, so he went over as soon as the call came in.'

'Good. Call Dottor Rizzardi and ask him to meet me there.'

'Yes, sir, I was going to call him as soon as I spoke to you.'

'Good,' Brunetti said, swinging his feet out and putting them on the floor. 'I should be there in about twenty minutes. We'll need a team to photograph and take prints.'

'Yes, sir. I'll call Pavese and Foscolo as soon as I've spoken to Dottor Rizzardi.'

'All right. Twenty minutes,' Brunetti said and hung up. Was it possible to be shocked and still not be surprised? A violent death, and only four days after Brett was attacked with similar brutality. While he pulled on his clothing and tied his shoes, he warned himself against jumping to conclusions. He walked around to Paola's side of the bed, leaned down, and shook her gently by the shoulder.

She opened her eyes and looked up at him over the top of the glasses she had begun, that year, to use for reading. She wore a ragged old flannel dressing gown she had bought in Scotland more than ten years ago and, pulled over it, an Irish knit cardigan her parents had given her for Christmas almost as long ago. Seeing her like that, momentarily confused by his having pulled her from her first deep sleep and peering myopically at him, he thought how much she looked like the homeless and apparently mad women who passed their winter nights in the railway station. Feeling traitorous for the thought, he leaned into the circle of light created by her reading lamp and bent down to kiss her forehead.

'Was that the sovereign call of duty?' she asked, immediately awake.

'Yes. Semenzato. The cleaning woman found him in his office at the Palazzo Ducale.'

'Dead?'

'Yes.'

'Murdered?'

'It looks that way.'

She removed her glasses and placed them on the papers that spilled across the covers in front of her. 'Have you sent a guard to the American's room?'

she asked, leaving it to him to follow the swift logic of what she said.

'No,' he admitted, 'but I will as soon as I get to the Palazzo. I don't think they'd risk two in the same night, but I'll send a man over.' How easily 'they' had come into existence, created by his refusal to believe in coincidence and Paola's to believe in human goodness.

'Who called?' she asked.

'Monico.'

'Good,' she said, recognizing the name and familiar with the man. 'I'll call him and tell him about the guard.'

'Thanks,' he said. 'Don't wait up. I'm afraid this will take a long time.'

'So will this,' she said, leaning forward and gathering up the papers.

He bent again and this time kissed her on the lips. She returned his kiss and turned it into a real one. He straightened up and she surprised him by wrapping her arms around his waist and pressing her face into his stomach. She said something that was too mumbled to understand. Gently, he stroked her hair, but his mind was on Semenzato and Chinese ceramics.

She pulled herself away and reached for her glasses. Putting them on, she said, 'Remember to take your boots.'

Chapter Nine

WHEN COMMISSARIO Brunetti of the Venice police arrived at the scene of the murder of the director of the most important museum in the city, he carried in his right hand a white plastic shopping bag which bore in red letters the name of a super-market. Inside the bag were a pair of size ten rubber boots, black, which he had bought at Standa three years before. The first thing he did when he arrived at the guards' station at the bottom of the staircase that led up to the museum was hand the bag to the guard he found there, saying he'd pick it up when he left.

As he placed the bag on the floor beside his desk, the guard said, 'One of your men is upstairs, sir.'

'Good. More will be coming soon. And the coroner. Has the press showed up yet?'

'No, sir.'

'What about the cleaning woman?'

'They had to take her home, sir. She couldn't stop crying after she saw him.'

'That bad, is it?'

The guard nodded. 'There's an awful lot of blood.'

A head wound, Brunetti remembered. Yes, there'd be a lot of blood. 'She's bound to make a stir when she gets there, and that means someone will call *Il Gazzetino*. Try to keep the reporters down here when they arrive, will you?'

'I'll try, sir, but I don't know if it'll do any good.'

'Keep them here,' Brunetti said.

'Yes, sir.'

Brunetti looked down the long corridor that led to a flight of stairs at the end. 'Is the office up there?' he asked.

'Yes, sir. Turn left at the top. You'll see the light at the end of the passage. I think your man is in the office.'

Brunetti turned away and started down the corridor. His steps echoed eerily, reverberating back at him from both sides and from the staircase at the end. Cold, the penetrating damp cold of winter, seeped out from the pavement below him and from the brick walls of the corridor. Behind him, he heard the sharp clang of metal on stone, but no one called out, so he continued down the corridor. The night mist had set in, painting a slippery film of condensation on the broad stone steps under his feet.

At the top, he turned left and made towards the light pouring from an open door at the end of the passage. Halfway there, he called out, 'Vianello?' Instantly, the sergeant appeared at the door, dressed in a heavy woollen overcoat, from under the bottom of which protruded a pair of bright yellow rubber boots.

'*Buona sera*, signore,' he said, and raised a hand in a gesture that was part salute, part greeting.

'*Buona sera*, Vianello,' Brunetti said. 'What's it like in there?'

Vianello's lined face remained impassive when he answered, 'Pretty bad, sir. It looks like there was a struggle: the place is a mess, chairs turned over, lamps knocked down. He was a big man, so I'd say there had to be two of them. But that's just first impressions. I'm sure the lab boys can tell us more.' He stepped back as he spoke, leaving room for Brunetti to follow him inside.

It was just as Vianello said: a floor lamp pitched forward against the desk, its glass dome shattered across the surface; a chair sprawled on its side behind the desk; a silk carpet lying in a bunched heap in front of the desk, its long fringe caught around the ankle of the man who lay dead on the floor beside it. He lay on his stomach, one arm trapped under the weight of his body, the other flung out ahead of him, fingers cupped upward, as if already begging mercy at the gate of heaven.

Brunetti looked at his head, at the grotesque halo of blood that surrounded it, and he quickly looked away. But wherever his eye rested, he saw

111

blood: drops of it had fallen on the desk, a thin trickle of it led from the desk to the carpet, and more of it covered the cobalt blue brick which lay on the floor half a metre from the dead man.

'The guard downstairs said it's Dottor Semenzato,' Vianello explained into the silence that radiated out from Brunetti. 'The cleaning lady found him at about ten thirty. The office was locked from the outside, but she had a key, so she came in to check that the windows were closed and to clean the room, and she found him here. Like that.'

Brunetti still said nothing, merely moved over to one of the windows and looked down into the courtyard of the Palazzo Ducale. All was quiet; the statues of the giants continued to guard the staircase; not even a cat moved to disturb the moonlit scene.

'How long have you been here?' Brunetti asked.

Vianello shot back his cuff and looked at his watch. 'Eighteen minutes, sir. I touched his pulse, but it was gone, and he was cold. I'd say he'd been dead at least a couple of hours, but the doctor can tell us better.'

From off to the left, Brunetti heard a siren shriek out and shatter the tranquillity of the night, and for a moment he thought it was the lab team, arriving in a boat and being stupid about it. But the siren rose in pitch, its insistent whine ever louder and more strident, and then it wailed its slow way down to the original note. It was the siren at San Marco, calling out to the sleeping city the news that the waters were rising: *acqua alta* had begun.

The noise of their actual arrival camouflaged by the siren, the two men of the lab crew set their equipment down in the hall outside the room. Pavese, the photographer, stuck his head into the room and saw the dead man on the floor. Apparently unmoved by what he saw, he called across to the other two, voice raised to be heard above the siren, 'You want a whole set, Commissario?'

Brunetti turned from the window at the sound of the voice and walked over towards him, careful not to go near the body until it had been photographed and the floor around it checked for fibres and hairs or possible scuff marks. He wondered if this caution served any real purpose: Semenzato's body had been approached by too many people, and the scene was already contaminated.

'Yes, and as soon as you're done with them, see what there is in the way of fibres and hairs, then we'll have a look.'

Pavese displayed no irritation at having his superior tell him to do the obvious and asked, 'Do you want a separate set of the head?'

'Yes.'

The photographer busied himself with his equipment. Foscolo, the second member of the team, had already assembled the heavy tripod and was attaching the camera to it. Pavese bent down and rummaged in his equipment bag, pushing aside rolls of film and slim packets of filters, and finally pulled out a portable flash that trailed a heavy electrical cord. He handed the flash to Foscolo and picked up the tripod. His quick professional glance at the body had been enough. 'I'll get a couple of the whole room from here, Luca, then from the other side. There's an electrical outlet under the window. When I'm done with the shot of the entire room, we'll set up there, between the window and the head. I want to get a few of the whole body, then we'll switch to the Nikon and do the head. I think the angle from the left would be better.' He paused for a moment, considering. 'We won't need the filters. The flash is enough to get the blood.'

Brunetti and Vianello waited outside the door, through which burst the intermittent glow of the flash. 'You think they used that brick?' Vianello finally asked.

Brunetti nodded. 'You saw his head.'

'They wanted to make sure, didn't they?'

Brunetti thought of Brett's face and suggested, 'Or perhaps they liked doing it.'

'I hadn't thought of that,' Vianello said. 'I suppose it's possible.'

A few minutes later, Pavese stuck his head out. 'We're finished with the photos, Dottore.'

'When will you have them?' Brunetti asked.

114

'This afternoon, about four, I'd say.'

Brunetti's acknowledgement of this was cut off by the arrival of Ettore Rizzardi, *medico legale*, there to represent the state in declaring the evident, that the man was dead, and then to suggest the probable cause of death, in this case not hard to determine.

Like Vianello, he was wearing rubber boots, though his were a conservative black and came only to the hem of his overcoat. 'Good evening, Guido,' he said, as he came in. 'The man downstairs said it's Semenzato.' When Brunetti nodded, the doctor asked, 'What happened?'

Rather than answer, Brunetti stepped aside, allowing Rizzardi to see the unnatural posture of the body and the bright splashes of blood. The technicians had been at work, and now strips of bright yellow tape surrounded two rectangles the size of phone books in which faint scuff marks were visible.

'Can we touch him?' Brunetti asked Foscolo, who was now busy sprinkling black powder on the surface of Semenzato's desk.

The technician exchanged a quick glance with his partner, who was placing tape around the blue brick. Pavese nodded.

Rizzardi approached the body first. He set his bag down on the seat of a chair, opened it, and removed a pair of thin rubber gloves. He slipped them on, crouched beside the body, and stretched his hand towards the dead man's neck, but, seeing the blood that covered Semenzato's head, he changed his mind and reached, instead, for the outflung wrist. The flesh he touched was cold, the blood inside it for ever stilled. Automatically, Rizzardi shot back his starched cuff and looked at the time.

The cause of death was not far to seek: two deep indentations penetrated the side of his head, and there seemed to be a third on his forehead, though Semenzato's hair had fallen forward in death to cover it partially. Bending closer, Rizzardi could see jagged pieces of bone within one of the holes, just behind the ear.

Rizzardi dropped on to both knees to get greater leverage and reached under the body to shift it over on to its back. The third indentation was now clearly visible, the flesh around it bruised and blue. Rizzardi reached down and lifted first one dead hand and then the other. 'Guido, look at this,' he said, indicating the back of the right hand. Brunetti knelt beside him and looked at the back of Semenzato's hand. The skin on the knuckles was scraped raw, and one of the fingers was swollen and bent brokenly to one side.

'He tried to defend himself,' Rizzardi said, then looked down the length of the body that lay below him. 'How tall would you say he is, Guido?'

'One-ninety, certainly taller than either of us.'

'And heavier, too,' Rizzardi added. 'There'd have to have been two of them.'

Brunetti grunted in agreement.

'I'd say the blows came from the front, so he wasn't surprised by them, not if he was hit with that,' Rizzardi said, pointing to the bright blue brick that lay inside its taped rectangle less than a metre from the body. 'What about noise?' Rizzardi asked.

'There's a television in the guards' office downstairs,' Brunetti answered. 'It wasn't on when I came in.'

'I should think not,' Rizzardi said, getting to his feet. He stripped the gloves from his hands and stuffed them carelessly in the pocket of his overcoat. 'That's all I can do tonight. If your boys can get him out to San Michele for me, I'll take a closer look tomorrow morning. But it seems pretty clear to me. Three hard blows to the head with the corner of that brick. Wouldn't take more than that.'

Vianello, who had been silent through all of this, suddenly asked, 'Would it have been quick, Dottore?'

Before he answered, Rizzardi looked down at the body of the dead man. 'It would depend on where they hit him first. And how hard. It's possible that he could have fought them off, but not for long. I'll check to see if there's anything under his nails. My guess is that it was fast, but I'll see what shows up.'

Vianello nodded and Brunetti said, 'Thanks, Ettore. I'll have them take him out tonight.'

'Not to the hospital, remember. To San Michele.'

'Of course,' Brunetti answered, wondering if his insistence meant some new chapter in the doctor's on-going battle with the directors of the Ospedale Civile.

'I'll say goodnight then, Guido. I should have something for you by tomorrow afternoon, but I don't think there are going to be any surprises here.'

Brunetti agreed. The physical causes of violent death seldom revealed secrets: they lay, if anywhere, in the motive.

Rizzardi exchanged a nod with Vianello and turned to go. Suddenly he turned back and looked down at Brunetti's feet. 'Didn't you wear boots?' he asked with real concern.

'I left them downstairs.'

'Good thing you brought them. It was already way above my ankles in Calle della Mandola when I came. Lazy bastards hadn't got the boards up yet, so I'm going to have to go back to Rialto to get home. It'll be above my knees by now.'

'Why don't you take the Number One and get off at Sant'Angelo?' Brunetti suggested. Rizzardi lived, he knew, by the Cinema Rossini, and he could get there quickly from that boat stop without having to use Calle della Mandola, one of the lowest parts of the city.

Rizzardi looked at his watch and made quick

calculations. 'No. The next one leaves in three minutes. I'll never make it. And then I'd have to wait twenty minutes at this time of night. Might as well walk. Besides, who knows if they've bothered to put the boards up in the Piazza?' He started towards the door, but his real anger at this latest of the many inconveniences of living in Venice drew him back. 'We ought to elect a German mayor some time. Then things would work.'

Brunetti smiled and said goodnight and listened to the doctor's boots slapping on the stones of the corridor until the noise disappeared.

'I'll talk to the guards and have a look around downstairs, sir,' Vianello said and left the office.

Brunetti went over to Semenzato's desk. 'You finished with this?' he asked Pavese. The technician was busy with the telephone, which had ended up on the other side of the room, smashed against the wall with such force that it had gouged a chunk from the plaster before falling in pieces to the floor.

At Pavese's nod, Brunetti pulled open the first drawer. Pencils, pens, a roll of cellophane tape and a packet of mints.

The second held a box of stationery engraved with Semenzato's name and title and the name of the museum. Brunetti found it interesting that the name of the museum was in smaller type.

The bottom drawer held a few thick manila

119

files, which Brunetti pulled out. He opened the top file on the desk and began to leaf through the papers.

Fifteen minutes later, when the technicians called across the room that they were finished, Brunetti knew little more about Semenzato than he had when he came in, but he did know that the museum was planning to mount, two years from now, a major show of Renaissance drawings and had already arranged extensive borrowings from museums in Canada, Germany and the United States.

Brunetti replaced the files and closed the drawer. When he looked up, he saw a man standing in the doorway. Short and sturdily built, he wore a rubber parka which hung open to reveal the white jacket of the hospital staff. Below this, Brunetti saw that he wore high black rubber boots. 'You finished here, sir?' he asked, giving a vague nod in the direction of Semenzato's body. As he spoke, another man, similarly dressed and booted, appeared at his side, a rolled canvas stretcher balanced on his shoulder as casually as if it were a pair of oars.

A nod from one of the technicians confirmed this, and Brunetti said, 'Yes. You can take him now. Out to San Michele directly.'

'Not to the hospital?'

'No. Dottor Rizzardi wants him at San Michele.'

'Yes, sir,' the attendant said with a shrug. It was

all overtime for them, and San Michele was further than the hospital.

'Did you come through the Piazza?' Brunetti asked.

'Yes, sir. Our boat's over by the gondolas.'

'How high is it?'

'About thirty centimetres, I'd say. But the boards are up in the Piazza, so it wasn't too bad getting here. Which way are you going when you leave here, sir?'

'Over towards San Silvestro,' Brunetti answered. 'I wondered how bad Calle dei Fuseri is.'

The second attendant, taller and thinner, with wispy blond hair that stuck out under the edges of his watch cap, answered, 'It's always worse than the Piazza, and there weren't any boards there when I went through two hours ago, on the way to work.'

'We can go up the Grand Canal,' the first one said. 'We could drop you at San Silvestro,' he offered, smiling.

'That's very kind of you,' Brunetti said, returning his smile and, like them, not unaware of the existence of overtime. 'I've got to go back to the Questura,' he lied. 'And I've got my boots downstairs.' That was true enough, but even if he had not brought them, he would have refused their offer. He did not relish the company of the dead and would have preferred to ruin his shoes than to share his ride home with a corpse.

Vianello came back in then and reported that

there was nothing new to learn from the guards. One of them had admitted that they had been in the small office, watching television, when the cleaning lady came screaming down the stairs. And those steps, Vianello assured him, were the only access to this part of the museum.

They stayed until the body was removed, then waited in the corridor while the technicians locked the office and sealed it against unauthorized entry. The four of them went down the stairs together and stopped outside the open door of the guards' office. The guard who had been there when Brunetti came in looked up from reading *Quattro Ruote* when he heard them come in. It always surprised Brunetti that anyone who lived in a city where there were no cars would read an automobile magazine. Did some of his sea-locked fellow citizens dream of cars the way men in prison dreamed of women? In the midst of the absolute silence that reigned over Venice at night, did they long for the roar of traffic and the blare of horns? Perhaps, less fantastically, they wanted no more than the convenience of being able to drive home from the supermarket, park the car in front of the house and unload the groceries, rather than carry the heavy bags along crowded streets, up and down bridges, and then up the many flights of stairs that seemed, inevitably, to lurk in wait for all Venetians.

Recognizing Brunetti, he asked, 'Are you here for your boots, sir?'

'Yes.'

He reached under the desk to pull out the white shopping bag and handed it to Brunetti, who thanked him.

'Safe and sound,' the guard said and smiled again.

The director of the museum had just been beaten to death in his office and whoever did it had walked past the guards' station unseen, but at least Brunetti's boots were safe.

Chapter Ten

BECAUSE IT WAS after two when Brunetti got home that night, he slept until well past eight the next morning and woke only, and grudgingly, when Paola shook him lightly by the shoulder and told him coffee was beside him. He managed to fight off full consciousness for another few minutes, but then he smelled the coffee, gave up and seized the day. Paola had disappeared after bringing the coffee, a decision the wisdom of which had been taught to her over the years.

When he finished the coffee, he pushed back the covers and went to look out of the window. Rain. And he remembered that the moon had been almost full the night before, so that meant more *acqua alta* with the change of tide. He went down the corridor to the bathroom and took a long shower, trying to store up enough heat to last him the day. Back in the bedroom, he began to dress and, while knotting his tie, decided he had better wear a sweater under his jacket because the visits he had already planned to both Brett and

Lele would have him walking from one side of the city to the other. He opened the second drawer in the *armadio* and reached for his grey lambswool. Not finding it, he reached into the next drawer, then the one above it. Detective-like, he thought of the places where it could be, checked the remaining two, and then remembered that Raffi had borrowed the sweater last week. That meant, Brunetti was sure, that he would find it lying in a crumpled ball in the bottom of his son's closet or in a bunched heap at the back of a drawer. The recent improvement in his son's academic performance had not, alas, extended to habits of personal cleanliness or general neatness.

He went across the hall and, because the door was open, into his son's room. Raffi had already left for school, but Brunetti hoped he wasn't wearing the sweater. The more he thought about it, the more he wanted to wear that sweater, and the more irritated he became at being frustrated in that desire.

He opened the cupboard. Jackets, shirts, a ski parka, and on the floor assorted boots, tennis shoes and a pair of summer sandals. But no sweater. It wasn't draped over the chair, nor over the end of the bed. He opened the first drawer in the dresser and found an upheaval of underwear. The second held socks, none of them matching and, he feared, few of them clean. The third drawer looked more promising: it held a sweatshirt and two T-shirts that bore insignia Brunetti didn't bother to read. He wanted his sweater, not publicity for the rainforest. He pushed aside the second T-shirt, and his hand froze.

Lying below the T-shirts, half hidden, but lazily so, were two syringes, neatly wrapped in their sterile plastic wrappers. Brunetti felt his heartbeat quicken as he stared down at them. '*Madre di Dio*,' he said out loud and looked quickly over his shoulder, afraid that Raffi would come in and find his father searching his room. He pushed the T-shirts back over the needles and slipped the drawer closed.

Suddenly, he found himself remembering the Sunday afternoon, a decade ago, when he had gone to the Lido with Paola and the children. Raffi, running on the beach, had stepped on a piece of broken bottle and sliced open the sole of his foot. And Brunetti, mute in the face of his son's pain and his own aching love for him, had wrapped a towel around the cut, gathered him up in his arms and carried him, running all the way, the kilometre to the hospital that stood at the end of the beach. He had waited for two hours, dressed in his bathing suit and chilled to the bone by fear and the air conditioning, until a doctor came out and told him the boy was fine. Six stitches and crutches for a week, but he was fine.

What made Raffi do it? Was he too strict a father? He had never raised his hand to either child, seldom raised his voice; the memory of the violence of his own upbringing was enough to destroy any violent impulse he might have had towards them. Was he too busy with his work, too busy with the problems of society to worry about those of his own children? When was the last time he had helped either one with homework? And where did he get the drugs? And what was it? Please, let it not be heroin, not that.

Paola? She usually knew before he did what the kids were doing. Did she suspect? Could it be that she knew and hadn't told him? And if she didn't know, should he do the same, protect her from this?

He reached out an unsteady hand and lowered himself to the edge of Raffi's bed. He locked his hands together and stuck them between his knees, staring down at the floor. Vianello would know who sold drugs in this neighbourhood. Would Vianello tell him if he knew about Raffi? One of Raffi's shirts lay beside him on the bed. He reached out and pulled it towards him, pressed it to his face and smelled his son's odour, that same scent he had first smelled the day Paola came home from the hospital with Raffi and he pressed his face into the round belly of his naked son. His throat closed and he tasted salt.

He sat on the edge of the bed for a long time, remembering the past and shying away from any thought of the future beyond the conviction that he would have to tell Paola. Though he had already embraced his own guilt, he hoped she would deny it, assure him that he had been father enough to his two children. And what about Chiara? Did she know, or suspect? And what beyond that? He stood up at that thought and left the room, leaving the door open, as he had found it.

Paola sat on the sofa in the living room, feet propped up on the low marble table, reading that morning's paper. That meant she had already been out in the rain to get it.

He stood at the door and watched her turn a page. The radar of long marriage caused her to turn to him. 'Guido, will you make more coffee?' she asked and turned back to the paper.

'Paola,' he began. She registered the tone and lowered the paper to her lap. 'Paola,' he repeated, not knowing what he had to say or how to say this. 'I found two syringes in Raffi's room.'

She paused, waiting for him to say more, then picked up the paper and continued to read.

'Paola, did you hear what I said?'

'Hm?' she asked, head tilted back to read the headline at the top of the page.

'I said I found two syringes in Raffi's room. In the bottom of a drawer.' He moved towards her, possessed for an instant of the mad urge to rip the paper from her hands and hurl it to the floor.

'That's where they were, then,' she said, and turned the page.

He sat beside her on the sofa and, forcing the gesture to remain calm, placed his palm flat on the page in front of her and pushed the paper slowly on to her lap. 'What do you mean, "That's where they were"?' he asked, voice tight.

'Guido,' she asked, turning her full attention to him, now that the paper was gone, 'what's the matter with you? Don't you feel well?'

Entirely unaware of what he was doing, he contracted his hand into an angry fist, dragging the paper into a loose ball. 'I said I found two syringes in Raffi's room, Paola. Syringes. Don't you understand?'

She stared at him for a moment, eyes wide in confusion, and then she understood what the syringes meant to him. Their eyes locked, and he watched as Raffi's mother registered his own belief that their son was addicted to drugs. Her mouth contracted, her eyes opened wide, and then she put back her head and began to laugh. She laughed, exploded into peals of real mirth and fell away from him sideways on the sofa, tears filling her eyes. She wiped at them, but she couldn't stop laughing. 'Oh, Guido,' she said, hand to her mouth in a vain effort to stop herself. 'Oh, Guido, no, you can't be thinking that. Not drugs.' And she was gone in another fit of laughter.

Brunetti thought for a moment that this was the hysteria of real panic, but he knew Paola too well for that; this was the pure laughter of high comedy.

With a violent gesture, he grabbed the newspaper from her lap and hurled it to the floor. His rage sobered her instantly, and she pushed herself upright on the sofa.

'Guido. *I tarli*,' she said, as though that explained it all.

Was she drugged too? What did woodworm have to do with this?

'Guido,' she repeated, keeping her voice soft, her tone level, as if speaking to the dangerous or the mad. 'I told you last week. We've got wood-worm in the table in the kitchen. The legs are full of them. And the only way to get rid of them is to inject poison into the holes they leave. Remember, I asked you if you'd help me move it out on to the terrace the first sunny day we have, so the fumes won't kill us all?'

Yes, he remembered this, but vaguely. He hadn't been paying attention when she told him, but it came back now.

'I asked Raffi to get me the syringes and some rubber gloves so we can inject the poison into the table. I thought he'd forgotten them, but I suppose he just put them in his drawer. And then forgot to tell me he'd got them.' She reached out and placed her hand over his. 'It's all right, Guido. It isn't what you thought.'

He had to lean against the back of the sofa as a burning rush of relief swept over him. He rested his head back and closed his eyes. He wanted to laugh at the absurdity of it, wanted to be as free to make fun of his fear as Paola was, but that wasn't possible, not yet.

When he could finally speak, he turned to her and asked, 'Don't ever tell Raffi, please, Paola.'

She leaned towards him and placed her palm against his cheek, studying his face, and he thought she was going to promise, but then she collapsed helplessly on his chest, lost again to laughter.

The contact of her body freed him at last, and he began to laugh, beginning with a faint chuckle and a shake of his head, but then graduating into real laughter, shouts of it, wild hoots of relief and joy and pure delight. She tightened her arms around him and then inched her body up across his chest, seeking his lips with hers. Like a pair of adolescents, then, they made love there on the sofa, heedless of the clothes that ended up heaped on the floor below them, heaped with much the same abandon as were those in Raffi's cupboard.

Chapter Eleven

AT THE BOTTOM of the Rialto Bridge, he slipped under the covered passageway to the right of the statue of Goldoni, heading back towards SS. Giovanni e Paolo and Brett's apartment. He knew she was home because the officer who had sat outside her hospital room for a day and a half had reported back to the Questura when she checked herself out and returned to her apartment. No guard had been posted at her home because a uniformed policeman could not stand in one of the narrow *calli* of Venice without being asked by everyone who passed what he was doing there, nor could a detective who was not a resident of the neighbourhood stand around for more than half an hour without the Questura receiving phone calls reporting his suspicious presence. Non-Venetians thought of it as a city; residents knew it was just a sleepy little country town with an impulse towards gossip, curiosity and small-mindedness no different from that of the smallest *paese* in Calabria or Aspromonte.

Though it had been years since he had been in her apartment, he found it with little difficulty, on the right side of Calle dello Squero Vecchio, a street so small that the city had never bothered to paint its name on the wall. He rang the bell and, moments later, a voice came through the intercom asking who he was. He was glad they were taking at least this minimum precaution; too often the people of this peaceful city merely clicked open their doors without bothering to learn who was there.

Though the building had been restored within the last few years and the stairwells newly plastered and painted, salt and humidity had already begun their work, devouring the paint and scattering large droppings of it on the floor, like scraps under a table. As he turned into the fourth and final flight of steps, he looked up and saw that the heavy metal door to the apartment was open, held back by Flavia Petrelli. However nervous and strained it was, that actually did seem to be a smile.

They shook hands at the door, and she stepped back to allow him to enter. They spoke at the same time, she saying, 'I'm glad you came,' and he, '*Permesso*,' as he stepped inside.

She wore a black skirt and a low-necked sweater in a canary yellow that few women would risk. Flavia's olive complexion and nearly black eyes glowed in response to the colour. But on closer inspection he saw that the eyes, however beautiful,

133

were tired, and small lines of tension radiated from her mouth.

She asked for his coat and hung it in a large *armadio* that stood on the left of the hallway. He had read the report of the officers who responded to the attack, so he couldn't keep himself from looking down at the floor and at the brick wall. There was no sign of blood, but he could smell strong cleansers and, he thought, wax.

Flavia made no motion to go back into the living room but kept him there and asked, her voice low, 'Have you found out anything?'

'About Dottor Semenzato?'

She nodded.

Before he could answer, Brett called out from the living room, 'Stop plotting, Flavia, and bring him in here.'

She had the grace to smile and shrug, then turned and led him back into the living room. It was as he remembered it, filled, even on this dreary day, with light that filtered in from the six immense skylights cut into the roof. Brett sat, dressed in burgundy slacks and a black turtleneck sweater, on a sofa placed between two tall windows. Brunetti could see that parts of her face, though far less swollen than they had been in the hospital, were still angry blue. She shifted herself to the left, leaving him a space next to her, and extended her hand.

He took her hand and sat beside her, looking at her more closely.

'No more Frankenstein,' she said, smiling to show not only that her teeth were free of the wires that had bound them together for most of the time that she was in the hospital, but that the cut on her lip had healed sufficiently for her to be able to close her mouth.

Brunetti, familiar with the assumed omniscience of Italian doctors and their concomitant inflexibility, asked in real surprise, 'How did you get them to let you out?'

'I made a scene,' she said quite simply.

Offered no more than that, Brunetti glanced at Flavia, who covered her eyes with her hand and shook her head at the memory.

'And?' he asked.

'They said I could go if I'd eat, so now my diet has progressed to bananas and yoghurt.'

With the talk of food, Brunetti looked more closely at her and saw that, under the bruises and scrapes, her face was indeed thinner, the lines finer and more angular.

'You should eat more than that,' he said. From behind him, he heard Flavia laugh, but when he turned to her, she recalled him to the business at hand by asking, 'What about Semenzato? We read about it this morning.'

'It's pretty much as they wrote. He was killed in his office.'

'Who found him?' Brett asked.

'The cleaning woman.'

'What happened? How was he killed?'

'He was hit on the head.'

'With what?' asked Flavia.

'A brick.'

Suddenly curious, Brett asked, 'What kind of brick?'

Brunetti remembered where he had first seen it, beside the body. 'It's dark blue, about twice the size of my hand, but there are some markings on it, in gold.'

'What was it doing there?' Brett asked.

'The cleaning woman said he used it as a paperweight. Why do you want to know?'

She nodded as if in answer to a different question and pushed herself up from the sofa and walked across the room to the bookshelves. Brunetti winced at the gingerly way she walked, at how slowly she raised her arm to pull a thick book down from a high shelf. Tucking it under one arm, she came back towards them and placed the book on the low table that stood in front of the sofa. She flipped it open, riffled through a few pages, then pushed it open and held it there with both palms pressed down on the outer edge of the pages.

Brunetti bent forward and looked at the coloured photo on the page. It appeared to be an immense gate, but all scale was missing because it wasn't attached to walls of any sort; instead, it stood free in a room, perhaps a museum gallery. Immense winged bulls stood in protective posture on either side of the opening. The background was the same cobalt blue of the brick that had been used to kill Semenzato, the body of the animals the same vibrant gold. A closer look showed him that the wall was entirely constructed of rectangular bricks, the form of the bulls raised up upon its surface in low relief.

'What is it?' he asked, pointing down at the photo.

'The Ishtar Gate of Babylon,' she said. 'Much of it's been reconstructed, but that's where the brick came from. That or a structure like it, from the same place.' Before he could ask, she explained, 'I remember that some of the bricks were in the storerooms of the museum when we were working there.'

'But how did it get on to his desk?' Brunetti asked.

Brett smiled again. 'The perks of the job, I suppose. He was the director, so he could have pretty well anything he wanted from the permanent collection brought up to his office.'

'Is that normal?' Brunetti asked.

'Yes, it is. Of course, they can't have a Leonardo or a Bellini hanging there just for them to look at, but it's not unusual for pieces from a museum's holdings to be used to decorate an office, especially the director's.'

137

'Are records kept of this kind of borrowing?' he asked.

From the other side of the table, Flavia crossed her legs with a slither of silk and said softly, 'Ah, so that's how it is.' Then she added, as if Brunetti had asked, 'I met him only once, but I didn't like him.'

'When did you meet him, Flavia?' Brett asked, ignoring Brunetti's question.

'About a half hour before I met you, *cara*. At your exhibition at the Palazzo Ducale.'

Almost automatically, Brett corrected her, 'It wasn't my exhibition.' Brunetti had the feeling that this same correction had been made many times before.

'Well, whosever it was, then,' Flavia said. 'It had just opened, and I was being shown around the city, given the full treatment – visiting diva and all that.' Her tone made the idea of her fame sound faintly ridiculous. Since Brett must know this story of their meeting, Brunetti assumed the explanation was directed at him.

'Semenzato showed me through the galleries, but I had a rehearsal that afternoon, and I suppose I might have been a bit brusque with him.' Brusque? Brunetti had seen Flavia's ill humour, and brusque was hardly an adequate term to describe it.

'He kept telling me how much he admired my talent.' She paused and leaned towards Brunetti, placing a hand on his arm while she explained,

138

'That always means they've never heard me sing and probably wouldn't like it if they did, but they've heard enough to know that I'm famous, so they feel they have to flatter me.' That explanation given, she removed her hand and sat back in her chair. 'I had the feeling that, while he was showing me how wonderful the exhibition was—' here she turned to Brett and added, 'and it was,' then turned her attention back to Brunetti and continued – 'what I was supposed to be registering was how wonderful he was for having thought of it. Though he didn't. Well, I didn't know that at the time – that it was Brett's show – but he was pushy about it, and I didn't like it.'

Brunetti could well imagine that she wouldn't like the competition of pushy people. No, that was unfair, for she didn't push herself forward. He had to admit that he had been wrong the last time he met her. There was no vanity here, only the calm acceptance of her own worth and of her own talent, and he knew enough about her past to realize how hard that must have been to achieve.

'But then you came by with a glass of champagne and rescued me from him,' she said, smiling at Brett.

'That's not a bad idea, champagne,' Brett said, cutting short Flavia's flow of memory, and Brunetti was struck at how very similar her reaction was to Paola's whenever he began to tell people about the way they met, crashing into one another at the end of one of the aisles in the library of the university. How many times in their years together had she asked him to get her a drink or otherwise interrupted his story by asking someone else a question? And why did the telling of that story bring him such joy? Mysteries. Mysteries.

Taking the hint, Flavia got out of her chair and went across the room. It was only eleven thirty in the morning, but if they felt like drinking champagne, he hardly thought it his place to contradict or try to prevent them.

Brett flipped a page in the book, then sat back in the sofa, and the pages floated back into place, showing Brunetti the gold bull, part of which had killed Semenzato.

'How did you meet him?' Brunetti asked.

'I worked with him on the China show, five years ago. Most of our contact was through letters because I was in China while most of the arrangements were being made. I wrote and suggested a number of pieces, sending photos and dimensions, and weights, since they all had to be air-freighted from Xian and Beijing to New York and London for the exhibition there, and then to Milan, and then trucked and boated here.' She paused for a moment and then added, 'I didn't meet him until I got here to set the show up.'

'Who decided what pieces would come here from China?'

This question caused her to grimace in remembered exasperation. 'Who knows?' When he failed to understand, she tried to explain. 'Involved in this were the Chinese government, their ministries of antiquities and foreign affairs, and, on our side' – he noticed that Venice was, unconsciously, 'our side' – 'the museum, the department of antiquities, the finance police, the ministry of culture, and a few other bureaus I've forced myself to forget about.' She allowed the memory of officialdom to flow across her. 'Here, it was awful, far worse than for New York or London. And I had to do all this from Xian, with letters delayed in the mail, or held up by the censors. Finally, after three months of it – this was about a year before it opened – I came here for two weeks and got most of it done, though I had to fly down to Rome twice to do it.'

'And Semenzato?' Brunetti asked.

'I think, first, you have to understand that his was pretty much a political appointment.' She saw Brunetti's surprise and smiled. 'He had museum experience, I forget where. But his selection was a political payoff. Anyway, there were—' she corrected herself immediately – 'there are curators at the museum who actually take care of the collection. His job was primarily administrative, and he did that very well.'

'What about the exhibition here? Did he help you set it up?' From the other side of the apartment, he could hear Flavia moving around, hear drawers and cabinets being opened and closed, the clink of glasses.

'To a small degree. I told you how I more or less commuted back and forth from Xian for the openings in New York and London, but I came here for the opening.' He thought she was finished, but then she added, 'And I stayed on for about a month after it.'

'How much contact did you have with him?'

'Very little. He was on vacation for much of the time it was being set up, and then when he got back, he had to go to Rome for conferences with the Minister, trying to arrange an exchange with the Brera in Milan for another exhibition they were planning.'

'But certainly you dealt with him personally at some time during all of this?'

'Yes, I did. He was utterly charming and, when he could be, very helpful. He gave me carte blanche with the exhibition, allowed me to set it up as I pleased. And then, when it closed, he did the same for my assistant.'

'Your assistant?' Brunetti asked.

Brett glanced across towards the kitchen and then answered, 'Matsuko Shibata. She was my assistant in Xian, on loan from the Tokyo Museum, in an exchange policy between the Japanese and Chinese governments. She'd studied at Berkeley but gone back to Tokyo after she got her degree.'

'Where is she now?' Brunetti asked.

She bent down over the book and turned a block of pages, her hand coming to rest beside a delicate Japanese screen painting that showed herons in flight above a tall growth of bamboo. 'She's dead. She was killed in an accident on the site.'

'What happened?' Brunetti spoke very softly, aware that Semenzato's death made this accident into something that Brett had already begun to examine in an entirely new fashion.

'She fell. The dig in Xian is little more than an open pit covered by an aeroplane hangar. All of the statues were buried, part of the army that the emperor would take into eternity with him. In some places, we've had to dig down three or four metres to reach them. There's an outer perimeter above the dig, and there's a low wall that protects tourists from falling into it or from kicking dirt down on us when we're working. In some areas, where tourists aren't permitted, there's no wall. Matsuko fell,' she began, but Brunetti watched as she continued to process new possibilities and adjusted her language accordingly. She restated this. 'Matsuko's body was found at the bottom of one of these places. She'd fallen about three metres and broken her neck.' She glanced across at Brunetti and made open admission of her new doubts by changing that last sentence. 'She was found at the bottom, with a broken neck.'

'When was she killed?'

A loud shot rang out from the kitchen. Entirely without thinking, Brunetti pivoted out of his chair and crouched in front of Brett, his body placed between her and the open door to the kitchen. His hand was underneath his jacket, pulling at his revolver, when they heard Flavia shout, '*Porco vacca*,' and then both of them heard the unmistakable sound of champagne splashing from the neck of a bottle on to the floor.

He released his hold on the pistol and moved back into his seat without saying anything to Brett. In different circumstances, it might have been funny, but neither of them laughed. By silent consent, they decided to ignore it, and Brunetti repeated his question: 'When was she killed?'

Deciding to save time and answer all of his questions at once, she said, 'It happened about three weeks after I'd sent my first letter to Semenzato.'

'When was that?'

'In the middle of December. I took her body back to Tokyo. That is, I went with it. With her.' She stopped, voice dried up by memory that she was not going to let Brunetti have any part of.

'I was going to San Francisco for Christmas,' she continued. 'So I left early and spent three days in Tokyo. I saw her family.' Again, a long pause. 'Then I went to San Francisco.'

Flavia came back from the kitchen, balancing a silver tray with three tall champagne flutes on one hand, the other wrapped around the neck of a bottle of Dom Perignon as if she were carrying a tennis racquet. No stinting here, not on the after-breakfast champagne.

She had heard Brett's last words and asked, 'Are you telling Guido about our happy Christmas?' The use of his first name did not go unnoticed by any of them, nor did her emphasis on 'happy'.

Brunetti took the tray and set it down on the table; Flavia poured champagne liberally into the glasses. Bubbles rushed over the rim of one of them, spilled down the side and over the edge of the tray, racing towards the book that still lay open on the table. Brett flipped it closed and placed it on the sofa beside her. Flavia handed Brunetti a glass, put one on the table in front of the place where she had been sitting, and passed the third to Brett.

'*Cin Cin*,' Flavia toasted with bright artificiality, and they raised their glasses to one another. 'If we're going to talk about San Francisco, then I think I need at least champagne.' She sat down facing them and took something too big to be called a sip from her glass.

Brunetti gave her an inquiring glance, and she rushed to explain. 'I was singing there. Tosca. God, what a disaster.' In a gesture so consciously theatrical it mocked itself, she placed the back of her hand to her forehead, closed her eyes for a moment, then continued, 'We had a German director who had a "concept". Unfortunately, his concept was to update the opera to make it relevant,' which word she pronounced with special contempt, 'and stage it during the Romanian Revolution, and Scarpia was supposed to be Ceaucescu, or however that terrible man pronounced his name. I was still supposed to be the reigning diva, but of Bucharest, not Rome.' She draped the hand over her eyes at the memory but forged ahead. 'I remember that there were tanks and machine guns, and at one point I had to hide a hand grenade in my cleavage.'

'Don't forget the telephone,' Brett said, covering her mouth and pressing her lips closed so as not to laugh.

'Oh, sweet heavens, the telephone. It tells you how much I've tried to put it out of my memory that I didn't remember it.' She turned to Brunetti, took a mouthful far more suited to mineral water than champagne, and continued, eyes alive at the memory. 'In the middle of "*Visse d'arte*", the director wanted me to try to telephone for help. So there I was, stretched across a sofa, trying to convince God that I didn't deserve any of this, and I didn't, when the Scarpia – I think he was a real Romanian – I certainly never understood a word he said.' She paused a moment and then added, 'Or sang.'

Brett interrupted to correct her. 'He was Bulgarian, Flavia.'

Flavia's wave, even encumbered with the glass, was airily dismissive. 'Same thing, *cara*. They all look like potatoes and stink of paprika. And they all shout so, especially the sopranos.' She finished her champagne and paused long enough to refill her glass. 'Where was I?'

'On the sofa, I think, pleading with God,' Brett suggested.

'Ah, yes. And then the Scarpia, a great, lumbering clod of a man, he tripped over the telephone wire and pulled it out of the wall. So there I lay on the sofa, line to God cut off, and, beyond the baritone, I could see the director in the wings, waving at me like a madman. I think he wanted me to plug it back in and use it, put the call through any way I could.' She sipped, smiled at Brunetti with a warmth that drove him to sip at his own champagne, and continued. 'But an artist has to have some standards,' glancing now at Brett, 'or as you Americans say, has to draw a line in the sand.'

She stopped and Brunetti picked up his cue. He said it. 'What did you do?'

'I picked up the receiver and sang into it, just as if I had someone on the other end, just as if no one had seen it pulled from the wall.' She set her glass down on the table, stood and stretched her arms out in agonized cruciform, then, utterly without warning, she began to sing the last phrases of the aria. ' "*Nell'ora del dolor perchè, Signor, ah perchè me ne rimuneri così?*" ' How did she do it? From a normal speaking voice, with no preparation, right up to those solidly floated notes?

Brunetti laughed outright, spilling some champagne down the front of his shirt. Brett set her glass on the table and clapped both hands to the sides of her mouth.

Flavia, as calmly as if she'd just gone into the kitchen to check on the roast and found it done, sat back down in her chair and continued her story. 'Scarpia had to turn his back on the audience, he was laughing so hard. It was the first thing he'd done in a month that made me like him. I almost regretted having to kill him a few minutes later. The director was hysterical during the intermission, screaming at me that I'd ruined his production, swearing he'd never work with me again. Well, that's certain, isn't it? The reviews were terrible.'

'Flavia,' Brett chided, 'it was the reviews of the production that were terrible; your reviews were wonderful.'

As if explaining something to a child, Flavia said, 'My reviews are always wonderful, *cara*.' Just like that. She turned her attention to Brunetti. 'It was into this fiasco that she came,' she said, pointing to Brett, 'for Christmas with me and my children.' She shook her head a few times. 'She came in from taking that young woman's body to Tokyo. No, it wasn't a happy Christmas.'

Brunetti decided that, champagne or not, he still wanted to know more about the death of Brett's assistant. 'Was there any question at the time that it might not have been an accident?'

Brett shook her head, glass forgotten in front of her. 'No. At one time or another, almost all of us had slipped when walking on the edge of the dig. One of the Chinese archaeologists had fallen and broken his ankle about a month before. So at the time we all believed that it was an accident. It might have been,' she added with an absolute lack of conviction.

'She worked on the exhibition here?' he asked.

'Not the opening. I came here alone for that. But Matsuko oversaw the packing, when the pieces left for China.'

'Were you here?' Brunetti asked.

Brett hesitated a long time, glanced across at Flavia, bowed her head, and answered, 'No, I wasn't.'

Flavia reached again for the bottle and poured more champagne into their glasses, though hers was the only glass that needed filling.

No one spoke for a while, and then Flavia asked Brett, making it a statement, not a question, 'She didn't speak Italian, did she?'

'No, she didn't,' Brett answered.

'But both she and Semenzato spoke English, as I remember.'

'What difference does that make?' Brett asked,

her voice edged with an anger Brunetti sensed but couldn't fathom.

Flavia made a tsking sound with her tongue and turned in feigned exasperation to Brunetti. 'Maybe it's true what people say about us Italians, and we do have a greater sympathy with dishonesty than other people. You see, don't you?'

He nodded. 'It means,' he explained to Brett when he saw that Flavia would not, 'that she couldn't deal with people here except through Semenzato. They had a common language.'

'Wait a minute,' Brett said. She understood now what they meant, but that didn't mean she liked it. 'So now Semenzato is guilty, just like that, and Matsuko is, too? Just because they both spoke English?'

Neither Brunetti nor Flavia said a word.

'I worked with Matsuko for three years,' Brett insisted. 'She was an archaeologist, a curator. You two can't just decide she was a thief, you can't sit there and play judge and jury and decide she's guilty without any information, any proof.' Brunetti noted that she seemed to have no problem with their equal assumption of Semenzato's guilt.

Still, neither of them answered her. Almost a full minute passed. Finally, Brett sat back in the sofa, then reached forward and picked up her glass. But she didn't drink, merely swirled the champagne around in the glass and then put it back down on the table. 'Occam's Razor,' she finally said in English, voice resigned.

Brunetti waited for Flavia to speak, thinking this might make some sense to her, but Flavia said nothing. So he asked, 'Whose razor?'

'William of Occam,' Brett repeated, though she kept her eyes on her glass. 'He was a medieval philosopher. English, I think. He had a theory that said the correct explanation to any problem was usually the one that made the simplest use of the available information.'

Signor William, Brunetti caught himself thinking, was clearly not an Italian. He glanced across at Flavia and would have sworn that her raised eyebrow carried the same message.

'Flavia, could I have something different to drink?' Brett asked, holding out the half-full glass. Brunetti noticed Flavia's initial hesitation, the suspicious glance she cast at him, then back at Brett, and he thought how very similar it was to the look Chiara gave him when she was told to do something that would take her out of the room where he and Paola were talking about something they wanted to keep secret from her. With a fluid motion, she got up from her chair, took Brett's glass, and walked towards the kitchen. At the door, she paused long enough to call back over her shoulder, 'I'll get you some mineral water. I'll see that it takes me a long time to open the bottle.' The door slammed and she was gone.

151

What was that all about? Brunetti wondered.

When Flavia was gone, Brett told him. 'Matsuko and I were lovers. I never told Flavia, but she knows anyway.' A hard clang from the kitchen confirmed the truth of this.

'It began in Xian, about a year after she got to the dig.' Then, to make things clearer, 'We worked on the exhibition together, and she wrote a chapter for the catalogue.'

'Whose idea was it that she collaborate on the show?' Brunetti asked.

Brett made no attempt to hide her embarrassment. 'Mine? Hers? I don't remember. It just happened. We were talking about it one night.' Under the bruises, she blushed. 'And, in the morning, it had been decided that she would write the article and come to New York to help set up the show.'

'But you came to Venice alone?' he asked.

She nodded. 'We both went back to China after the New York opening. I went back to New York to close things down there and then Matsuko came to London to help me set up for the opening. We both went back to China right after that. Then I went back to pack it up for Venice. I thought she'd join me here for the opening, but she refused. She said she wanted . . .' Brett's voice dried up. She cleared her throat and repeated, 'She said she wanted at least this part of the show to be all mine, so she wouldn't come.'

'But she came when it was over? When the pieces were sent back to China?'

'She came from Xian for three weeks,' Brett said. Brett stopped speaking and looked down at her clasped hands, muttering, 'I don't believe this. I don't believe this,' which, to Brunetti, suggested that she did.

'Things were over between us by then, when she came here. I'd met Flavia at the opening. I told Matsuko when I got back to Xian about a month after the show opened here.'

'How did she react when you told her?'

'How would you expect her to react, Guido? She was gay, little more than a kid, caught between two cultures, raised in Japan and educated in America. When I went back to Xian after the Venice opening – I'd been away almost two months – she cried when I showed her the Italian catalogue with her article in it. She'd helped mount the most important show in our field in decades, and she was in love with her boss, and she thought her boss was in love with her. And there I was, breezing in from Venice to tell her everything was over, that I was in love with someone else, and when she asked why, I stupidly said something about culture, about the difficulty of ever really understanding someone from a different culture. I told her that she and I didn't share it but that Flavia and I had a common culture.' Another loud crash from the kitchen was enough to show this up as the lie it was.

'How did she react?' Brunetti asked.

'If it had been Flavia, I suppose she would have killed me. But Matsuko was Japanese, no matter how long she had been in America. She bowed very deeply and left my room.'

'And after that?'

'After that, she was the perfect assistant. Very formal and distant and very efficient. She was gifted in what she did.' She paused for a long time and then said, 'I don't like what I did to her, Guido,' in a soft voice.

'Why did she come here to send things back to China?'

'I was in New York,' Brett said, as if that explained things. To Brunetti, it didn't, but he decided to leave that until later. 'I called Matsuko and asked her if she would oversee the closing here and send things back to China.'

'And she agreed?'

'I told you, she was my assistant. The exhibition meant as much to her as it did to me.' Hearing how that sounded, Brett added, 'At least I thought it did.'

'What about her family?' he asked.

Obviously surprised by the question, Brett asked, 'What about them?'

'Are they rich?'

'*Ricca sfondata,*' she explained. Bottomless wealth. 'Why do you ask that?'

'To understand if she did it for money,' he explained.

'I don't like the way you simply assume that she was involved in this,' Brett protested, but weakly.

'Is it safe to come back?' Flavia asked in a loud voice from the kitchen.

'Stop it, Flavia,' Brett shot back angrily.

Flavia came back, carrying a single glass of mineral water, bubbles swirling up happily from the bottom. She set it down in front of Brett, looked at her watch, and said, 'It's time for you to take your pills.' Silence. 'Do you want me to get them?'

With no warning, Brett slammed her fist down on the surface of the marble table, causing the tray to rattle and a jolt of bubbles to swirl up from the bottom of all the glasses. 'I'll get my own pills, damn it.' She pushed herself up from the sofa and walked quickly across the room. Seconds later, the sharp crack of another slammed door echoed back into the living room.

Flavia sat back in her chair, picked up her champagne glass, and took a sip. 'Warm,' she remarked. The champagne? The temperature of the room? Brett's temper? She poured the contents of her glass into Brett's champagne glass and emptied the bottle into her own. She took a tentative sip, then smiled across at Brunetti. 'Better.' She set the glass on the table.

155

Not knowing if this was a piece of theatre or not, Brunetti decided to wait her out. Companionably, they sipped at their drinks for a while, until Flavia finally asked, 'How necessary was the guard in the hospital?'

'Until I have some clearer idea of what's going on here, I won't know how necessary anything is,' he answered.

Her smile was broad. 'How refreshing it is to hear a public official admit to ignorance,' she said, reaching forward to place her empty glass on the table.

The champagne gone, her voice changed and grew more serious. 'Matsuko?' she asked.

'Probably.'

'But how would she know Semenzato? Or know enough about him to know he'd be the person to contact?'

Brunetti considered this. 'It seems he had a reputation, at least here.'

'The kind of reputation Matsuko would know about?'

'Perhaps. She'd worked with antiquities for years, so she probably heard things. And Brett said her family was very rich. Maybe the very rich know about this sort of thing.'

'Yes, we do,' she agreed with an offhandedness he was sure was real. 'It's almost a private club, as if we'd taken a vow to keep one another's secrets. And it's always easy, very easy, to know where to find a crooked tax lawyer – not that there's any other type, at least not in this country – or someone who can get drugs, or boys, or girls, or someone who's willing to see that a painting gets from one country to another, and no questions asked. Of course, I'm not sure how these things work in Japan, but I don't see why there should be any difference. Wealth carries its own passport.'

'Had you heard anything about Semenzato?'

'I told you, I met him only that one time, and I didn't like him, so I wasn't interested in anything that was said about him. And it's too late to find out now, since everyone will be busy talking well of him.' She reached forward and took Brett's drink and sipped at it. 'Of course, that will change in a few weeks, and people will go back to telling the truth about him. But now's not the time to try to find that out.' She set the glass back on the table.

Though he thought he knew what the answer would be, he still asked, 'Has Brett said anything about Matsuko? That is, since Semenzato was killed?'

Flavia shook her head. 'She hasn't said much about anything. Not since this began.' She leaned forward and shifted the glass a few millimetres to the left. 'Brett is afraid of violence. That doesn't make any sense to me because she's very brave. We Italian women aren't, you know. We're brash and brazen, but we have little physical courage. She's off in China, living in a tent half of the time, roaming around the country. She even went to Tibet on a bus. She told me that when the Chinese officials refused to give her a visa, she simply forged the papers and went. She's not afraid of that sort of thing, of the things that most people are terrified of, of getting into official trouble or being arrested. But actual physical violence terrifies her. I think it's because she lives in her mind so much, solving things there and working them out there. She hasn't been the same since this happened. She doesn't want to answer the door. She pretends she doesn't hear or she waits for me to go and do it. But the reason is that she's afraid.'

Brunetti wondered why Flavia was telling him all of this. 'I've got to leave next week,' she said, answering his question. 'My children have been skiing with their father for two weeks, and they come home then. I've cancelled three performances, but I can't cancel any more. And I don't want to. I've asked her to come with me, but she refuses.'

'Why?'

'I don't know. She won't say. Or she can't.'

'Why are you telling me this?'

'I think she'd listen to you.'

'If I said what?'

'If you asked her to go with me.'

'To Milan?'

'Yes. Then, in March, I have to go to Munich for a month. She could come with me.'

'What about China? Isn't she supposed to go back there?'

'And end up with her neck broken on the floor of that pit?' Even though he knew her anger wasn't directed at him, he still winced at the sound of it.

'Has she talked about going back?' he asked.

'She hasn't talked about anything.'

'Do you know when she was supposed to leave?'

'I don't think she had any plan. When she arrived, she said she didn't have a return reservation.' She met Brunetti's inquisitive look. 'That depended on what she learned from Semenzato.' From her tone, it was clear that this was only part of the explanation. He waited for her to finish it. 'But part of it depended on me, I suppose.' She paused, looked away from Brunetti, then quickly back. 'She's managed to get me an invitation to teach master classes there, in Beijing. She wanted me to go back with her.'

'And?' Brunettti asked.

Flavia dismissed the idea with a wave of her hand but said only, 'We hadn't discussed it before this happened.'

'And not since?'

She shook her head.

All of this talk of Brett made Brunetti suddenly realize that she had been gone from the room for a long time. 'Is that the only door?' he asked.

His question was so sudden that Flavia took a

moment to understand it and then to understand everything it meant.

'Yes. There's no other way out. Or in. And the roof is separate. There's no access to it.' She got up. 'I'll go and see how she is.'

She was gone a long time, during which Brunetti picked up the book that Brett had left on the sofa and paged through it. He stared at the photo of the Ishtar Gate for a long time, trying to see which part of the figure appeared on the brick that had killed Semenzato. It was like a jigsaw puzzle, but he proved incapable of fitting the single missing piece that lay in the police laboratory at the Questura into the whole picture of the gate that lay in front of him.

It was almost five minutes before Flavia came back. She stood by the table while she spoke, letting Brunetti know that their conversation was over. 'She's asleep. The pain pills she's taking are very strong, and I think there's a tranquillizer, too. The champagne didn't help things. She'll sleep until the afternoon.'

'I need to speak to her again,' he said.

'Can it wait until tomorrow?' It was a simple question, not an imperious demand.

It really couldn't, but he had no choice. 'Yes. Is it all right if I come at about the same time?'

'Of course. I'll tell her you're coming. And I'll try to limit the champagne.' The conversation might be over, but the truce apparently held.

Brunetti, who had decided that Dom Perignon was an excellent mid-morning drink, thought this an unnecessary precaution and hoped that Flavia might change her mind by the next day.

Chapter Twelve

WAS THIS THE beginning of alcoholism, Brunetti wondered, as he found himself wanting to stop in a bar on the way back to the Questura and have another glass of champagne? Or was it merely the inescapable response to the certainty that he would have to speak to Patta that morning? The first explanation seemed preferable.

When he opened the door to his office, a wave of heat swept across him, so palpable that he turned to see if he could watch it roll down the corridor, perhaps to engulf some innocent soul unfamiliar with the vagaries of the heating system. Each year, on or about the feast day of Saint Agatha, 5 February, heat flared out of all the rooms on the north side of the fourth floor of the Questura at the same time as it disappeared from the corridors and the offices on the south side of the third floor. It remained this way for about three weeks, generally until the feast of Saint Leandro, whom most people in the building tended to thank for their deliverance. No one had ever been able to understand or correct this phenomenon, though it had gone on for five years or more. The main heating unit had, at various times and by various technicians, been worked on, inspected, adjusted, tinkered with, sworn at and kicked, but it had never been repaired. By now, people who worked on these two floors were resigned and took the necessary measures, some removing jackets while others wore gloves in the office.

So closely did Brunetti associate this phenomenon with the feast of Saint Agatha that he could never see an image of that martyr, invariably pictured holding her two severed breasts on a plate, but he imagined she was carrying thereon, instead, two matching pieces from the central heating unit: large washers, perhaps.

He walked across the room, stripping off coat and jacket as he went, and threw open both the tall windows. He was as suddenly chilled and went back to take his jacket from his desk, where he had tossed it. Over the course of the years, he had developed a rhythm for opening and closing the windows, one that not only effectively controlled the temperature in the room but also prevented him from concentrating on anything at all. Could the caretaker be in the pay of the Mafia? Each time he read the paper, it seemed that almost every other person who worked for the police was, so why not the caretaker?

On his desk lay the usual personnel reports and

requests for information from police in other cities as well as letters from people in the city. There was one from a woman on the small island of Torcello, asking him personally to look for her son, whom she knew had been kidnapped by the Syrians. The woman was mad, and different members of the police received a letter from her each month: it was always the same non-existent son, but the kidnappers changed according to the winds of world politics.

If he went now, he could see Patta before lunch. With this beacon shining out its bright hope, he took the slim file of papers on the Semenzato and Lynch crimes and went down to Patta's office.

Though fresh iris abounded, Signorina Elettra was not at her desk. Probably out at the landscaper's. He knocked and was told to enter. Spared the vagaries of the heating system, Patta's office was a perfect 22 degrees, the ideal temperature to allow him the luxury of removing his jacket, should the pace of work grow too frenetic. Having so far been spared that necessity, he sat behind his desk, his mohair jacket buttoned, diamond tie-pin neatly in place. As always, Patta looked as if he had just slipped off a Roman coin, his large brown eyes perfectly set among the other perfections of his face.

'Good morning, sir,' Brunetti said, taking the seat that Patta gestured him to.

'Good morning, Brunetti.' When Brunetti

leaned forward to place the folder on Patta's desk, his superior waved it away with his hand. 'I've read it. Carefully. I take it you're working on the assumption that the beating of Dottoressa Lynch and the murder of Dottor Semenzato are related?'

'Yes, sir, I am. I don't see how they can't be.'

He thought for a moment that Patta, as was usual with him, would object to any expressed certainty that was not his own, but he surprised Brunetti by nodding his head and saying, 'Yes, you're probably right. What have you done so far?'

'I've interviewed Dottoressa Lynch,' he began, but Patta broke in.

'I hope you were polite with her.'

Brunetti contented himself with a simple, 'Yes, sir.'

'Good, good. She's an important benefactress of the city, and she's to be treated accordingly.'

Brunetti allowed that to trickle away and then resumed. 'There was a Japanese assistant who came here to close the exhibition and send the pieces back to China.'

'Dottoressa Lynch's assistant?'

'Yes, sir.'

'A woman?' Patta asked sharply.

Patta's tone so dirtied the word that Brunetti had to pause for a moment before he replied, 'Yes, sir. A woman.'

'Ah, I see.'

'Shall I go on, sir?'

'Yes, yes. Of course.'

'Dottoressa Lynch told me that the woman was killed in an accident in China.'

'What kind of accident?' Patta asked, as if this would turn out to have been an inescapable consequence of her sexual proclivities.

'In a fall at the archaeological site where they were working.'

'When did this happen?'

'Three months ago. It was after Dottoressa Lynch wrote to Semenzato to say that she thought some of the pieces that had been returned to China were false.'

'And this woman who was killed was the one who packed them?'

'It would seem so, sir.'

'Did you ask Dottoressa Lynch what her relationship was to this woman?'

Well, he hadn't, had he? 'No, sir. I didn't. The Dottoressa seemed troubled by her death and by the possibility of the young woman's involvement in whatever is going on here, but there was no more than that.'

'Are you sure of that, Brunetti?' Patta's eyes actually narrowed when he asked this.

'Absolutely, sir. I'd stake my reputation on it.' As he always did when he lied to Patta, he stared him directly in the eyes, careful to keep his own open fully, his gaze level. 'Shall I go on, sir?' As soon as he said it, Brunetti realized he didn't have

166

anything else to say – well, anything else he wanted to say to Patta. Surely not that the Japanese girl's family was so wealthy that she would, presumably, have had no financial interest in the substitution of pieces. The thought of the way Patta would respond to the idea of sexual jealousy as a motive made Brunetti feel faintly queasy.

'Do you think this Japanese woman knew that false pieces were sent back to China?'

'It's possible, sir.'

'But it is not possible,' Patta said with heavy emphasis, 'that she could have organized it herself. She must have had help here, here in Venice.'

'It would seem so, sir. That's a possibility I'm pursuing.'

'How?'

'I've initiated an investigation of Dottor Semen-zato's finances.'

'On whose authority?' Patta snapped.

'My own, sir.'

Patta let that stand as said. 'What else?'

'I've already spoken to some people about Semenzato, and I expect to get information about his real reputation.'

'What do you mean, "real reputation"?'

Oh, so seldom does fate cast our enemy into our hands, to do with as we will. 'Don't you think, sir, that every bureaucrat has an official reputation, what people say about him publicly, and then the real reputation, what people know to be true and say about him in private?'

Patta turned his right palm upward on his desk and moved his pinkie ring around on his finger with his thumb, examining it to see that he got the motion right. 'Perhaps. Perhaps.' He looked up from his palm. 'Go on, Brunetti.'

'I thought I'd begin with these things and see where they lead me.'

'Yes, that sounds fair enough to me,' Patta said. 'Remember, I want to know about anything you do or find out.' He consulted his Rolex Oyster. 'I don't want to keep you from getting busy with this, Brunetti.'

Brunetti stood, recognizing Patta's lunch hour when it struck. He started towards the door, curious only about the way Patta would remind him to handle Brett with kid gloves.

'And Brunetti,' Patta said as Brunetti reached the door.

'Yes, sir?' he said, really curious, something he very seldom was with Patta.

'I want you to handle Dottoressa Lynch with kid gloves.' Ah, so that's how he'd say it.

Chapter Thirteen

BACK IN HIS office, the first thing Brunetti did after he opened the window was call Lele. There was no answer at his house, so Brunetti tried the gallery, where the painter picked up the phone after six rings. '*Pronto.*'

'*Ciao*, Lele, it's Guido. I thought I'd call and see if you'd managed to find out anything.'

'About that person?' Lele answered, making it clear that he couldn't talk freely.

'Yes. Is someone there?'

'Ah, yes, now that you mention it, I think that's true. Are you going to be in your office for a while, Signor Scarpa?'

'Yes, I will be. For another hour or so.'

'Good, then, Signor Scarpa. I'll call you there when I'm free.'

'Thanks, Lele,' Brunetti said and hung up.

Who was it that Lele didn't want to know he was talking with a commissario of police?

He turned to the papers in the file, making a note here and there. He had been in contact with the special branch of police that dealt with art theft on several occasions in the past, but at this point all he had to give them was Semenzato's name and no proof of anything at all. Semenzato might indeed have a reputation that did not appear in official reports, the sort that never got written down.

Four years ago, he had dealt with one of the captains of the art branch in Rome, about a Gothic altarpiece stolen from the church of San Giacomo dell'Orio. Giulio something or other, but Brunetti couldn't remember his surname. He reached for the phone and dialled Signorina Elettra's number.

'Yes, Commissario?' she asked when he identified himself.

'Have you had any response from Heinegger or your friends at the bank?'

'This afternoon, sir.'

'Good. Until then, I'd like you to take a look in the files and see if you can find a name for me, a captain of the art theft bureau in Rome. Giulio something. He and I corresponded about a theft at San Giacomo dell'Orio. About four years ago. Perhaps five.'

'Have you any idea how it would be filed, sir?'

'Either under my name, since I wrote the original report, or under the name of the church, or perhaps under art theft.' He thought for a moment and then added, 'You might check the record of a certain Sandro – Alessandro, that is – Benelli, whose address used to be in San Lio. I think he's still in prison, but there might be some mention of the captain's name in there. I think he provided a deposition at the trial.'

'Certainly, sir. Today?'

'Yes, signorina, if you could.'

'I'll go down to the files and take a look now. Maybe I can find something before lunch.'

The optimism of youth. 'Thank you, signorina,' he said and hung up. As soon as he did, the phone rang, and it was Lele.

'I couldn't talk, Guido. I had someone in the gallery who I think might be useful to you in this.'

'Who?' When Lele didn't answer, Brunetti apologized, remembering that he needed the information, not its source. 'Sorry, Lele. Forget I asked that. What did he tell you?'

'It seems that Dottor Semenzato was a man of many interests. Not only was he the director of the museum, but he was also a silent partner in two antique shops, one here and one in Milan. The man I was talking to works in one of the shops.'

Brunetti resisted the urge to ask which one. Instead, he remained silent, knowing that Lele would tell him what he thought necessary.

'It seems that the owner of these shops − not Semenzato, the official owner − has access to pieces that never appear in the shops. The man I spoke to said that twice in the past certain pieces have been brought in and unpacked by mistake. As soon as the owner saw them, he had them repacked and taken away, said that they were for his private collection.'

'Did he tell you what these pieces were?'

'He said that one of them was a Chinese bronze, and the other was a piece of pre-Islamic ceramic. He also said, and I thought this might interest you, that he was fairly certain he had seen a photo of the ceramic in an article about the pieces taken from the Kuwait Museum.'

'When did this happen?' Brunetti asked.

'The first time, about a year ago, and then three months ago,' Lele answered.

'Did he tell you anything else?'

'He said that the owner has a number of clients who have access to this private collection.'

'How did he know that?'

'Sometimes, when he was talking to these clients, the owner would refer to pieces he had, but the pieces weren't in the shop. Or he'd telephone one of these clients and tell him he was getting a particular item on a certain date, but then the piece would never come into the shop. But, later, it would sound like a sale had taken place.'

'Why would he tell you this, Lele?' Brunetti asked, though he knew he wasn't supposed to.

'We worked together in London, years ago, and I did him some favours then.'

'And how did you know to ask him, of all people?'

172

Instead of being offended, Lele laughed. 'Oh, I asked some questions about Semenzato, and someone told me to speak to my friend.'

'Thanks, Lele.' Brunetti understood, as do all Italians, how the whole delicate web of personal favours enwrapped the social system. It all seemed so casual: someone spoke to a friend, had a word with a cousin, and some information was exchanged. And with that information a new balance was struck between debit and credit. Sooner or later, everything was repaid, all debts called in.

'Who's the owner of these shops?'

'Francesco Murino. He's a Neapolitan. I did some business with him when he first opened his shop here, years ago, and he's *un vero figlio di puttana*. If there's anything crooked going on here, he's in for his fair share.'

'Is he the one who has the shop in Santa Maria Formosa?'

'Yes, do you know him?'

'Only by sight. He's never been in any trouble, not that I know of.'

'Guido, I told you he's a Neapolitan. Of course he hasn't been in any trouble, but that doesn't mean he isn't as crooked as a viper.' The passion with which Lele spoke made Brunetti curious about the dealings he might have had with Murino in the past.

'Did anyone say anything else about Semenzato?'

Lele made a noise of disgust. 'You know how it is when a person dies. No one wants to tell the truth.'

'Yes, someone else told me that, just this morning.'

'What else did they tell you?' Lele asked with what seemed like real curiosity.

'That I should wait a couple of weeks, and then people will begin to tell the truth again.'

Lele laughed so loudly that Brunetti had to hold the phone away from his ear until he stopped. When he did, Lele said, 'How right they are. But I don't think it will take that long.'

'Does that mean there's more to tell about him?'

'No, I don't want to mislead you, Guido, but one or two people didn't seem terribly surprised that he was killed like this.' When Brunetti didn't ask him what he meant, Lele added, 'It would seem that he had connections with people from the South.'

'Are they getting interested in art now?' Brunetti asked.

'Yes, it seems drugs and prostitutes aren't enough any more.'

'I guess we'd better double the guards in the museums from now on.'

'Guido, who do you think they buy the paintings from?'

Was this to be yet another consequence of upward mobility, Brunetti wondered, the Mafia in

174

competition with Sotheby's? 'Lele, how trust-worthy are these people you've spoken to?'

'You can believe what they say, Guido.'

'Thanks, Lele. If you hear anything more about him, please let me know.'

'Of course. And Guido, if these gentlemen from the South are involved in this, then you'd better be very careful, all right?' It was a sign of the power it had already garnered here in the North that people were reluctant to pronounce the name of the Mafia.

'Of course, Lele, and thanks again.'

'I'm serious,' Lele said before he hung up.

Brunetti replaced his phone and, almost without thinking, went and opened the window to allow some cold air into the room. Work on the façade of the church of San Lorenzo opposite his office had stopped for the winter, and the scaffolding stood there deserted. One large piece of the plastic wrapping that encased it had been torn loose and, even at this distance, Brunetti could hear it snap-ping angrily in the wind. Above the church and rolling in from the south, Brunetti could see the dark clouds that would surely bring more rain by the end of the afternoon.

He glanced at his watch. There was no time to visit Signor Murino before lunch, but Brunetti decided to stop by his shop that afternoon and see how he reacted to having a commissario of police come in and announce himself. The Mafia. Stolen art. He knew that more than half of the museums in the country were more or less permanently closed, but he had never before stopped to consider what this could mean in terms of pilfering, theft or, in the case of the Chinese exhibits, substitution. Guards were badly paid, yet their unions were so strong that they prevented volunteers from being allowed to work as guards in the museums. He remembered hearing, years ago, a suggestion that young men who chose two years of social service in lieu of a year and a half of military service be allowed to serve as museum guards. The idea had not even made it to the floor of the Senate.

Assuming that the substitution of false pieces was something Semenzato had a part in, who better to dispose of the originals than an antique dealer? He would have not only the clientele and the expertise to make an accurate appraisal, but, if necessary, he would know how to make delivery without interference from either the police of the Finance Department or the Fine Arts Commission. Getting pieces into or out of the country was child's play. A glance at the map of Italy showed how permeable the borders were. Thousands of kilometres of bays, coves, inlets, beaches. Or, for the well organized or well connected, there were the ports and the airports, through which anything could pass with impunity. It was not only those who guarded the museums who were badly paid.

His reverie was broken by a knock on the door.

'*Avanti*,' he shouted and closed the window. Time to resume roasting.

Signorina Elettra came into the room, a note-book in one hand, a file in the other. 'I found the captain's name in the file, sir. It's Carrara, Giulio Carrara. He's still in Rome, but he was promoted to *maggiore* last year.'

'How did you find that out, signorina?'

'I called his office in Rome and spoke to his secretary. I asked her to tell him to expect a call from you this afternoon. He's already gone to lunch and won't be back until three thirty.' Brunetti knew what three thirty could mean in Rome.

He might as well have spoken the thought, for Signorina Elettra answered it. 'I asked. She said he actually gets back then, so I'm sure you could call him.'

'Thank you, signorina,' he said and once again gave silent thanks that this marvel had managed to resist the daily assault of Patta's reign. 'If I might ask, how did you manage to find his name so quickly?'

'Oh, I've been familiarizing myself with the files for months. I've made some changes because there doesn't seem to be any inner logic to the system as it is now. I hope no one will mind.'

'No, I don't think so. No one's ever able to find anything, so I don't think you can do the system any harm. It's all supposed to be put on computer.'

She gave him the look of one who had spent

time among the accumulated records; he would not repeat the remark. She came up to his desk and placed the folder on it. He noticed that she was wearing a black woollen dress today, tied with a bold red belt pulled tight around a very narrow waist. She took a handkerchief from her pocket and wiped at her forehead. 'Is it always so hot in here, sir?' she asked.

'No, signorina, it's something that happens for a few weeks in early February. It's usually over by the end of the month. It doesn't affect your office.'

'Is it the *scirocco*?' It was a sensible enough question. If the hot wind that blew up from Africa could bring *acqua alta*, there was certainly no reason it couldn't raise the temperature in his office.

'No, signorina. It's something in the heating system. No one's ever been able to figure it out. You'll get used to it, and it really will be gone by the end of the month.'

'I hope so,' she said, wiping again at her brow. 'If there's nothing else, sir, I'll go to lunch now.'

Brunetti looked at his watch and saw that it was almost one. 'Take an umbrella with you when you go out,' he said. 'It looks like it's going to rain again.'

Brunetti went home for lunch with his family, and Paola kept her promise not to tell Raffi about the syringes and what his father had feared when he found them. She did, however, manage to use her silence to pry from Brunetti a firm promise that he would not only help her carry the table out on to the terrace at the first sign of sun but would also help her use the syringes to inject poison into each of the many holes made by the woodworms as they bored their way out of the legs where they spent their winter lethargy.

Raffi closed himself in his room after lunch, saying that he had to do his Greek homework, ten pages of Homer to translate for the next morning. Two years ago, when he had fancied himself an anarchist, he had closed himself in his room to think dark thoughts about capitalism, in the doing perhaps to hasten its fall. But this year he had not only found a girlfriend but, apparently, the desire to be accepted at the university. In either case, he disappeared into his room directly after meals, leaving Brunetti to conclude that his wish for solitude had something to do with adolescence, not political orientation.

Paola threatened dark things to Chiara if she didn't help with the dishes, and while they were busy there, Brunetti stuck his head into the kitchen and told them he was going back to work.

When he left the house, the threatened rain was falling, still light but with the promise of much worse to come. He raised his umbrella and turned right into Rugetta, making his way back towards the Rialto Bridge. Within a few minutes, he was glad he had remembered to wear his boots, for large puddles covered the pavement, tempting him to step heavily into them. By the time he got to the other side of the bridge, it was raining more heavily, and by the time he got to the Questura, his trousers were soaked from calf to knee above where they were protected by the boots.

In his office, he removed his jacket and wished for a moment that he could take off his trousers, too, and hang them to dry above the heater: they'd be dry in minutes. Instead, he held the window open long enough to cool off the office then sat behind his desk, dialled the operator and asked to be connected to the office of the art theft squad at police headquarters in Rome. When he was through, he gave his name and asked for Maggiore Carrara.

'*Buon giorno*, Commissario.'

'Congratulations, Maggiore.'

'Thanks, and it was about time they did it.'

'You're still a kid. You've got plenty of time to become a general.'

'By the time I'm a general, there won't be a single painting left in any of the museums in this country,' he said. Carrara's laugh, when it came, was delayed just so long that Brunetti was unsure whether the remark was meant to be a joke or not.

'That's what I'm calling you about, Giulio.'

'What? Paintings?'

'I'm not sure about that, museums, at any rate.'

180

'Yes, what is it?' he asked with the sharp curiosity that Brunetti remembered he felt for his work.

'We've had a murder here.'

'Yes, I know, Semenzato, at the Palazzo Ducale.' His voice was neutral.

'You know anything about him, Giulio?'

'Officially or unofficially?'

'Officially.'

'Absolutely not. Nothing. No. Not a thing.' Before Brunetti could do it, Carrara broke into his own litany and asked, 'Is that enough to make you ask the next question, Guido?'

Brunetti smiled into the phone. 'All right. Unofficially?'

'How strange of you to ask that. In fact, I have a note here on my desk to call you. I didn't know you were handling the case until I read your name in the papers this morning, so I thought I'd give you a call and suggest a few things. And ask a few favours, as well. I think there are a number of things we might both be interested in.'

'Like what?'

'Like his bank statements.'

'Semenzato's?'

'Isn't that who we're talking about?'

'Sorry, Giulio, but I've had people telling me all day that I ought not to talk ill of the dead.'

'If we can't talk ill of the dead, who can we talk ill of?' Carrara asked with surprising good sense.

'I've already got someone working on them. I ought to have them by tomorrow. Anything else?'

'I'd like to have a look at records of his long–distance calls, both from his home and from the office at the museum. Do you think you could get them?'

'This still unofficial?'

'Yes.'

'I'll have them.'

'Good.'

'What else?'

'Have you spoken to his widow yet?'

'No, I haven't, not personally. One of my men has spoken to her. Why?'

'She might have some idea of where he travelled to during the last few months.'

'Why do you want to know that?' Brunetti asked, honestly curious.

'No special reason, Guido. But we like to know this sort of thing, once a person's name has come under our noses more than once.'

'And his had?'

'Yes.'

'Why?'

'Nothing specific, if I have to tell the truth.' Carrara sounded disappointed that he didn't have a definite accusation to pass on to Brunetti. 'Two men we arrested at the airport here, more than a year ago, with Chinese jade figurines, said only that they had heard him named in conversation.

They were only carriers; they didn't know much at all, didn't even know the value of what they were carrying.'

'And that was?' Brunetti asked.

'Billions. The statues were traced back to the National Museum in Taiwan. They'd disappeared three years before; no one ever learned how.'

'Were those the only things taken?'

'No, but they're the only things recovered. So far.'

'When else did you hear his name?'

'Oh, from one of the little people we keep on a string down here. We can get him for drugs or for breaking and entering any time we want him, so we let him run loose, and in return he brings us back a piece of information now and again. He said that he had overheard Semenzato's name mentioned on the phone by one of the men he sells things to.'

'Stolen things?'

'Of course. He has nothing else to sell.'

'Was the man speaking to Semenzato, or about him?'

'About him.'

'Did he tell you what he heard?'

'The man who was speaking said only that the other person should try to speak to Semenzato. At first, we assumed the reference to him was innocent. After all, the man was a museum director. But then we caught the two men at the airport, and then Semenzato turned up dead in his office. So I thought it was time to call and tell you.' Carrara paused long enough to signal that he was finished with what he had to give, and now it was time to see what he could get. 'What have you found out about him there?'

'Remember the Chinese exhibition a few years ago?'

Carrara grunted in assent.

'Some of the pieces that were sent back to China were copies.'

Carrara's whistle, either of surprise or admiration for such a feat, came clearly through the line.

'And it seems he was silent partner in a pair of antique shops, one here and one in Milan,' Brunetti continued.

'Whose?'

'Francesco Murino. Do you know him?'

Carrara's voice was slow, measured. 'Only in the way we knew Semenzato, unofficially. But his name has turned up more than a few times.'

'Anything definite?'

'No, nothing. It looks like he covers himself very well.' There was a long pause, and then Carrara added, in a voice suddenly grown more serious, 'Or someone covers things for him.'

'Like that, is it?' Brunetti asked. It could mean anything: some branch of the government, Mafia, a foreign government, even the Church.

'Yes. Every lead we get turns to nothing. We

184

hear his name, and then we don't. The finance police have checked him three times in the last two years, and he's clean.'

'Has his name ever been linked to Semenzato's?'

'Not by anyone here. What else have you got?'

'Are you familiar with Dottoressa Lynch?'

'*L'americana?*' Carrara asked.

'Yes.'

'Of course I'm familiar with her. I have a degree in art history, Guido, after all.'

'Is she that well known?'

'Her book on Chinese art is the best one around. She's still in China, isn't she?'

'No, she's here.'

'In Venice? What's she doing there?'

Brunetti had asked himself the same question. Trying to decide whether to go back to China, whether to stay here because of her lover, or, now, waiting to see if her former lover had been murdered. 'She came here to talk to Semenzato about the pieces that were sent back to China. Two toughs beat her up last week. Cracked her jaw and broke some ribs. It was in the papers here.'

Again, Carrara's whistle came across the line from Rome, but this one somehow managed to convey compassion. 'There was nothing here,' he said.

'Her assistant in China, a Japanese woman who came here to oversee the return of the exhibits to China, died in an accident out there.'

'Freud says somewhere that there are no accidents, doesn't he?' Carrara asked.

'I don't know if Freud meant to include China when he said that, but, no, it doesn't sound like it was an accident.'

Carrara's grunt could have meant anything. Brunetti chose to interpret it as assent and said, 'I'm going to talk to Dottoressa Lynch tomorrow morning.'

'Why?'

'I want to try to convince her to leave the city for a while, and I want to learn more about the pieces that were substituted. What they were, whether they have a market value—'

Carrara interrupted him. 'Of course they have a market value.'

'Yes, I understand that, Giulio. But I want to get some idea of what the market would be, whether they could be sold openly.'

'Sorry. I didn't understand what you meant, Guido.' His pause could have been read as an apology, and then he added, 'If it's coming out of a dig in China, you can pretty much put any price you want on it.'

'That rare?' Brunetti asked.

'That rare. But what do you want to know about it?'

'Chiefly, I want to know where or how the copies could have been made.'

Carrara interrupted again. 'Italy is full of studios

that make copies, Guido. Everything: Greek statues, Etruscan jewellery, Ming pottery, Renaissance paintings. You name it, and there's an Italian artisan who can make you one that will fool the experts.'

'But haven't you people down there got all sorts of ways to detect them? Surely I've read that. Carbon-14 and things like that.'

Carrara laughed. 'Talk to Dottoressa Lynch, Guido. She has a whole chapter on it in her book, so I'm sure she can tell you things that will keep you awake on long winter nights.' Brunetti heard noise from the other end, then silence as Carrara covered the phone with his hand. In a moment, he was back. 'Sorry, Guido, but I've got a call coming in from Vietnam; it's taken two days to get it through. Call me if you hear anything, and I'll call you if I do.' Before Brunetti could agree, Carrara was gone and the line was dead.

Chapter Fourteen

ENTIRELY UNCONSCIOUS of how hot his office had become, Brunetti sat at his desk and considered what Carrara had told him. Take a museum director, add guards, labour unions, stir in a bit of the Mafia, and the result was a cocktail strong enough to give the art theft branch a bad hangover. He drew a piece of paper from his drawer and began to make a list of the information he needed to get from Brett. He wanted complete descriptions of the pieces she had discovered to be false. He needed more information about how the switch could have been done and where and how the false pieces could have been made. And he needed a complete account of her every conversation or exchange with Semenzato.

He stopped writing and allowed his thoughts to veer towards the personal: would she go back? As he thought of her, called up a picture of her as he had last seen her, slamming her hand down on the table and walking angrily from the room, he was struck by a discrepancy he had previously overlooked. Why had she received only a beating while Semenzato had been killed? He had no doubt that the men sent to her had been ordered only to deliver their violent warning that she not keep the meeting. But why would they have bothered with that if Semenzato was going to be killed anyway? Had Flavia's interference upset the balance of things, or had Semenzato somehow precipitated the violence that led to his death?

Practical things first. He called down and asked Vianello to come up, and he told him to stop outside Patta's office to request Signorina Elettra to come up with him. The Interpol report had not arrived, so he thought it was time to begin ferreting about on his own. He went and opened the window while he waited for them to arrive.

They came in together a few minutes later, Vianello holding the door open to allow her to pass in before him. As soon as they were inside, Brunetti closed the window, and the sergeant, ever gruff and bear-like Vianello, pulled a chair up to Brunetti's desk and held it while Signorina Elettra took her place on it. Vianello?

As she sat down, Signorina Elettra slipped a single sheet of paper on to Brunetti's desk. 'This came in from Rome, sir.' In response to his unspoken question, she added, 'They've traced the fingerprints.'

Under the letterhead of the Carabinieri, the letter, bearing an indecipherable signature, stated that fingerprints taken from Semenzato's telephone corresponded to those of Salvatore La Capra, age twenty-three, resident in Palermo. Despite his youth, La Capra had amassed a significant number of arrests and charges: extortion, rape, assault, attempted murder, and association with known members of the Mafia. All of these charges, at various times during the long legal processes that led from arrest to trial, had been dropped. Three witnesses in the extortion case had disappeared; the woman who brought the charge of rape had retracted her *denuncia*. The only conviction that stood against La Capra's name was for speeding, for which infraction he had paid a four-hundred-and-twenty-thousand-lire fine. The report went on to state that La Capra, who was not employed, lived with his father.

When he finished reading the report, Brunetti looked up at Vianello. 'Have you seen this?'

Vianello nodded.

'Why does the name sound familiar?' Brunetto asked, addressing them both with the question.

Signorina Elettra and Vianello started to speak at the same time, but Vianello, when he heard her, stopped and waved at her to proceed.

When she did not, Brunetti prodded, 'Well?' impatient for an answer in the midst of all of this chivalry.

'The architect?' Signorina Elettra asked, and Vianello nodded in agreement.

It was enough to remind Brunetti. Five months ago, the architect in charge of extensive restorations to a *palazzo* on the Grand Canal had sworn out a complaint against the son of the owner of the *palazzo*, claiming that the son had threatened him with violence if there were any more delays to the restoration project, already in its eighth month. The architect's attempt to explain about the difficulty in obtaining building permits was brushed aside by the son, who warned him that his father was not a man who was accustomed to being kept waiting and that bad things often happened to people who displeased him or his father. The following day, and before there had been a chance for the police to act on the complaint, the architect was back in the Questura, claiming that the whole thing had been a misunderstanding and no actual threats had been made. The charges had been withdrawn, but the report of the original *denuncia* had been made out and read by all three of them, and all of them now remembered that it had been made against Salvatore La Capra.

'I think we should see if Signorino La Capra or his father is at home,' Brunetti suggested. 'And, signorina,' he added, turning to her, 'perhaps you could see what you can find out about his father, if you're not busy with anything.'

'Of course, Dottore,' she said. 'I've already made the Vice-Questore's dinner reservation, so I'll begin on this immediately.' Smiling, she stood, and

Vianello, shadow-like, drifted to the door in front of her. He held it for her while she left the office, then came back to his seat.

'I've seen the wife, sir. The widow, that is.'

'Yes. I read your report. It seemed very brief.'

'It was brief, sir,' Vianello said, voice level. 'There wasn't much to say. She was sick with grief for him, could barely talk. I asked her a few questions, but she cried through all of it, so I had to stop. I'm not sure she understood why I was there or why I was asking her the questions.'

'Was it real grief?' Brunetti asked. Both policemen for many years, they had seen more than enough of both kinds, real and feigned, to last many lifetimes.

'I think so, sir.'

'What was she like?'

'She's about forty, ten years younger than he was. There weren't any children, so he was all she had. I don't think she fitted in here very well.'

'Why not?' Brunetti asked.

'Semenzato was Venetian, but she's from the South. Sicily. And she's never liked it here. She said she wanted to go home after all of this was over.'

How many threads in this were going to pull towards the South, Brunetti wondered. Surely, the place of the woman's birth shouldn't cause him to suspect her of criminal involvement. Telling himself this, he said, 'I want to get a tap on her phone.'

'On Signora Semenzato's?' Vianello's surprise was audible.

'Who else have we been talking about, Vianello?'

'But I just talked to her, and she's hardly capable of standing up by herself. She's not faking that grief, sir. I'm sure of it.'

'Her grief isn't in question, Vianello. It's her husband.' Brunetti was also curious about what the widow might have known of her husband's behaviour, but with Vianello in an uncharacteristically gallant mood, this was best left unsaid.

Vianello's assent was grudging. 'Even if that's the reason—'

Brunetti cut him off. 'What about the staff at the museum?'

Vianello allowed himself to be herded back into line. 'They seemed to like Semenzato. He was efficient, dealt well with the unions, and he was apparently very good at delegating authority, at least to the extent that the Ministry would let him.'

'What does that mean?'

'He let the curators decide which paintings needed to go to restoration, let them decide what techniques to use, when to call in outside experts. From what I gathered from the people I talked to, the man who had the job before he did insisted on keeping everything under his control, and that meant things got slowed down, since he wanted to know all the details. Most of them preferred Semenzato.'

'Anything else?'

'I went back up to the hallway where Semenzato's office is and took another look around in the daylight. There's a door that leads into that corridor from the left wing, but it's nailed shut. And there's no way anyone could have come across the roof. So they went up the stairs.'

'Right past the guards' office,' Brunetti finished for him.

'And past it again on the way down,' Vianello added, not kindly.

'What was on television that night?'

Vianello answered, 'Reruns of *Colpo Grosso*,' with an immediacy that forced Brunetti to wonder if the sergeant had been at home that night, with half of Italy, watching demi-celebrities remove their clothing piece by piece to the excited shrieks of a studio audience. If the breasts had been big enough, thieves could probably have gone into the Piazza and removed the Basilica, and no one would have noticed until the following morning.

This seemed a wise point to change the subject. 'All right, Vianello, see what you can do about getting her phone taken care of.' His tone couldn't be described as dismissive, not quite.

By mutual assent, the conversation was over. Vianello stood, still not pleased with this further invasion of the grief of the widow Semenzato, but

194

agreed to see that it was done. 'Anything else, sir?'

'No, I don't think so.' Ordinarily, Brunetti would ask to be informed when the tap was in place, but he left it to Vianello. The sergeant moved his chair a few centimetres forward and placed it squarely in front of Brunetti's desk, waved a vague salute, and left the office without another word. Brunetti thought it was enough that he had one prima donna to deal with over in Cannaregio. He didn't need another one here at the Questura.

Chapter Fifteen

WHEN BRUNETTI left the Questura fifteen minutes later, he wore his boots and carried his umbrella. He cut back to his left, heading in the general direction of Rialto, but then turned to the right, suddenly to the left, and soon found himself coming down off the bridge that led into Campo Santa Maria Formosa. Directly in front of him, on the other side of the *campo*, stood Palazzo Priuli, abandoned for as long as he could remember, the central prize of vicious litigation over a contested will. As the heirs and presumptive heirs fought over whose it was or should be, the *palazzo* went about its business of deteriorating with a single-mindedness that ignored heirs, claims and legality. Long smears of rust trickled down the stone walls from the iron gratings that tried to protect it from unlawful entry, and the roof pitched and sagged, opening up fissures here and there, allowing the curious sun to peek into the attic, closed up these many years. Brunetti the dreamer had often considered that Palazzo Priuli would be the ideal place to imprison a mad aunt, a recalcitrant wife or a reluctant heiress at the same time as his more sober and practical Venetian self viewed it as a prime piece of real estate and studied the windows, dividing the space beyond into apartments, offices and studios.

Murino's shop, he had the vague semi-memory, stood on the north side, between a pizzeria and a mask shop. The pizzeria was closed for the season, awaiting the return of the tourists, but both the mask shop and the antique shop were open, their lights burning brightly through the late winter rain.

As Brunetti pushed open the door to the shop, a bell sounded in a room somewhere off behind a pair of damasked velvet curtains that hung in a doorway that led to the back. The room radiated the subdued glow of wealth, the wealth of ages and stability. There were, surprisingly, few pieces on display, yet each called for the complete attention of the viewer. At the back stood a walnut credenza with a row of five drawers down the left side, the wood aglow with centuries of attentive care. Just beneath his hand stood a long oak table, probably taken from the refectory of some religious house. It, too, had been polished to a shimmering glow, but no attempt had been made to disguise or remove the chips and stains of long use. At his feet crouched a pair of marble lions, teeth bared in a threat which had perhaps once been terrifying.

But age had worn away their teeth and softened their features until now they faced their enemies with a yawn rather than a growl.

'*C'è qualcuno?*' Brunetti called towards the back. He looked down and noticed that his folded umbrella had already left a large puddle on the parquet floor of the shop. Signor Murino must surely be an optimist, as well as a non-Venetian, to have covered a floor in this part of the city with parquet, for the zone lay low, and the first serious *acqua alta* was sure to flow in here, destroying the wood and sweeping out both glue and varnish when the tide changed.

'*Buon giorno?*' he called again, taking a few steps towards the doorway and leaving a trail of raindrops on the floor behind him.

A hand appeared at the curtain and pushed it aside. The man who stepped into the room was the same one Brunetti remembered having seen in the city and who had been pointed out to him – he could no longer remember by whom – as the antique dealer from Santa Maria Formosa. Murino was short, as were many Southerners, with lustrous black hair which he wore in a crown of loose ringlets hanging down to his collar. His colouring was dark, his skin smooth, his features small and well proportioned. What was disconcerting, in the midst of this cliché of Mediterranean good looks, were the eyes, a clear opaline green. Though they gazed out at the world from behind round gold-framed glasses which partially obscured them and were shadowed by lashes as long as they were black, they remained the dominant feature of his face. The French, Brunetti knew, had conquered Naples centuries ago, but the usual genetic souvenir of their long occupation was the red hair sometimes seen in the city, not these clear, Nordic eyes.

'Signor Murino?' he asked, extending his hand.

'*Sì*,' the antique dealer answered, taking Brunetti's hand and returning his grip firmly.

'I'm Guido Brunetti, Commissario of Police. I'd like to have a few words with you.'

Murino's expression remained one of polite curiosity.

'I'd like to ask you some questions about your partner. Or should I say, your late partner?'

Brunetti watched as Murino absorbed this information, then waited as the other man began to consider what his visible response should be. All of this took only seconds, but Brunetti had been observing the process for decades and was familiar with it. The people to whom he presented himself had a drawer of responses which they thought appropriate, and part of his job was to watch them as they sifted through them one at a time, seeking the right fit. Surprise? Fear? Innocence? Curiosity? He watched Murino flip through them, studied his face as he considered, then discarded, various possibilities. He decided, apparently, on the last.

'Yes? And what would you like to know, Commissario?' His smile was polite, his tone friendly. He looked down and noticed Brunetti's umbrella. 'Here, let me take that, please,' he said, managing to sound more concerned with Brunetti's inconvenience than with any damage the dripping water might be doing to his floor. He carried the umbrella over to a flower-painted porcelain umbrella stand that stood next to the door. He slipped it in and turned back to Brunetti. 'May I take your coat?'

Brunetti realized that Murino was attempting to set the tone of their interview, and the tone he aimed for was friendly and relaxed, the verbal manifestation of his own innocence. 'Thank you, don't bother,' Brunetti answered, and with his response grabbed the tone back into his own command. 'Could you tell me how long he was a partner in your business?'

Murino gave no sign that he had registered the struggle for dominance of the conversation. 'Five years,' he answered, 'from when I opened this shop.'

'And what about your shop in Milan? Did his partnership extend to that?'

'Oh, no. They're kept as separate businesses. His partnership pertained only to this one.'

'And how is it that he became a partner?'

'You know how it is. Word travels.'

'No, I'm afraid I don't know how it is, Signor Murino. How did he become your partner?'

Murino's smile was consistently relaxed; he was willing to ignore Brunetti's rudeness. 'When I was given the opportunity to rent this space, I contacted some friends of mine here in the city and tried to borrow money from them. I had most of my capital tied up in the stock in the Milan shop, and the market for antiques was very slow at that time.'

'But still you wanted to open a second shop?'

Murino's smile was cherubic. 'I had hope in the future. People might stop buying for a period, but that always comes to an end, and people will always return to buying beautiful things.'

If Murino had been a woman, Brunetti would have said he was fishing for a compliment and nudging Brunetti to admire the pieces in the shop and, with that, relax the tension created by the questions.

'And was your optimism rewarded, Signor Murino?'

'Oh, I can't complain.'

'And your partner? How was it that he found out about your interest in borrowing money?'

'Oh, voices travel. Word spreads.' That, apparently, was as much of an explanation as Signor Murino was prepared to give.

'And so he appeared, money in hand, asking to become a partner?'

Murino walked over to a Renaissance wedding chest and wiped at a fingerprint with his handkerchief. He bent down to get his eyes horizontal with the surface of the chest and wiped repeatedly at the smear until it was gone. He folded his handkerchief into a neat rectangle, put it back into the pocket of his jacket, and leaned back against the edge of the chest. 'Yes, I suppose you could say that.'

'And what did he get in return for his investment?'

'Fifty per cent of the profits for ten years.'

'And who kept the books?'

'We have *un contabile* who takes care of all that for us.'

'Who does the buying for the shop?'

'I do.'

'And the selling?'

'I. Or my daughter. She works here two days a week.'

'So it's you and your daughter who know what gets bought, and at what price, and what gets sold, and at what price?'

'I have receipts for all purchases and sales, Dottor Brunetti,' Murino said, voice just short of indignation.

Brunetti considered for a moment the option of telling Murino that everyone in Italy had receipts for everything and that all of those receipts were utterly meaningless as anything other than evidence faked to avoid paying taxes. But one did not point out that rain fell from the sky to the earth

below or that it was in the spring that trees blossom-
ed. Just so, one did not have to point out the
existence of tax fraud, especially not to an antique
dealer, and most especially not to a Neapolitan
antique dealer.

'Yes, I'm sure you have, Signor Murino,' Brunetti said, and changed the subject. 'When was the
last time you saw him?'

Murino had apparently been expecting this
question, for his answer was immediate. 'Two
weeks ago. We met for a drink, and I told him I
was planning a buying trip up into Lombardy at
the end of the month. I told him I wanted to
close the shop for a week and asked him if he had
any objection if I did so.'

'And did he?'

'No, none at all.'

'What about your daughter?'

'She's busy studying for her exams. She's studying law. And whole days pass when no one comes
into the shop. So I thought this was a good time
to close for a while. We also needed to get some
work done.'

'What sort of work?'

'We've got a door that opens to the canal, and
it's come off its hinges. So if we want to use it, a
whole new frame has to be built,' he said, gesturing
towards the velvet curtains. 'Would you like to
see?' Murino asked.

'No, thank you,' Brunetti answered. 'Signor

Murino, did it ever occur to you that there might be a certain conflict of interest for your partner?'

Murino smiled inquisitively. 'I'm afraid I don't understand.'

'Then let me try to make it clearer. His other position might have served to, let us say, work to the advantage of your joint investment here.'

'I must apologize, but I still don't understand what you mean.' Murino's smile would not have seemed out of place on the face of an angel.

Brunetti gave examples. 'Using you, perhaps, as a consultant or learning that certain pieces or collections were going to come up for sale. Perhaps recommending the shop to people who expressed an interest in a particular sort of item.'

'No, that never occurred to me.'

'Did it occur to your partner?'

Murino took his handkerchief and leaned over to wipe at another smudge. When he was satisfied that the surface was clean, he said, 'I was his business partner, Commissario, not his confessor. I'm afraid that's a question only he could answer.'

'But that, alas, is not to be.'

Murino shook his head sadly. 'No, that is not to be.'

'What will happen to his share of the shop now?'

Murino's face was all astonished innocence. 'Oh, I'll continue dividing the profits with his widow.'

'And you and your daughter will continue to do the buying and selling?'

Murino's answer was slow in coming, but when it came, it was no more than an acknowledgement of the self-evident. 'Yes, of course.'

'Of course,' Brunetti echoed, though the words neither sounded the same nor conveyed the same idea when he said them.

Murino's face suffused with sudden anger, but before he could speak, Brunetti said, 'Thank you for your time, Signor Murino. I hope you have a successful trip to Lombardy.'

Murino pushed himself away from the chest and went over to the door to retrieve Brunetti's umbrella. He held it by the still-wet cloth and offered it, handle first, to Brunetti. He opened the door and held it politely for Brunetti, then closed it softly behind him. Brunetti stood in the rain and raised his umbrella. As he did, a sudden gust of wind tried to pull it from his hands, but he tightened his grip and turned towards home. During the entire conversation, neither of them had once used Semenzato's name.

Chapter Sixteen

AS HE MADE HIS way across the rain-swept *campo*, Brunetti found himself wondering if Semenzato would have trusted a man like Murino to keep the records of all purchases and sales. Brunetti had certainly known odder business arrangements, and he kept in mind the fact that he knew Semenzato, as it were, only in retrospect, a vision that seldom encouraged clarity. But still, who would be so dull as to believe the word of an antiquarian, as slippery a bunch as he could imagine? Here a voice stronger than his attempt to suppress it asked, 'And a Neapolitan, to boot?' No one would accept what they said as face value, without question. But if the major business of their partnership was in stolen or false pieces, then the earnings from the legitimate business of the shop wouldn't matter. In that case, Semenzato would never have had to question Murino's receipts or his word that an *armadio* or a table had been purchased for a certain price, sold for so much more. When he thought of the idea of profit, loss, price, he realized he had no base figures here, no idea whatsoever of the market value of the pieces Brett said were missing. For that matter, he didn't even know what those pieces were. Tomorrow.

Because of the ever-increasing rain and the threat of *acqua alta*, the streets were strangely deserted, even though this was the time when most people would be hurrying home from work or out to do some last-minute shopping before the stores closed. Instead, Brunetti found that he could pass easily through the narrow streets without the repeated bother of turning his umbrella sideways to allow shorter people to pass under it with theirs. Even the broad top of the Rialto Bridge was strangely deserted, something he could not remember ever having seen before. Many of the stalls were empty, boxes of fruit and vegetables whisked away before closing time, owners escaped from the grinding cold and the rain that continued to pound down.

He slammed the door of his building behind him: in wet weather, the lock tended to stick, and only violence would get the massive door to close or open. He shook his umbrella a few times, then furled it and stuck it under his arm. With his right hand, he grabbed the handrail and began the long climb to their apartment. On the first floor, Signora Bussola, the deaf widow of a lawyer, was watching the *telegiornale*, which meant that everyone on the floor got to listen to the news.

Predictably, she watched the news on RAI Uno; not for her those radical leftists and communist scum on RAI Due. On the second floor, the Rossis were quiet: that meant their argument was over and they were in the back of the house, in the bedroom. The third floor was silent. A young couple had moved in there two years ago and bought the entire floor, but Brunetti could count on one hand the times he had met either one of them on the stairs. He was said to work for the city, though no one was sure what he did. The wife left every morning and came home at five thirty every afternoon, but no one knew where she went or what she did, a fact which Brunetti thought miraculous. On the fourth floor, there were only scents. The Amabiles seldom emerged, but the stairwell was always awash with the glorious, tempting smells of food. Tonight it appeared to be *capriolo* and, if he wasn't wrong, artichokes, though it might be fried aubergine.

And then there was his own door and the promise of peace. Which lasted only as long as it took him to open the door and step inside. From the back of the apartment, he could hear Chiara sobbing. This was his little Spartan, the child who almost never cried, the girl who could be punished by being deprived of the things she most desired and who would never shed a tear, this the child who had once broken her wrist but had sat tearless, however pale, while it was being set. And she was not merely crying; she was sobbing.

He walked quickly down the hall and into her room. Paola sat on the side of the bed, cradling Chiara in her arms. 'But, baby, I don't think there's anything we can do. I've got the ice on it, but you're just going to have to wait until it stops hurting.'

'But, *Mamma*, it hurts. It hurts so much. Can't you make it stop?'

'I can give you more aspirin, Chiara. Maybe that will help.'

Chiara gulped back her tears and repeated, her voice gone strangely high, '*Mamma*, please do something.'

'Paola, what is it?' he asked, keeping his voice very calm, very level.

'Oh, Guido,' Paola said, turning to him but keeping firm hold of Chiara. 'Chiara dropped the table on her toe.'

'What table?' he asked, rather than what toe.

'The one in the kitchen.' That was the one with the woodworm. What had they done, tried to move it themselves? But why do that when it was raining? They couldn't take it out on to the terrace; it was too heavy for them.

'What happened?'

'She didn't believe me that there were so many holes, so she turned it on its side to look, and it slipped out of her hands and landed on her toe.'

'Let me see,' he said and, as soon as he spoke, saw that her right foot lay on top of the coverlet, wrapped in a bath towel that held a plastic bag of ice against the injured toe to work against the swelling.

It proved to be just as he imagined, and the toe proved to be worse. It was the big toe of her right foot, swollen, the entire nail red with the promise of the blue that would emerge with time.

'Is it broken?' he asked.

'No, *Papà*, I can bend it and that doesn't hurt. But it throbs and throbs,' Chiara said. She had stopped sobbing, but he could see from her face that the pain was still strong. '*Papà*, please do something.'

'There's nothing *Papà* can do, Chiara,' Paola said, pushing the foot a bit to the side and placing the bag of ice back on top of it.

'When did it happen?' he asked.

'This afternoon, right after you left,' Paola answered.

'And she's been like that all day?'

'No, *Papà*,' Chiara said, defending herself from the unspoken accusation that she had spent the entire afternoon in tears. 'It hurt at the beginning, and then it was all right for a while, but now it hurts a lot.' She had already asked once if he could do something; Chiara was not the sort of person who repeated a request.

He remembered something he had learned years

ago, when he was doing his military service and one of the men in his unit had dropped a manhole cover on his toe. Somehow, he had managed not to break it because it had caught his toe just at the end, but it had, like Chiara's, gone red and swollen.

'There is one thing,' he began. Paola and Chiara swung their heads to look at him.

'What?' they asked in unison.

'It's disgusting,' he said, 'but it will help.'

'What is it, *Papà*?' Chiara asked through lips that were beginning to tremble again with pain.

'I have to stick a needle through the nail and let the blood out.'

'No,' Paola shouted, tightening her grip around Chiara's shoulder.

'Does it work, *Papà*?'

'It worked the one time I saw it done, but that was years ago. I've never done it, but I watched the doctor do it.'

'Do you think you could do it, *Papà*?'

He removed his coat and laid it across the foot of her bed. 'I think so, angel. Do you want me to try?'

'Will it make it stop hurting?'

'I think so.'

'All right, *Papà*.'

He glanced across at Paola, asking her opinion. She bent and kissed the top of Chiara's head, wrapped her in an even tighter embrace, then nodded to Brunetti and tried to smile.

He went down the hall and took a candle from the third drawer to the right of the kitchen sink. He jammed it down into a ceramic candle-holder, grabbed a box of matches and went back into the bedroom. He set the candle down on Chiara's desk, lit it and went down the hall into Paola's study. From her top drawer he took a paper clip and bent it open into a straight rod as he went back towards Chiara's room. He'd said 'needle', but then he'd remembered that the doctor had used a paper clip, saying a needle was too thin to burn through the nail quickly.

Back in Chiara's room, he took the candle and set it at the foot of the bed, behind Paola's back. 'I think it might be better if you didn't watch, angel,' he told Chiara. To assure that, he sat on the edge of the bed, next to Paola, his back turned to hers, and uncovered Chiara's foot.

When he touched it, she pulled it away instinctively, said 'Sorry' into her mother's shoulder, and pushed her foot back near him. He took it with his left hand and moved the ice bag away from it. He had to change his position on the bed, careful not to let the candle spill over, until he was sitting facing the two of them. He took her heel and wedged it between his knees, pressing them together to hold it steady.

'It's all right, baby. It's just going to take a second,' he said, reaching for the candle with one hand and holding the end of the paper clip in the other. When the heat seared his fingers, he dropped the paper clip and spilled wax over the coverlet. Both his wife and his daughter winced away from his sudden motion.

'One moment, one moment,' he said and went back into the kitchen, muttering darkly under his breath. He took a pair of pliers from the bottom drawer and went back into the bedroom. When the candle was relit and everything was as it had been before, he grasped one end of the paper clip in the pliers and stuck the other into the flame. He waited until it glowed red and then, so quickly that he would not have time to think about what he was doing, he pressed the glowing end of the paper clip into the centre of the nail on Chiara's toe. He held it there while the toenail began to smoke, grabbed her ankle with his left hand to prevent her from pulling her foot back.

Suddenly, the resistance disappeared from under the paper clip, and dark blood flooded up out of her toe and across his fingers. He pulled the paper clip out and, acting more from instinct than from anything he might have remembered, he pressed at the bottom of her toe, forcing the dark blood to flow out of the hole in the nail.

Through all of this, Chiara had wrapped herself around Paola, and she, in her turn, had kept her eyes turned away from what Brunetti was doing. When he glanced up, however, he saw that Chiara was looking at him over her mother's shoulder and then down at her foot. 'Is that all?' she asked.

'Yes,' he answered. 'How does it feel?'

'It's better already, *Papà*. All the pressure's gone, and it doesn't throb any more.' She studied the tools of his trade: candle, pliers, paper clips. 'That's all you need to do it?' she asked with real curiosity, tears forgotten.

'That's all,' he said, giving her ankle a squeeze.

'Do you think I could do it?' she asked.

'Do you mean on yourself or on someone else?' he asked.

'Either.'

'I don't see why not.'

Paola, whose daughter seemed to have forgotten about her in the fascination of this new scientific discovery, removed her arms from that no-longer-suffering daughter and picked up the ice bag and towel from the bed. She stood, looked down at the two of them for a moment, as if studying some alien life form, and went down the hall towards the kitchen.

Chapter Seventeen

THE FOLLOWING morning, Chiara's foot felt good enough for her to go to school, though she opted to wear three pairs of woollen socks and her high rubber boots, not only because of the still-pounding rain and threatened *acqua alta*, but because the boots were wide and large enough to allow her healing toe plenty of room. She was gone by the time he was dressed and ready to leave for work, but at his place on the kitchen table he found a large sheet of paper with an immense red heart drawn on it and, under it, in her precise block print, '*Grazie, Papà.*' He folded the drawing into a neat rectangle and sipped it into his wallet.

He hadn't bothered to phone to tell Flavia and Brett – he assumed both of them were there – he was coming, but it was almost ten when he rang the bell, and he believed that was a sufficiently respectable hour to arrive to speak of murder.

He told the voice on the intercom who he was and pushed the heavy door open when the switch from upstairs released the lock. He propped his umbrella in a corner of the entrance, shook himself much in the manner of a dog, and began to climb the steps.

Today it was Brett who stood by the open door, she who let him into the apartment. She smiled when she saw him, and he saw again only the white flash of her teeth.

'Where's Signora Petrelli?' he asked as she led him into the living room.

'Flavia is seldom presentable before eleven. Never human before ten.' As she led the way across the living room, he noticed that she walked more easily and seemed to be less concerned about caus-ing pain to her body by some entirely natural movement or gesture.

She motioned him to a seat and took her place on the sofa; what little light came into the room entered behind her and partially shadowed her face. When they were seated, he pulled from his pocket the paper on which he had made notes the day before, though he was fairly clear about what he needed to know.

'I'd like you to tell me about the pieces you found in China, the ones you think are false,' he began with no introduction.

'What do you want to know?'

'Everything.'

'That's rather a lot.'

'I need to know about the pieces you think have

been stolen. And then I need to know something about how it could have been done.'

She began to answer immediately. 'I'm sure now about four, but the other is genuine.' Here her expression changed and the look she gave him was a confused one. 'But I have no idea how it was done.'

It was his turn not to understand. 'But someone told me yesterday that you have a whole chapter on it in a book you wrote.'

'Oh,' she said with audible relief, 'that's what you mean, how they were made. I thought you meant how they were stolen. I have no idea about that, but I can tell you how the false pieces were manufactured.'

Brunetti didn't want to bring up the idea of Matsuko's involvement, at least not yet, and so he merely asked, 'How?'

'It's a simple enough process.' Her voice changed, taking on the quick certainty of the expert. 'Do you know anything about pottery or ceramics?'

'Very little,' he admitted.

'The pieces that were stolen were all from the second century before Christ,' she began by way of explanation, but he interrupted her.

'Over two thousand years ago?' Brunetti asked.

'Yes. The Chinese had very beautiful pottery, even then, and very sophisticated means of making it. But the pieces that were taken were simple things, at least then, when they were made. They're unglazed, hand-painted, and they usually have the figures of animals. Primary colours: red and white, often on a black background.' She pushed herself up from the sofa and walked over to the bookcase, where she stood for a few minutes, considering, turning her head rhythmically as she studied the titles in front of her. Finally she took a book from a shelf directly in front of her and brought it back to Brunetti. She turned to the index, then opened it and flipped through the pages until she found the one she wanted. She passed the open book to Brunetti.

He saw a photo of a gourd-shaped, squat, covered jar, no idea given of its scale. The decoration on the jar was divided up into three horizontal bands: the neck and cover, a broad centre field, and a third band that ran to the bottom. In the broad central field, placed just on the widest part of the vase, he saw a wide view of an open-mouthed animal figure that might have been a stylized wolf, or a fox, even a dog, his white body standing upright and lurching to the left, back legs spread wide and raised forelegs stretched out on either side. The sense of motion created by his limbs was reflected in a series of geometric curves and swirls sketched in a repeated pattern across the front of the vase and, presumably, around to its unpictured back. The rim, he could see, was pitted and chipped, but the central image was intact, and it was very beautiful. The inscription said only that it was Han Dynasty, which meant nothing to Brunetti.

'Is this the sort of thing you find in Xian?' he asked.

'It's from Western China, yes, but not from Xian. It's a rare piece; I doubt we'll find anything like it.'

'Why?'

'Because two thousand years have passed.' That, she seemed to believe, was more than sufficient explanation.

'Tell me about how you'd copy it,' he said, keeping his eyes on the photo.

'First, you'd need an expert potter, someone who had actually had time and opportunity to study the ones that have been found, seen them close up, worked with them, perhaps worked at finding them, or worked at displaying them. That would allow him to have seen actual fragments, so he would have a clear idea of the thickness of the different parts. Then you'd need a very good painter, someone who could copy a style, catch the mood in a vase like this, and then reproduce it so closely that it would appear to be the same piece that had been in the exhibition.'

'How hard would that be to do?'

'Very hard. But there are men, and women, who are trained for it and who do it superbly well.'

Brunetti placed the point of his finger just above

the central figure. 'This one looks worn; it looks really old. How do they copy that?'

'Oh, that's relatively easy. They bury the piece in the ground; some of them use raw sewage and bury it there.' Seeing Brunetti's instinctive disgust, she explained. 'It corrodes the paint and wears it away faster. Then they chip tiny pieces away, usually from the edges or from the bottom.' To explain, she pointed to a small chip on the top rim of the vase in the photo, just where it met the cylindrical cover, and on the bottom, where the vase touched the ground.

'Is it difficult?' Brunetti asked.

'No, not to make a piece that will fool the layman. It's much harder to make something that will fool an expert.'

'Like you?' he asked.

'Yes,' she said, not bothering with the pretence of false modesty.

'How can you tell?' he asked, then expanded the question. 'What are some of the things that tell you it's a fake? Things that other people wouldn't see?'

Before she answered, she flipped through a few pages of the book, pausing now and again to look at a photo. Finally she snapped it closed and looked across at him. 'There's the paint, whether the colour is right for the period when the vase was supposed to have been made. And the line, if it shows hesitation in the execution. That suggests that the painter was trying to copy something and had to think about it, pause while drawing to get it right. The original artists didn't have to meet a standard; they just painted what they pleased, so their line is always fluid. If they didn't like it, they probably broke the pot.'

He picked up immediately on the use of the casual word. 'Pot or vase?'

She laughed outright at his question. 'They're vases now, two thousand years later, but I think they were just pots to the people who made them and used them.'

'What did they use them for?' Brunetti asked. 'Originally.'

She shrugged. 'For whatever people ever used pots for: storing rice, carrying water, storing grain. That one with the animal has a top, so they wanted whatever they kept in it to be safe, probably from mice. That suggests rice or wheat.'

'How valuable are they?' Brunetti asked.

She sat back in the sofa and crossed her legs. 'I don't know how to answer that.'

'Why not?'

'Because you have to have a market to have a price.'

'And?'

'And there's no market in these pieces.'

'Why not?'

'Because there are so few of them. The one in the book is at the Metropolitan in New York.

221

There might be three or four in other museums in different parts of the world.' She closed her eyes for a moment, and Brunetti could picture her running through lists and catalogues. When she opened them, she said, 'I can think of three: two in Taiwan, and one in a private collection.'

'No others?' Brunetti asked.

She shook her head. 'None.' But then she added, 'At least none that are on display or in a collection that is known about.'

'And private collections?' he asked.

'Perhaps, but one of us would probably have heard about it, and there's nothing in the literature that mentions any others. So I think it's a pretty safe guess there are no more than those.'

'What would one of the museum pieces be worth?' he asked, then explained when he saw her begin to shake her head, 'I know, I know, from what you've said, it would be impossible to put an exact price on it, but can you give me some idea of what the value would be?'

It took her a while to think of an answer. When she did, she said, 'The price would be whatever the seller asked or whatever the buyer was willing to pay. The market prices are in dollars – a hundred thousand? Two? More? But there really are no prices because there are so few pieces of this quality. It would depend entirely on how much the buyer wanted to have the piece, and on how much money he had.'

Brunetti translated her prices into millions of lire: two hundred million, three? Before he could complete this speculation, she continued.

'But that's only for the pottery, the vases. To the best of my knowledge, none of the statues of the soldiers has disappeared, but if that were to happen, there really is no price that could be put on it.'

'But there's also no way the owner could show it publicly, is there?' Brunetti asked.

She smiled. 'I'm afraid there are people who don't care about showing things publicly. They just want to possess, be sure that a certain piece is theirs. I've no idea if they're prompted by love of beauty or the desire of ownership, but, believe me, there are people who simply want to have a piece in their collection, even if no one ever sees it. Aside from themselves, that is.' She saw how sceptical he looked at this, so she added, 'Remember that Japanese billionaire, the one who wanted to be buried with his Van Gogh?'

Brunetti remembered having read something about it, last year. The man was said to have bought the painting at auction and then had it written in his will that he was to be buried with the painting, or, to put things in the proper order of importance, the painting was to be buried with him. He remembered something about a storm in the art world over this. 'In the end, he gave up and said he wouldn't do it, didn't he?'

'Well, that's what was reported,' she agreed. 'I never believed the story, but I mention him to give you an idea of how some people feel about their possessions, how they believe that their right of ownership is the absolute measure or the chief purpose of collecting, not the beauty of the object.' She shook her head. 'I'm afraid I'm not explaining this very well, but, as I said, it doesn't make any sense to me.'

Brunetti realized he still didn't have a sufficient answer to his original question. 'But I still don't understand how you know that something is an original or a copy.' Before she could answer, he added, 'A friend of mine told me about that sixth sense you get, that something just looks right or wrong to you. But that's very subjective. What I mean is this: if two experts disagree, one saying the piece is original and another saying it isn't, how do you resolve the difference? Call in a third expert and take a vote?' He smiled to show he was joking, but he could think of no other way out of the situation.

Her answering smile showed she got the joke. 'No, we call in the technicians. There are a number of tests we can perform to prove the age of an object.' With a change of voice, she asked, 'Are you sure you want to listen to all of this?'

'Yes, I do.'

'I'll try not to be too pedantic about it,' she said, pulling her feet up under her on the sofa. 'There are all sorts of tests that we can do on paintings: analysis of the chemical composition of paints to see if they're right for the time when the picture is said to have been painted, X-rays to see what's underneath the surface layer of a painting, even Carbon-14 dating.' He nodded to show that he was familiar with all of these.

'But we're not talking about paintings,' he said.

'No, we're not. The Chinese never worked in oils, at least not in the periods covered in the show. Most of the objects were ceramic or metal. I've never been interested in the metal pieces, well, not very much, but I do know it's almost impossible to check them scientifically. For them, you need the eye.'

'But not for ceramic?'

'Of course you need the expert eye, but, luckily, the techniques for checking authenticity are as sophisticated as they are for painting.' She paused a moment and asked again, 'Do you want me to be technical?'

'Yes, I do,' he said, finding his pen and, in the doing, feeling very much like a student.

'The chief technique we use – and the most reliable – is called thermoluminescence. All we have to do is extract about thirty milligrams of ceramic from any piece we want to test.' She anticipated his question by explaining, 'It's easy. We take it from the back of a plate or from the underside of a vase or a statue. The amount we need is barely noticeable, just enough to get a sample. Then a photo multiplier will tell us, with an accuracy of about ten to fifteen per cent, the age of the material.'

'How does it work?' Brunetti asked. 'I mean, on what principle?'

'When clay is fired, well, if it's fired above about 300 degrees centigrade, then all the electrons in the material it's made out of will be – I suppose there's no better word for it – they'll be erased. The heat destroys their electric charges. Then, from that point on, they begin to pick up new electrical charges. That's what the photo multiplier measures, how much energy they've absorbed. The older the material is, the brighter it glows.'

'And this is accurate?'

'As I said, to about fifteen per cent. That means, with a piece that's supposed to be two thousand years old, we can get a reading that will tell us, to within about three hundred years, when it was made – well, when it was last fired.'

'And did you do this test on the pieces while you were in China?'

She shook her head. 'No, there's no equipment like that in Xian.'

'So how can you be sure?'

She smiled when she answered him. 'The eye. I looked at them, and I was fairly sure they were fake.'

'But to be sure? Did you ask anyone else?'

'I told you. I wrote to Semenzato. And when I didn't get an answer, I came back here.' She saved him the question. 'Yes, I brought samples with me, samples from the three pieces I was most suspicious of and from the other two that I think might be false.'

'Did Semenzato know you had these samples?'

'No. I never mentioned it to him.'

'Where are they?'

'I stopped in California on the way here and left one set with a friend of mine who's a curator at the Getty. They have the equipment, so I asked him to run them through for me.'

'And did he?'

'Yes.'

'And?'

'I called him when I got home from the hospital. All three of the pieces that I thought were fake were made within the last few years.'

'And the other two?'

'One of them is genuine. The other is a fake.'

'Is one test enough?' Brunetti asked.

'Yes.'

Even if it weren't sufficient proof, Brunetti realized, what had happened to her and Semenzato was.

After a moment, Brett asked, 'Now what?'

'We try to find out who killed Semenzato and who the two men who came here were.'

Her look was level and very sceptical. Finally, she asked, 'And what are the chances of that?'

227

He pulled from his inner pocket the police photos of Salvatore La Capra and passed them over to Brett. 'Was this one of them?'

She took the photos and studied them for a minute. 'No,' she said simply and handed them back to Brunetti.

'They're Sicilian,' she said. 'They're probably back home now, paid off and happy with the wife and kids. Their trip was a success; they did both things they were sent to do, scare me and kill Semenzato.'

'That doesn't make any sense, does it?' he asked.

'What doesn't make any sense?'

'I've been talking to people who knew him and knew about him, and it seems that Semenzato was mixed up in a number of things that a museum director shouldn't have had anything to do with.'

'Like what?'

'He was a silent partner in an antique business. Other people have told me his professional opinion was for sale.' Brett apparently needed no explanation of what the second meant.

'Why is that important?'

'If their intention had been to kill him, they would have done that first, then warned you to keep quiet or the same thing would happen to you. But they didn't do that; they went to you first. And if that had worked, then Semenzato would never have known, at least not officially, about the substitution.'

'You're still assuming that he was part of this,' Brett said. When Brunetti nodded his agreement, she added, 'I think that's a big assumption.'

'It doesn't make sense any other way,' Brunetti explained. 'How else would they have known to come to you, known about the appointment?'

'And if I had still told him, even after they did this to me?' He was surprised that she wouldn't have seen this and was reluctant to explain it to her now. He didn't answer.

'Well?' she insisted.

'If Semenzato was a part of this, it's pretty clear what would have happened if you spoke to him,' Brunetti said, still reluctant to be the one to give it voice.

'I still don't understand.'

'They would have killed you, not him,' he said simply.

He watched her face as he spoke, saw it reach her eyes, first as shock and disbelief. After a moment, she understood, and her expression stiffened, her lips compressing and drawing her mouth tight.

Luckily, Flavia chose that time to come into the living room, bringing with her the flowery scent of soap or shampoo or one of those things women use to make themselves smell wonderful at the wrong time of the day. Why the morning and not the night?

She was wearing a simple brown woollen dress tied by a bright orange scarf wrapped around her waist a few times and knotted at her side, its end hanging below her knees and swinging as she walked. She wore no make-up and, seeing her without it, Brunetti wondered why she ever bothered with it.

'*Buon giorno*,' she said, smiling and offering him her hand.

He stood to take it. Glancing at Brett, she included her in her next remark. 'I'm going to make coffee. Would either of you like some?' Then with a smile, 'A bit early for champagne.'

Brunetti nodded but Brett shook her head. Flavia turned and disappeared into the kitchen. Her arrival and departure had, however moment-arily, deflected his last remark, but now they had no choice but to return to it.

'Why did they kill him?' Brett asked.

'I don't know. An argument with the other people involved with him? A disagreement about what to do, perhaps what to do about you?'

'Are you sure he was killed because of all of this?'

'I think it's best to work on that assumption,' he answered blandly, not surprised at her reluctance to see it this way. To do so, obviously, would be to admit her own peril: with Matsuko and Semenzato

230

both dead, she was the only one who knew about the theft. Whoever had killed Semenzato could have no idea that she had brought proof, as well as suspicions, back from China with her, and so they would have to believe that his death would effectively end the trail. If the fraud should ever be detected some time in the future, it was not likely that the government of the People's Republic of China could be moved to interest itself in the murderous greed of Western capitalists; it would probably search for the thieves nearer to home.

'While they were still in China, who was in charge of the pieces selected for the show?'

'We dealt with a man from the Beijing Museum, Xu Lin. He's one of their leading archaeologists and a very good art historian.'

'Did he accompany the exhibits out of China?'

She shook her head. 'No, his political past prevented that.'

'Why?'

'His grandfather was a landlord, so he was considered politically undesirable or, at least, suspect.' She saw Brunetti's open look of surprise and explained. 'I know it sounds irrational.' Then, after a pause, she added, 'It *is* irrational, but that's the way it is. He spent ten years during the Cultural Revolution herding pigs and spreading dung on cabbage fields. But as soon as the Revolution was over, he returned to the university, and since he was a brilliant student, he couldn't be kept from winning the job in Beijing. But they wouldn't let him leave the country. The only people who travelled with the exhibition were party hacks who wanted to go abroad to go shopping.'

'And you.'

'Yes, and me.' After a moment, she added in a low voice, 'And Matsuko.'

'So you're the one who will be held responsible for the theft?'

'Of course, I'm responsible. They clearly aren't going to accuse the party cadres who came along for the ride, not when they have a Westerner to take the blame for the whole thing.'

'What do you think happened?'

She shook her head. 'Nothing makes sense. Or I can't believe what does make sense.'

'Which is?' He was interrupted by Flavia, who came back into the room carrying a tray. She walked past him, went to sit beside Brett on the sofa, and placed the tray on the table in front of them. On it were two cups of coffee. She handed one of the cups to Brunetti, took the other, and sat back in the sofa. 'There are two sugars in it. I think that's what you take.'

Ignoring this interruption, Brett continued. 'One of the party cadres must have been approached by someone here.' Though Flavia had missed the question that prompted this explanation, she made no attempt to disguise her response to the answer. She turned and stared at

Brett in stony silence, then glared over at Brunetti and met his eyes. When neither of them said anything, Brett continued, 'All right. All right. Or Matsuko. Maybe it was Matsuko.'

Sooner or later, Brunetti was sure, she would be forced to remove that 'maybe'.

'And Semenzato?' Brunetti asked.

'Possibly. At any rate, someone at the museum.'

He interrupted her. 'Did these people, the ones you call cadres, did any of them speak Italian?'

'Yes, two or three of them.'

'Two or three?' he repeated. 'How many of them were there?'

'Six,' Brett answered. 'The party takes care of its own.'

Flavia sniffed.

'How well did they speak Italian? Do you remember?' Brunetti asked.

'Well enough,' was her terse reply. She paused and then admitted, 'No, not well enough for that. I was the only one who was able to speak to the Italians. If it was done, it would have to have been done in English.' Matsuko, Brunetti recalled, had taken her degree at Berkeley.

Exasperated, Flavia snapped out, 'Brett, when are you going to stop being stupid about this and take a look at what happened? I don't care about you and the Japanese girl, but you've got to look at this clearly. This is your life you're playing with.' As suddenly as she had started, she stopped, sipped at her coffee but, finding the cup empty, set it roughly down on the table in front of her.

No one spoke for a long time until Brunetti finally asked, 'When would the switch have been done?'

'After the closing of the exhibition,' Brett answered in a shaky voice.

Brunetti shifted his glance to Flavia. She remained silent, glancing down at her hands, clasped loosely in her lap.

Brett sighed deeply and whispered, 'All right. All right.' She sat back in the sofa and watched the rain drive down against the glass of the skylights. Finally, she said, 'She was here for the packing. She had to verify each object before the Italian customs police sealed the package and then sealed the crate that the boxes were put into.'

'Would she have recognized a fake?' Brunetti asked.

Brett's answer was a long time coming. 'Yes, she would have seen the difference.' For a moment, he thought she was going to add something to that, but she didn't. She watched the rain.

'How long would it have taken them to pack everything?'

Brett considered for a moment and then answered, 'Four days? Five?'

'And then what? Where did the crates go from here?'

'They were flown to Rome on Alitalia, but then

they were held up there for more than a week by a strike at the airport. From there, they went to New York, and they were held up there by American customs. Finally, they were put on the Chinese airline and taken back to Beijing. The seals on the crates were checked every time they were put on or taken off a plane, and guards stayed with them while they were in the foreign airports.'

'How long was it from the time they left Venice until they got to Beijing?'

'More than a month.'

'How long was it before you saw them?'

She shifted around on the sofa before she answered him, but she still didn't look at him. 'I told you, not until this winter.'

'Where were you when they were being packed?'

'I told you. In New York.'

Flavia interrupted. 'With me. I was making my debut at the Met. Opening night was two days before the exhibition closed here. I asked Brett to go with me, and she did.'

Brett finally looked away from the rain and across at Flavia. 'And I left Matsuko in charge of the shipment.' She put her head back on the sofa and looked up at the skylights. 'I went to New York for a week, and I stayed three. Then I went back to Beijing to wait for the shipment. When it didn't arrive, I went back to New York and got it through US customs. But then,' she continued,

'I decided to stay in New York. I called Matsuko and told her I was delayed, and she offered to go to Beijing to check the collection when it finally got back to China.'

'Was it her job to verify the objects in the shipment?' Brunetti asked.

Brett nodded.

'If you had been in China,' Brunetti asked, 'then you would have unpacked the collection yourself?'

'I've just told you that,' Brett snapped.

'And you would have noticed the substitution then?'

'Of course.'

'Did you see any of the pieces before this winter?'

'No. When they first got back to China, they disappeared into some sort of bureaucratic limbo for six months, then they were put on display in a warehouse, and then they were finally sent back to the museums they had originally been borrowed from.'

'And that's when you saw that they had been changed?'

'Yes, and that's when I wrote to Semenzato. About three months ago.' With no warning, she raised her hand and slammed it down on the arm of the sofa. 'The bastards,' she said, voice guttural with rage. 'The filthy bastards.'

Flavia put a calming hand on her knee. 'Brett, there's nothing you can do about it.'

With no change in her voice, Brett turned to her. 'It's not your career that's over, Flavia. People will come and hear you sing no matter what you do, but they've just destroyed the last ten years of my life.' She stopped for a moment and then added, voice softer, 'And all of Matsuko's.'

When Flavia tried to object, she continued, 'It's over. Once the Chinese find out about this, they'll never let me go back. I'm responsible for those pieces. Matsuko brought the papers back from Beijing with her, and I signed them when I got back to Xian. I verified that they were all there, in the same condition as when they left the country. I should have been there, should have checked them all, but I let her go instead because I was in New York with you, listening to you sing. And it's cost me my career.'

Brunetti looked at Flavia, saw the flush that had come into her face at the sound of Brett's growing anger. He saw the graceful line her shoulder and arm made as she sat turned towards Brett, studied the curve of her neck and jaw. Perhaps she was worth a career.

'The Chinese don't have to find out about it,' he said.

'What?' both of them asked.

'Did you tell your friends who did the tests what the samples were?' he asked Brett.

'No, I didn't. Why?'

'Then we seem to be the only people who know

about it. Of course, unless you told anyone in China.'

She shook her head from side to side. 'No, I told no one. Only Semenzato.'

Flavia interrupted here and said, 'And I doubt we have to worry he told anyone, aside from the person he sold them to.'

'But I have to tell them,' Brett insisted.

Instead of looking at her, Flavia and Brunetti glanced across the table at each other, understanding instantly what could be done, and it was only with the exercise of great force of will that each of them resisted the impulse to mutter, 'Americans.'

Flavia decided to explain things to her. 'So long as the Chinese don't know, then nothing has happened to your career.'

To Brett, it was as if Flavia hadn't spoken. 'They can't keep those pieces on display. They're fakes.'

'Brett,' Flavia asked, 'how long have they been back in China?'

'Almost three years.'

'And no one has noticed they aren't genuine?'

'No,' Brett conceded.

Brunetti picked it up here. 'Then it's not likely that anyone will. Besides, the substitution could have happened any time during the last four years, couldn't it?'

'But we know it didn't,' Brett insisted.

'That's just it, *cara*.' Flavia decided to try to explain it to her again. 'Aside from the people who stole the vases, we're the only people who know about it.'

'That doesn't make any difference,' Brett said, her voice once more rising towards anger. 'Besides, sooner or later, someone is going to realize they're fake.'

'And the later it is,' Flavia explained with a broad smile, 'the less likely it is that anyone will link you to it.' She paused to let this sink in, then added, 'Unless, of course, you want to toss away ten years' work.'

For a long time, Brett didn't say anything, just sat while the others watched her consider what had been said. Brunetti studied her face, feeling that he could read the play of emotion and idea. When she was about to speak, he suddenly said, 'Of course, if we find out who killed Semenzato it's likely that we'll get the original vases back.' He had no way of knowing if this was true, but he had seen Brett's face and knew she had been about to refuse the idea of remaining silent.

'But they'd still have to get back to China, and that's impossible.'

'Hardly,' Flavia interrupted and laughed outright. Realizing that Brunetti would be more receptive, she turned to him to explain. 'The master classes.'

Brett's response was instant. 'But you said no, you turned them down.'

'That was last month. What's the good of my

being a prima donna if I can't change my mind? You told me yourself that they'd give me royal treatment if I accepted. They'd hardly go through my bags when I got to the Beijing airport, not with the Minister of Culture there to meet me. I'm a diva, so they'll be expecting me to travel with eleven suitcases. I'd hate to disappoint them.'

'And what if they open your bags?' Brett asked, but there was no fear in her voice.

Flavia's response was immediate, 'If memory serves, one of our cabinet ministers was caught with drugs at some airport in Africa, and nothing came of it. Certainly, in China, a diva ought to be far more important than a cabinet minister. Besides, it's your reputation we're worrying about, not mine.'

'Be serious, Flavia,' Brett said.

'I am serious. There is absolutely no chance that they'd search my luggage, at least not when I'm going in. You've told me they've never searched yours, and you've been going in and out of China for years.'

'There's always the chance, Flavia,' Brett said, but it was audible to Brunetti that she didn't believe it.

'There's more of a chance, from what you've told me about their ideas of maintenance, that my plane will crash, but that's no reason not to go. Besides, it might be interesting to go. It might give me some ideas about Turandot.' Brunetti thought she was finished, but then she added, 'But why are we wasting time talking about this?' She looked at Brunetti, as if she held him responsible for the missing vases.

It surprised Brunetti to realize he had no idea if she was serious or not about trying to take the pieces back to China. He spoke to Brett. 'In any case, you can't say anything now. Whoever killed Semenzato doesn't know what you told us, doesn't even know if we've managed to come up with a reason for his murder. And I want to keep it that way.'

'But you've been here, and you came to the hospital,' Brett said.

'Brett, you said they weren't Venetian. I could be anyone: a friend, a relative. And I haven't been followed.' It was true. Only a native could successfully follow another person through the narrow streets of the city; only a native would know the sudden stops, the hidden turns, the dead ends.

'So what should I do?' Brett asked.

'Nothing,' he answered.

'And what does that mean?'

'Just that. Nothing. In fact, it would be wise if you were to leave the city for a while.'

'I'm not sure I want to take this face anywhere,' she said, but she said it with humour, a good sign.

Turning to Brunetti, Flavia said, 'I've tried to get her to come to Milan with me.'

A team player, Brunetti asked her, 'When are you going?'

'Monday. I've already told them I'll sing Thursday night. They've scheduled a piano rehearsal for Tuesday afternoon.'

He turned back to Brett. 'Are you going to go?' When she didn't answer, he added, 'I think it's a good idea.'

'I'll think about it,' was as much as Brett would say, and he decided to leave it at that. If she was going to be convinced, it was Flavia who could do it, not he.

'If you decide to go, please let me know.'

'Do you think there's any danger?' Flavia asked.

Brett answered the question before he could. 'There's probably less danger if they think I've spoken to the police. Then they don't have to stop me from doing so.' Then, to Brunetti, 'That's right, isn't it?'

He was not in the habit of lying, even to women. 'Yes, I'm afraid it is. Once the Chinese are notified about the fakes, whoever killed Semenzato will no longer have a reason to try to silence you. They'll know the warning failed to stop you.' Or, he realized, they could try to silence her permanently, but he chose to say nothing of this.

'Wonderful,' Brett said. 'I can tell the Chinese and save my neck, but I ruin my career. Or I keep quiet, save my career, and then all I have to worry about is my neck.'

Flavia leaned across the table and placed her

242

hand on Brett's knee. 'That's the first time you've sounded like yourself since this began.'

Brett smiled in response and said, 'Nothing like the fear of death to wake a person up, is there?'

Flavia sat back in her chair again and asked Brunetti, 'Do you think the Chinese are involved in this?'

Brunetti was no more inclined than any other Italian to believe in conspiracy theories, which meant he often saw them even in the most innocent of coincidences. 'I don't believe your friend's death was accidental,' he said to Brett. 'That means they have someone in China.'

'Whoever "they" are,' Flavia interrupted with heavy emphasis.

'Because I don't know who they are doesn't mean they don't exist,' Brunetti said, turning to her.

'Precisely,' agreed Flavia and smiled.

To Brett, he said, 'That's why I think it might be better if you were to leave the city for a while.'

She nodded vaguely, surely not in agreement. 'If I do go, I'll let you know.' Hardly a pledge of good faith. She leaned back again and rested her head on the back of the sofa. From above them all, the sound of the rain pounded down.

He turned his attention to Flavia, who signalled towards the door with her eyes, then made a small gesture with her chin, telling him it was time to leave.

He realized that there was little more to say, so he got to his feet. Brett, seeing him, pulled her feet out from beneath her and started to rise.

'No, don't bother,' Flavia said, standing and moving off towards the entrance hall. 'I'll see him out.'

He leaned down and shook Brett's hand. Neither said anything.

At the door, Flavia took his hand and pressed it with real warmth. 'Thank you,' was all she said, and then she held the door while he passed in front of her and started down the steps. The closing door cut off the sound of the falling rain.

Chapter Eighteen

EVEN THOUGH he had assured Brett that he had not been followed, when he left her apartment, Brunetti paused before turning into Calle della Testa and looked both ways, searching for anyone he might remember having seen when he entered. No one looked familiar. He started to turn right, but then he recalled something he had been told when he came to the area some years ago, searching for Brett's apartment.

He turned left and walked down to the first large cross street, Calle Giacinto Gallina, and there he found, just as he remembered from his first visit, the news stand that stood at the corner, in front of the grammar school, facing on to the street that was the main artery of this neighbourhood. And, as though she hadn't moved from where he had seen her last, he found Signora Maria, seated on a high stool inside the newsstand, her upper body wrapped in a hand-knitted scarf that made at least three passes around her neck. Her face was red, either with cold or an early morning brandy, perhaps both, and her short hair seemed even whiter by the contrast.

'*Buon giorno*, Signora Maria,' he said, smiling up at her ensconced behind the papers and magazines.

'*Buon giorno*, Commissario,' she answered, as casually as if he were an old customer.

'Signora, since you know who I am, you probably know why I'm here.'

'*L'americana?*' she asked, but it really wasn't a question.

He sensed motion behind him; suddenly a hand shot forward and took a newspaper from one of the stacks in front of Maria, extending a ten-thousand-lire note. 'Tell your mother the plumber will come at four this afternoon,' Maria said, handing back change.

'*Grazie*, Maria,' the young woman said and was gone.

'How can I help you?' Maria asked him.

'You must see whoever passes this way, signora.' She nodded. 'If you see anyone lingering in the neighbourhood who shouldn't be here, would you call the Questura?'

'Of course, Commissario. I've been keeping an eye on things since she got home, but there's been no one.'

Once again a hand, this one clearly male, shot in front of Brunetti and pulled down a copy of *La Nuova*. It disappeared for a moment, then returned

246

with a thousand-lire note and some small change, which Maria took with a muttered '*Grazie*'.

'Maria, have you seen Piero?' the man asked.

'He's down at your sister's house. He said he'd wait for you there.'

'*Grazie*,' the man said and was gone.

He had come to the right person. 'If you call, just ask for me,' he said, reaching for his wallet to give her one of his cards.

'That's all right, Dottor Brunetti,' she said. 'I've got the number. I'll call if I see anything.' She raised a hand in a friendly gesture, and he noticed that the tips of her woollen gloves were cut off, leaving her fingers free to handle change.

'Can I offer you something, signora?' he asked, nodding with his head to the bar that stood on the opposite corner.

'A coffee would help against the cold,' she answered. '*Un caffè corretto*,' she suggested, and he nodded. If he spent the entire morning sitting motionless in this damp cold, he'd want a shot of grappa in his coffee, too. He thanked her again and went into the bar, where he paid for the *caffè corretto* and asked that it be taken out to Signora Maria. It was clear from the barman's response that this was standard procedure in the neighbourhood. Brunetti couldn't remember if there was a Minister of Information in the current government; if so, Signora Maria was a natural for the job.

At the Questura, he went quickly up to his

office and found it, surprisingly, neither tropical nor arctic. For a moment he entertained the fantasy that the heating system had finally been fixed, but then a shriek of escaping steam from the radiator under his window put an end to it. The explanation, he realized, lay in the thick sheaf of papers on his desk. Signorina Elettra must have put them there recently, opened the window for a moment, then closed it before she left.

He hung his overcoat behind the door and walked over to his desk. He sat, picked up the papers and began to read through them. The first was a copy of Semenzato's bank statements, going back four years. Brunetti had no idea how much the museum director had been paid and made a note to find out, but he did know the bank statement of a rich man when he saw one. Large deposits had been made with no apparent regularity; just so, amounts of fifty million and more had been taken out, again, with no apparent pattern. At his death, Semenzato's balance had been two hundred million lire, an enormous amount to keep in a savings account. The second page of the statement noted that he also had double that amount invested in government bonds. A wealthy wife? Good luck on the stock market? Or something else?

The next pages listed foreign calls made from his office number. There were scores of them, but, again, no pattern that Brunetti could discern.

248

The last three pages were copies of Semenzato's credit card receipts for the last two years, and from them Brunetti got an idea of the airline tickets he had paid for. He ran his eye quickly down the list, amazed at the frequency and distance of the trips. The museum director, it seemed, would spend a weekend in Bangkok as casually as another man might go to his beach house, would go to Taipei for three days and stop in London for the night on his way back to Venice. A copy of the statements from his two charge cards accompanied the itinerary and gave proof that Semenzato did not stint himself in any way when he travelled.

Beneath these, he found a sheaf of fax papers, clipped together at the top. All of these related to Carmello La Capra. On the first sheet, Signorina Elettra had pencilled the observation, 'Interesting man, this one.' Salvatore's father, it appeared, had no visible means of support; that is, he appeared to have no job or fixed employment. Instead, on his tax return for the last three years, he listed his profession as 'consultant', a term which, when added to the fact that he was from Palermo, sounded alarm bells in Brunetti's mind. His bank statement showed that large transfers had been made to his various accounts in interesting, one might even say suspicious, currencies: Colombian pesos, Ecuadorean escudos, and Pakistani rupees. Brunetti found copies of the bill of sale of the *palazzo* La Capra had bought two years ago; he must have paid in cash, for there was no corresponding withdrawal from any of his accounts.

Not only had Signorina Elettra succeeded in getting copies of La Capra's bank statements, but she had also managed to provide copies of his credit card receipts as complete as those she had obtained for Semenzato. Well aware of how long it took to obtain this information through legal channels, Brunetti had no choice but to accept the fact that she must be doing it unofficially, which probably meant illegally. He admitted this, and he read on. Sotheby's and the Metropolitan Opera box office while in New York, Christie's and Covent Garden in London, and the Sydney Opera House, apparently while on the way back from a weekend in Taipei. La Capra had stayed, of course, at the Oriental in Bangkok, where he had gone, it seemed, for a weekend. Seeing that, Brunetti shuffled back through the papers until he found the list of Semenzato's travels and his credit card receipts. He put the papers side by side: La Capra and Semenzato had spent the same two nights at the Oriental. Brunetti separated the papers and laid the separate sheets in two vertical columns on his desk. On at least five occasions, Semenzato and La Capra had been in a foreign city on the same dates, often staying in the same hotel.

Did hunters feel this rush of excitement when they saw the first prints in the snow or when they heard a rustling in the trees behind them and turned to see the bright rush of wings? La Capra and his new *palazzo*, La Capra and his purchases at Sotheby's, La Capra and his trips to the Orient and the Middle East. The trajectory of his life crossed repeatedly with that of Semenzato, and Brunetti suspected the reason lay in their shared interest in things of great beauty and even greater price. And Murino? How many objects had his shop provided for Signor La Capra's new home?

He decided to go down and thank her in person, telling himself that he would make no inquiries about the source of her information. The door to her office was open, and she sat behind her desk, typing into her computer, head turned aside to watch the screen. He noticed that today's flowers were red roses, at least two dozen of them, flowers which proclaimed love and longing.

She sensed his presence and glanced up at him, smiled, and stopped typing. '*Buon giorno*, Commissario,' she said. 'How can I help you?'

'I've come to thank you, *bravissima* Elettra,' he said. 'For the papers you left on my desk.'

She smiled at the use of her first name, as if she saw it as a tribute, not a liberty. 'Ah, you're welcome. Interesting coincidences, aren't they?' she asked, making no attempt to disguise her satisfaction at having noticed them.

'Yes. How about the phone records? Did you get them?'

'They're cross-checking them now to see if they

251

called one another. They've got the records on Signor La Capra's phone in Palermo as well as the phone and fax lines he had installed here. I told them to check for any that might have come from Semenzato's home or office, but that will take a bit longer and probably won't be ready until tomorrow.'

'Do we owe all of this to your friend Giorgio?' Brunetti asked.

'No, he's in Rome on some sort of training programme. So I called and said Vice-Questore Patta needed the information immediately.'

'Did they ask you what it was for?'

'Of course they did, sir. You wouldn't want them to give this sort of information out without the proper authorization, would you?'

'No, of course not. And what did you tell them?'

'That it was classified. A government matter. That will make them work faster.'

'And what if the Vice-Questore finds out about this? What if they mention this to him, say you used his name?'

Her smile grew even warmer. 'Oh, I told them that he would have to deny all knowledge of it, so he wouldn't like their mentioning it to him. Besides, I'm afraid they're rather used to doing things like this, checking on private phones and keeping records of the calls that people make.'

'Yes, so am I,' Brunetti agreed. He was afraid that a record was also kept of what some people said during those phone calls, a flight of paranoia in which he was probably joined by a large part of the population, but he didn't bother to mention this to Signorina Elettra. Instead, he asked, 'Any chance we could get them today?'

'I'll give them a call. Perhaps this afternoon.'

'Would you bring them up to me if they come in, signorina?'

'Of course,' she answered and turned back to her keyboard.

He went to the door but before reaching it, he turned, hoping to capitalize on the intimacy of the last minutes. 'Signorina, excuse me if I ask, but I've always been curious about why you decided to come to work for us. Not everyone gives up a job at Banca d'Italia.'

She stopped typing but kept her fingers poised over the keys. 'Oh, I wanted a change,' she answered casually and turned her attention back to her typing.

And fish flew, Brunetti thought to himself as he left her office and went back up to his own. The heat had become tropical in his absence, so he opened the windows for a few minutes, holding them only partially open to prevent the rain from driving in, then closed them and went back to his desk.

La Capra and Semenzato, the mysterious man from the South and the museum director. The man with expensive taste and the money to indulge it, and the museum director with the contacts that might be necessary to indulge that taste to its fullest. They were an interesting pair. What other objects would Signor La Capra have in his possession, and were they to be found in his *palazzo*? Was the restoration completed, and, if so, what sort of changes had been made? That was easily discovered; all he had to do was go down to city hall and ask to see the plans. Of course, what was to be read in the plans and the work that had actually been done might not bear too close a resemblance to each other, but to discover the truth of that, all he had to do was learn which of the city inspectors had signed off on the final papers, and he would have a fairly good idea of how close the relationship was likely to be.

There remained the question of what objects might be contained in the newly restored *palazzo*, but that demanded a different sort of answer. The magistrate who would issue a search warrant on the basis of hotel receipts for the same dates didn't exist in Venice, a city where *palazzi* such as La Capra's sold for seven million lire per square metre.

He decided to try official means first, which meant a call to the other side of the city and the offices of the *catasto*, where all plans, projects and transfers of ownership had to be registered. It took him a long time to get through to the proper office, as his call was shunted back and forth between uninterested civil servants who were sure, even before Brunetti had a chance to explain what he wanted, that it was another office which could give him the information. A few times, he tried speaking in Veneziano, sure that the use of dialect would ease things by assuring the person on the other end of the line that he was not only a police official but, more importantly, a native Venetian. The first three people he spoke to answered his every question in Italian, apparently not themselves Venetian, and the fourth slipped into thoroughly incomprehensible Sardinian until Brunetti relented and spoke in Italian. That, however, didn't get him what he wanted, but it did get him, finally, transferred to the correct office.

He felt a surge of joy when the woman who answered the phone spoke in purest veneziano – what's more, with the strongest of Castello accents. Forget what Dante said about Tuscan being sweet in the mouth. No, this was the language to bring delight.

During the long wait for officialdom to make up its mind to speak to him, he had abandoned all hope of getting a copy of the plans and so asked, instead, for the name of the firm that had done the restorations. Brunetti recognized the name, Scattalon, and knew that they were among the best and most expensive companies in the city. In fact, it was they who had the more-or-less eternal contract to maintain his father-in-law's *palazzo* against the equally eternal ravages of time and tide.

Arturo, the oldest Scattalon son, was in the office but was unwilling to discuss a client's affairs with the police. 'I'm sorry, Commissario, but that is privileged information.'

'All I'd like is a general idea of how much the work cost, perhaps rounded out to the nearest ten million,' Brunetti explained, failing to see how such information could be privileged or in any way private.

'I'm sorry, but that's absolutely impossible.' The sound from the other end of the line disappeared, and Brunetti imagined Scattalon was covering the mouthpiece with his hand in order to speak to someone there with him. In a moment he was back. 'You'd have to give us an official request from a judge before we would reveal information like that.'

'Would it help if I had my father-in-law call and ask your father about this?' Brunetti asked.

'And who is your father-in-law?' Scatta-lon asked.

'Count Orazio Falier,' Brunetti said, savouring, for the first time in his life, the rich sound of each syllable as it fell trippingly from his tongue.

Again, the sound at the other end grew muffled, but Brunetti could still make out the deep rumble of male voices. The phone was set down on a hard surface, he heard noises in the background, and then another voice spoke, 'Buon giorno, Dottor Brunetti. You must excuse my son. He's new to the business. A university graduate, so perhaps he isn't familiar with the trade, not yet.'

'Of course, Signor Scattalon. I understand completely.'

'What information was it you said you needed, Dottor Brunetti?' Scattalon asked.

'I'd like a rough estimate of how much Signor La Capra has spent on the restoration of his *palazzo*.'

'Of course, Dottore, of course. Let me just get the file.' The phone was set down again, but Scattalon was quickly back. He said he didn't know how much the original purchase price had been, but he estimated that, during the last year, his company had charged La Capra at least five hundred million, including both labour and materials. Brunetti assumed that this was the price '*in bianco*', the official price that would be reported to the government as what had been spent and earned. He didn't know Scattalon well enough to feel himself free to ask about this, but it was a safe conclusion that a great deal, perhaps the major part, of the work had been paid for '*in nero*', unofficially and at a cheaper rate, the better for Scattalon to avoid having to declare it as income and hence be forced to pay taxes on it. Brunetti considered it a safe assumption that he could factor in another five hundred million lire, if not for Scattalon, then for other workers and expenses that would have been paid '*in nero*'.

As to what had actually been done in the *palazzo*, Scattalon was more than forthcoming. New roof and ceilings, structural reinforcement with steel beams (and the fine paid for that), all walls stripped down to the original brick and re-plastered, new plumbing and wiring, a complete heating system, central air conditioning, three new stairways, parquet floors in the central salons, and double-glazed windows throughout. No expert, Brunetti could still calculate that this work would cost enormously more than the sum Scattalon had quoted. Well, that was between Scattalon and the tax people.

'I thought he was planning a room where he could put his collection,' Brunetti fabricated. 'Did you work on that, a room for paintings or,' and here he hoped as he paused, 'ceramics?'

After a brief hesitation during which Scattalon must have been weighing his obligation to La Capra against that to the Count, he said, 'There was one room on the third floor that might have served as a kind of gallery. We put bullet-proof glass and iron gratings on all the windows,' Scattalon continued. 'It's at the back of the *palazzo*, and the windows face north, so it gets indirect light, but the windows are large enough to allow a fair amount to come in.'

'A gallery?'

'Well, he never said that, but it would certainly seem that's what it is. Only one door, reinforced with steel, and he had us cut a number of indentations in the wall. They would be perfect for showing statues, so long as they were small, or perhaps for ceramics.'

'What about an alarm system? Did you install one?'

'No, we didn't, but that's not work we're prepared to do. If he had it done, he would have had to hire a different company.'

'Do you know if he did?'

'I've no idea.'

'What sort of man did he seem to you, Signor Scattalon?'

'A wonderful man to work for. Very reasonable. And very inventive. He has excellent taste.'

Brunetti understood this to mean that La Capra was extravagant, probably given to the sort of extravagance that did not quibble over bills or examine them too closely.

'Do you know if Signor La Capra is living in the *palazzo* now?'

'Yes, he is. In fact, he's called us in a few times to take care of details that were overlooked in the last weeks of work.' Ah, Brunetti thought, the ever-useful passive voice: the details had been 'overlooked'; Scattalon's workmen had not overlooked them. What a wondrous thing was language.

'And do you know if any details were overlooked in the room you call the gallery?'

Scattalon's answer was immediate. 'I didn't call it that, Dottor Brunetti. I said it might serve that function. And, no, there were no details overlooked there.'

'Do you know if your workmen had reason to go into that room when they went back to the *palazzo* for the last pieces of work?'

'If there was no work to be done in the room, then there would be no reason for my men to enter it, so I'm sure they would not.'

'Of course, of course, Signor Scattalon. I'm sure that's true.' His sense of the conversation suggested that Scattalon had patience for one more question, no more. 'Is the door the only means of access to that room?'

'Yes. That, and the air-conditioning duct.'

'And do the gratings open?'

'No.' Simple, monosyllabic, and quite audibly terminal.

'Thank you for your help, Signor Scattalon. I'll be sure to mention it to my father-in-law.' Brunetti concluded, giving no more explanation at the end of the conversation than he had at the beginning but reasonably certain that Scattalon, like most Italians, would be sufficiently suspicious of anything having to do with a police investigation not to mention it to anyone, most assuredly not to a client who might not yet have paid him in full.

Chapter Nineteen

WOULD SIGNOR La Capra, he wondered, turn out to be yet another of those well-protected men who were appearing on the scene with unsettling frequency? Rich, but with a wealth that had no roots, at least none that were traceable, they seemed to be moving north, coming up from Sicily and Calabria, immigrants in their own land. For years, people in Lombardy and the Veneto, the wealthiest parts of the country, had thought themselves free from *la piovra*, the many-tentacled octopus that the Mafia had become. It was all *roba dal Sud*, stuff from the South, those killings, the bombings of bars and restaurants whose owners refused to pay protection money, the shoot-outs in city centres. And, he had to admit, as long as it had remained, all that violence and blood, down in the South, no one had felt much concern with it; the government had shrugged it off as just another quaint custom of the *meridione*. But in the last few years, just like an agricultural blight that couldn't be stopped, the violence had moved north: Florence,

Bologna, and now the heartland of industrialized Italy found themselves infected and looked in vain for a way to contain the disease.

Along with the violence, along with the hired killers who shot twelve-year-olds as messages to their parents, had come the men with the brief-cases, the soft-spoken patrons of the opera and the arts, with their university-educated children, their wine cellars and their fierce desire to be perceived as patrons, epicures and gentlemen, not as the thugs they were, prating and posturing with their talk of *omertà* and loyalty.

For a moment, he had to stop himself and accept the fact that Signor La Capra might well be no more than what he appeared to be: a man of wealth who had bought and restored a *palazzo* on the Grand Canal. But even as he thought this, he thought of the presence of Salvatore La Capra's fingerprints in Semenzato's office and saw again the names of those cities and the identical dates when La Capra and Semenzato had visited them. Coincidence? Absurd.

Scattalon had said La Capra was living in the *palazzo*; perhaps it was time for a representative of one of the official arms of the city to greet the new resident and have a word with him about the need for security in these sadly criminal times.

Since the *palazzo* was on the same side of the Grand Canal as his home, he had lunch there but had no coffee after it, thinking that Signor La Capra might be polite enough to offer it to him.

The *palazzo* stood at the end of Calle Dilera, a small street that dead-ended into the Grand Canal. As he approached, Brunetti could see the sure signs of newness. The exterior layer of *intonaco* plastered over the bricks from which the walls were constructed was still virgin and free of graffiti. Only near the bottom did it show the first signs of wear: the recent *acqua alta* had left its mark at about the height of Brunetti's knee, lightening the dull orange of the plaster, some of which had already begun to crumble away and now lay kicked or swept to the side of the narrow *calle*. Iron gratings were cemented into place on the four ground-level windows and thus prevented all chance of entry. Behind them, he saw new wooden shutters, tightly closed. He moved to the other side of the narrow *calle* and put his head back to study the upper floors. All of them had the same dark green wooden shutters, these thrown back, and windows of double-glazed glass. The gutters that hung under the new terracotta tiles of the roof were copper, as were the pipes that carried the run-off water from them. At the second floor, however, the pipes changed to far less tempting tin and ran down to the ground.

The nameplate by the single bell was taste itself:

a simple italic script with only the name, 'La Capra'. He rang the bell and stood near the intercom.

'*Sì, chi è?*' a male voice asked.

'*Polizia,*' he answered, having decided not to waste time with subtlety.

'*Sì. Arrivo,*' the voice said, and then Brunetti heard only a mechanical click. He waited.

After a few minutes, the door was opened by a young man in a dark blue suit. Clean-shaven and dark-eyed, he was handsome enough to be a model but perhaps a bit too stocky to photograph well. '*Sì?*' he asked, not smiling but not seeming any more unfriendly than the average citizen would be if asked to come to the door by the police.

'*Buon giorno,*' Brunetti said. 'I'm Commissario Brunetti; I'd like to speak to Signor La Capra.'

'About what?'

'About crime in the city.'

The young man remained where he was, standing a bit outside the door, and made no move to open it or allow Brunetti to enter. He waited for Brunetti to explain more fully, and when it became obvious this was not about to happen, he said, 'I thought there wasn't supposed to be any crime in Venice.' His Sicilian accent became audible in the longer sentence, his belligerence in the tone.

'Is Signor La Capra at home?' Brunetti asked, tired of sparring and beginning to feel the cold.

'Yes.' The young man stepped back inside the

door and held it open for Brunetti. He found himself in a large courtyard with a circular well in the centre. Off to the left, marble pillars supported a flight of steps that led up to the first floor of the building that enclosed the courtyard on all sides. At the top, the stairs turned back upon themselves, still hugging the exterior wall of the building, and climbed to the second and then the third floor. The carved heads of stone lions stood at equal distances on the marble banister that ran along the stairs. Tucked below the stairs were the signs of recent work: a wheelbarrow filled with paper bags of cement, a roll of heavy-duty plastic sheeting, and large tins dripping different colours of paint down their sides.

At the top of the first flight of steps, the young man opened a door and stepped back to allow Brunetti to pass into the *palazzo*. The moment he stepped inside, Brunetti heard music filtering down from the floors above. As he followed the young man up the steps, the sound grew louder, until he could distinguish the presence of a single soprano voice in the midst of it. The accompaniment, it seemed, was strings, but the sound was muffled, coming from another part of the house. The young man opened another door, and just at that moment the voice soared up above the instruments and hung suspended in beauty for the space of five heartbeats, then dropped back to the lesser world of the instruments.

They passed down a marble hallway and started up an inner stairway, and as they went, the music grew louder and louder, the voice clearer and brighter, the nearer they came to its source. The young man seemed not to hear, though the world in which they moved was filled only with that sound, nothing more. At the top of the second flight of stairs, the young man opened another door and stood back again, nodding Brunetti into a long corridor. He could only nod; there was no way Brunetti could have heard him.

Brunetti walked in front of him and along the corridor. The young man caught up with him and opened a door on the right; this time he bowed as Brunetti passed in front of him and closed the door behind him, leaving Brunetti inside, all but deafened by the music.

Robbed of every sense but sight, Brunetti saw in four corners wide cloth-covered panels that reached from the floor to the height of a man, all turned to face the centre of the room. And there in the centre, a man lay on a chaise-longue covered with pale brown leather. His attention entirely given to a small square booklet in his hands, he gave no sign that he had noticed Brunetti's entrance. Brunetti stopped just inside the door and watched him. And he listened to the music.

The soprano's tone was absolutely pure, a sound that was generated in the heart and warmed there until it came swelling out with the apparent effortlessness that was achieved only by the greatest singers and then only with the greatest skill. Her voice paused upon a note, soared off from it, swelled, flirted with what he now realized was a harpsichord, and then rested for a moment while the strings spoke with the harpsichord. And then, as if it had always been there, the voice returned and swept the strings up with it, higher and higher still. Brunetti could make out words and phrases here and there, *'disprezzo'*, *'perchè'*, *'per pietade'*, *'fugge il mio bene'*, all of which spoke of love and longing and loss. Opera, then, though he had no idea which one it was.

The man on the chaise-longue looked to be in his late fifties and wore around his middle proof of good eating and soft living. His face was dominated by his nose, large and fleshy – the same nose Brunetti had seen on the mug shot of the accused rapist, his son – on which sat a pair of half-lens reading glasses. His eyes were large, limpid and dark enough to seem almost black. He was clean-shaven, but his beard was so heavy that a dark shadow was evident on his cheeks, though it was still early afternoon.

The music came to a chilling diminuendo and died away. It was only in the silence that radiated out to him that Brunetti became aware of just how perfect the quality of sound had been, the volume disguised by that perfection.

The man leaned back limply on his chaise-longue, and the booklet fell from his hand to the floor beside him. He closed his eyes, head back, his entire body slack. Though he had in no way acknowledged Brunetti's arrival, Brunetti had no doubt the man was very much aware of his presence in the room; moreover, he had the feeling that this display of aesthetic ravishment was being put on specifically for his edification.

Gently, much in the manner his mother-in-law used to applaud an aria she hadn't liked but had been told was very well sung, he patted the tips of his fingers together a few times, very lightly.

As if called back from realms where lesser mortals dared not enter, the man on the chaise-longue opened his eyes, shook his head in feigned astonishment, and turned to look at the source of the lukewarm response.

'Didn't you like the voice?' La Capra asked with real surprise.

'Oh, I liked the voice a great deal,' Brunetti answered, then added, 'but the performance seemed a bit forced.'

If La Capra caught the absence of possessive pronoun, he chose to ignore it. He picked up the libretto and waved it in the air. 'That was the best voice of our age, the only great singer,' he said, waving the small libretto for emphasis.

'Signora Petrelli?' Brunetti inquired.

The man's mouth twisted up as if he'd bitten into something unpleasant. 'Sing Handel? La Petrelli?' he asked with tired surprise. 'All she can sing is Verdi and Puccini.' He pronounced the names as a nun would say "sex" and "passion".

Brunetti began to offer that Flavia also sang Mozart, but instead he asked, 'Signor La Capra?'

At the sound of his name, the man pushed himself to his feet, suddenly recalled from aesthetic pronouncements to his duty as a host, and approached Brunetti, extending his hand. 'Yes. And whom do I have the honour of meeting?'

Brunetti took his hand and returned the very formal smile. 'Commissario Guido Brunetti.'

'Commissario?' One would think La Capra had never heard the word.

Brunetti nodded. 'Of the police.'

Momentary confusion crossed the other man's face, but this time Brunetti thought it might be a real emotion, not one manufactured for an audience. La Capra quickly recovered and asked, very politely, 'And what is it, if I might ask, that brings you to visit me, Commissario?'

Brunetti didn't want La Capra to suspect that the police connected him with Semenzato's death, so he had decided to say nothing about his son's fingerprints having been found at the scene of Semenzato's murder. And until he had a better sense of the man, he didn't want La Capra to know the police were curious about any link that might exist between him and Brett. 'Theft, Signor La Capra,' Brunetti said and then repeated, 'Theft.'

Signor La Capra was, in an instant, all polite attention. 'Yes, Commissario?'

Brunetti smiled his most friendly smile. 'I came to speak to you about the city, Signor La Capra, since you're a new resident, and about some of the risks of living here.'

'That's very kind of you, Dottore,' returned La Capra, matching him smile for smile. 'But, please, we can't stand here like two statues. Could I offer you a coffee? You've had lunch, haven't you?'

'Yes, I have. But a coffee would be welcome.'

'Ah, then come along with me. We'll go down to my study and I'll have us brought some.' Saying that, he led Brunetti from the room and back down the stairway. On the second floor, he opened a door and stood back politely to allow Brunetti to enter before him. Books lined two walls; paintings much in need of cleaning – and looking all the more expensive because of that – filled the third. Three ceiling-high windows looked out over the Grand Canal, where boats went about their boaty business. La Capra waved Brunetti to a satin-covered divan and went himself to a long oak desk, where he picked up the phone, pushed a button, and asked that coffee be brought to the study.

He came back across the room and sat down opposite Brunetti, careful first to pull gently at his trousers above the knees so as not to stretch them out when he sat. 'As I said, it's very thoughtful of you to come to speak to me, Dottor Brunetti. I'll be sure to thank Dottor Patta when I see him.'

'Are you a friend of the Vice-Questore's?' Brunetti asked.

La Capra raised his hands in a self-deprecating gesture, pushing away the possibility of such glory. 'No, I have no such honour. But we are both members of the Lions' Club, and so we have occasion to meet socially.' He paused a moment and then added, 'I'll be sure to thank him for your thoughtfulness.'

Brunetti nodded his gratitude, knowing just how thoughtful Patta would find it.

'But, tell me, Dottor Brunetti, what is it you wanted to warn me about?'

'There's no specific warning I can give you, Signor La Capra. It's more that I want to tell you that the appearances of this city are deceiving.'

'Yes?'

'It seems that we have a peaceful city here,' Brunetti began and then interrupted himself to ask, 'You know that there are only seventy thousand inhabitants?'

La Capra nodded.

'So it would seem, at first glance, that it is a sleepy little provincial town, that the streets are safe.' Here Brunetti hastened to add, 'And they are; people are still safe at all times of the day or night.' He paused a moment and then added, as if it had just come to him, 'And they are generally safe in their homes, as well.'

'If I might interrupt you here, Commissario, that's one of the reasons I chose to move here, to enjoy that safety, the tranquillity that seems to remain only in this city.'

'You are from . . .?' Brunetti asked, though the accent that bubbled up, no matter how La Capra fought to keep it down, left that in no doubt.

'Palermo,' La Capra responded.

Brunetti paused to allow that name to sink in and then continued, 'There is still, however, and it is this I came to speak to you about, there is still a risk of theft. There are many wealthy people in the city, and some of them, lulled, perhaps, by the apparent peacefulness of the city, are not as careful as they should be about the security they maintain within their homes.' He glanced around him and then followed with a graceful gesture of the hand. 'I can see that you have many beautiful things here.' Signor La Capra smiled but then quickly bowed his head in the appearance of modesty. 'I hope only that you have been provident enough to see to their best protection,' Brunetti concluded.

The door opened behind him and the same young man came into the room carrying a tray on which sat two cups of coffee and a silver sugar bowl resting on three delicate clawed feet. He stood silently beside Brunetti and waited while he took a cup and spooned two sugars into it. He repeated the process with Signor La Capra and left the room without having said a word, taking the tray with him.

As he stirred his coffee, Brunetti noticed that it was covered with the thin layer of froth that came only from the standard electric espresso machines: no screw-top Moka Espresso pot placed hurriedly on the back burner in Signor La Capra's kitchen.

'It's very thoughtful of you to come to tell me this, Commissario. I'm afraid it's true that many of us do see Venice as an oasis of peace in what is an increasingly criminal society.' Here, Signor La Capra shook his head from side to side. 'But I assure you that I have taken every precaution to see that my possessions remain safe.'

'I'm glad to learn that, Signor La Capra,' Brunetti said, placing his cup and saucer on top of a small marble-topped table that stood beside the divan. 'I'm sure you would want to be most prudent with the beautiful things you have here. After all, I'm sure you've gone to considerable trouble to acquire some of them.'

This time, Signor La Capra's smile, when it came, was in a lower key. He finished his coffee and leaned forward to place his cup and saucer beside Brunetti's. He said nothing.

'Would it be intrusive if I were to ask you what sort of protection you've provided, Signor La Capra?'

'Intrusive?' La Capra asked, opening his eyes

wide in surprise. 'But how could that be? I'm sure you ask only out of consideration for the citizens of the city.' He let that rest a moment and then explained, 'I had a burglar alarm installed. But more importantly, I have round-the-clock staff. One of them is always here. I tend to place greater trust in the loyalty of my staff than in any mechanical protection I might buy.' Here, Signor La Capra turned up the temperature of his smile. 'Perhaps this makes me old-fashioned, but I believe in these values – loyalty, honour.'

'Certainly,' Brunetti said blandly, but he smiled to show that he understood. 'Do you allow people to see the other pieces in your collection? If these,' Brunetti said, waving a hand lightly in a gesture that encompassed the entire room, 'are any indication, then it must be very impressive.'

'Ah, Commissario, I'm sorry,' La Capra said with a small shake of his head, 'but I'm afraid that would be impossible just now.'

'Yes?' Brunetti inquired politely.

'You see, the room where I plan to display them isn't finished to my satisfaction yet. The lighting, the tiles for the floor, even the ceiling panels – none of them makes me happy, so I would be embarrassed, yes, actually embarrassed, to allow anyone to see it now. But I'd be very happy to invite you back to see my collection when the room is finished and,' he paused, searching for the proper final word, and finding it, 'presentable.'

'That's very kind of you, signore. I'll plan, then, on seeing you again?'

La Capra nodded, but he did not smile.

'I'm sure you're a very busy man,' Brunetti said and got to his feet. How strange, he thought, for a lover of art to feel the least reluctance to show his collection to someone who displayed curiosity or enthusiasm for beautiful things. Brunetti had never known it to happen before. And even stranger that, during all this talk of crime in the city, La Capra had not seen fit to mention either of the two incidents which had, this very week, shattered the calm of Venice and the lives of people who, like himself, were lovers of beauty.

When he saw Brunetti stand, La Capra got up and accompanied him to the door. In fact, he went down the steps with him, across the open courtyard, and to the front door of the *palazzo*. He opened it himself and held it while Brunetti stepped outside. They shook hands cordially and Signor La Capra stood quietly at the open door while Brunetti made his way back up the narrow *calle* towards Campo San Polo.

Chapter Twenty

THE HALF HOUR spent with La Capra made Brunetti reluctant to risk having to speak to Patta on the same afternoon, but he decided to go back to the Questura anyway, to see what messages had come in for him. Two people had called: Giulio Carrara, asking that Brunetti call him in Rome, and Flavia Petrelli, saying she would call again later in the afternoon.

He had the operator put a call through to Rome and was soon speaking to the *maggiore*. Carrara wasted no time with personal conversation but began immediately with Semenzato. 'Guido, we've got something here that makes it look like he was involved in more than we thought.'

'What is it?'

'Two days ago, we stopped a shipment of alabaster ashtrays coming into Livorno from Hong Kong, on their way to a wholesaler in Verona. The usual thing – he gets the ashtrays, attaches labels to them, and sells them, "Made in Italy".'

'Why did you stop the shipment? That hardly

sounds like the sort of thing you people are interested in.'

'One of the little people in our stable told us that it might be a good idea to take a closer look at the shipment.'

'For labelling?' Brunetti asked, still not understanding. 'Isn't that the sort of thing the finance boys take care of?'

'Oh, they'd been paid off,' Carrara said dismissively, 'so the shipment would have been safe until it got to Verona. But it's what we found in with the ashtrays that made him call us.'

Brunetti knew a hint when he heard one. 'What did you find?'

'You know what Angkor Wat is, don't you?'

'In Cambodia?'

'If you ask that, then you know. Four of the crates had statues that had been taken from the temples there.'

'Are you sure?' As soon as he spoke, Brunetti wished he had phrased the question differently.

'It's our business to be sure,' Carrara said, but only in simple explanation. 'Three of the pieces were spotted in Bangkok a few years ago, but they disappeared from the market before the police there could confiscate them.'

'Giulio, I don't understand how you can be sure they come from Angkor Wat.'

'The French made pretty extensive drawings of the temple grounds when Cambodia was still a colony, and since then much of it has been photographed. Two of the statues we found had been, so we were sure.'

'When were the photographs taken?' Brunetti asked.

'In 1985. An archaeological team from some university in America spent a few months there, sketching and photographing, but then the fighting moved too close and they had to get out. But we've got copies of all the work they did. So we're sure, absolutely sure, about two of the pieces, and the other two are likely to have come from the same source.'

'Any idea where they're going?'

'No. The best we have is the address of the wholesaler in Verona.'

'Have you moved on this yet?'

'We've got two men watching the warehouse in Livorno. We've got a tap on the phone there and in the office in Verona.'

Though Brunetti thought this an extraordinary response to the finding of a mere four statues, he kept the idea to himself. 'What about the wholesaler? Do you know anything about him?'

'No, he's new to us. Nothing on him at all. Even the finance people don't have a file on him.'

'What do you think, then?'

Carrara considered for a moment before he answered. 'I'd say he was clean. And that probably means that someone will remove the statues before the shipment's delivered.'

'Where? How?' Brunetti asked. And then he added, 'Does anyone know you opened the crates?'

'I don't think so. We had the finance police close off the warehouse and make a big show of opening a shipment of lace that was coming in from the Philippines. While they were doing that, we took a look at the ashtrays, but we closed up the crates and left everything there.'

'What about the lace?'

'Oh, it was the usual stuff. Twice as much there as declared on the papers, so they confiscated the whole shipment, and they're trying to figure out how much the fines should be.'

'And the ashtrays?'

'They're still in the warehouse.'

'What are you going to do?'

'I'm not in charge of it, Guido. The Milan office gets to handle this. I spoke to the man in charge, and he said he wants to step in the minute the crates with the statues are picked up.'

'And you?'

'I'd let them pick up the shipment and then try to follow them.'

'If they take the crates,' Brunetti said.

'Even if they don't, we've got around-the-clock teams in the warehouse, so we'll know when they make their move. Besides, whoever gets sent to pick up the statues won't be important, and they probably won't know much, except where to take them, so there's no sense in stepping in and arresting them.'

Finally Brunetti asked, 'Giulio, isn't this an awfully complicated manoeuvre for four statues? And you still haven't said how Semenzato was involved in any of this.'

'We don't have a clear idea of that, either, but the man who made the original phone call told us that the people – he meant police, Guido – in Venice might be interested in this.' Even before Brunetti could interrupt him, Carrara went on, 'He wouldn't explain what that meant, but he did say that there were more shipments. This was only one of many.'

'All coming from the Orient?' Brunetti asked.

'He didn't say.'

'Is there a big market here for things like this?'

'Not here in Italy, but certainly in Germany, and it's easy enough to get the things there once they've arrived in Italy.'

No Italian would bother to ask why the shipments were not made directly to Germany. The Germans, it was rumoured, saw the law as something to be obeyed, unlike the Italians, who saw it as something first to be fathomed and then evaded.

'What about value, price?' Brunetti asked, feeling very much the stereotypical Venetian as he did so.

'Tremendous, not because of the beauty of the

statues themselves but because of the fact that they come from Angkor Wat.'

'Could they be sold on the open market?' Brunetti asked, thinking of the room Signor La Capra had built on the third floor of his *palazzo* and wondering how many more Signor La Capras there might be.

Again, Carrara paused while he considered how to answer the question. 'No, probably not. But that doesn't mean there isn't a market for them.'

'I understand.' It was only a possibility, but he asked, 'Giulio, do you have a file on a man named La Capra, Carmello La Capra? From Palermo.' He explained the coincidence of the foreign trips taken to the same places and on the same days as Semenzato.

After a short pause, Carrara replied, 'The name sounds faintly familiar, but nothing comes directly to mind. Give me an hour or so, and I'll tap into the computer and see what we have on him.'

Brunetti's question was prompted by the purest of professional curiosity. 'How much have you got in your computer down there?'

'Lots,' Carrara responded with audible pride. 'We've got listings by name, by city, by century, art form, artist, technique of reproduction. You name it, if it's been stolen or faked, we've got a breakdown in the computer. He'd be listed under his name or any aliases or nicknames he has.'

'Signor La Capra is not the sort of man who would permit a nickname,' Brunetti explained.

'Oh, one of them, huh? Well, we'd have him under "Palermo", in any case,' and then Carrara added, quite unnecessarily, 'Rather full, that file.' He paused a moment to allow Brunetti time to appreciate the remark and then asked, 'Is there any special sort of art he's interested in, any technique?'

'Chinese ceramics,' Brunetti supplied.

'Ah,' Carrara said on a long rising tone. 'That's where the name came from. I still can't remember exactly what it was, but if the connection sticks in my mind, it's in the computer. Can I call you back, Guido?'

'I'd appreciate it, Giulio.' Then, prompted by real curiosity, he asked, 'Is there any chance you'll be sent up to Verona?'

'No, I don't think so. The people in Milan are about the best we have. I'd come only if it turned out to be connected in some way to any of the cases I'm working on down here.'

'All right, then. Give me a call if you have anything on La Capra. I should be here all afternoon. And thanks, Giulio.'

'Don't thank me until you know what I have to tell you,' Carrara said but hung up before Brunetti could respond.

He rang down and asked Signorina Elettra if she had received the records of the phone calls of La Capra and Semenzato and was glad to learn that not only had the Telecom office sent over copies, but as well as between their homes and offices in

Italy she had also found a number of calls between those phones and the hotels in foreign countries when the other was staying there. 'Would you like me to bring them up to you, sir?'

'Yes, thank you, signorina.'

While he was waiting for her, he opened the file on Brett and dialled the number that was given there. He let the phone ring seven times, but there was no answer. Did this mean that she had taken his advice and left the city to go and stay in Milan? Perhaps that was what Flavia had called to tell him.

His musing was cut off by the arrival of Signorina Elettra, in sombre grey today; sombre, at least, until he glanced down and saw wildly patterned black stockings – were those flowers? – and red shoes with heels higher than any Paola had ever dared to wear. She came up to his desk and placed a brown folder in front of him. 'I've circled the phone calls that correspond,' she explained.

'Thank you, signorina. Did you keep a copy of this?'

She nodded.

'Good. I'd like you to get the phone listing for the antique shop of Francesco Murino, in Campo Santa Maria Formosa, and see if there's a record that either Semanzato or La Capra made calls to him. I'd also like to know if he called either one of them.'

'I took the liberty of calling AT&T in New York,' Signorina Elettra said, 'and asked if they would check to see if either of them has one of their international dialling cards. La Capra does. The man I spoke to said he'd fax us a list of his calls for the last two years. I might have it later this afternoon.'

'Signorina, did you speak to him yourself?' Brunetti asked, marvelling to himself. 'English? A friend in Banca d'Italia, and English, too?'

'Of course. He didn't speak Italian, even though he was working in the international section.' Was Brunetti meant to be shocked by this lapse? If so, then he would be shocked, for, surely, Signorina Elettra was.

'And how is it that you come to speak English?'

'That's what I did at Banca d'Italia, Dottore. I was in charge of translation from English and French.'

He spoke before he could stop himself. 'And you left?'

'I had no choice, sir,' she said, then, seeing his confusion, explained, 'The man I worked for asked me to translate a letter to a bank in Johannesburg into English.' She stopped speaking and bent down to pull out another paper. And was that all the explanation he was going to get?

'I'm sorry, signorina, but I'm afraid I don't understand. He asked you to translate a letter to Johannesburg?' She nodded. 'And you had to leave because of that?'

Her eyes opened wide. 'Well, of course, sir.'

He smiled. 'I'm afraid I still don't understand. Why did you have to leave?'

She looked at him very closely, as if she'd suddenly realized he didn't really understand Italian after all. Very clearly, she pronounced, 'The sanctions.'

'Sanctions?' he repeated.

'Against South Africa, sir. They were still in effect then, so I had no choice but to refuse to translate the letter.'

'Do you mean the sanctions against their government?' he asked.

'Of course, sir. They were declared by the UN, weren't they?'

'Yes, I think they were. And because of that, you wouldn't do the letter?'

'Well, there's no sense in declaring sanctions unless people are going to impose them, is there?' she asked with perfect logic.

'No, I imagine there isn't. And then what happened?'

'Oh, he became very unpleasant about it. Wrote a letter of reprimand. Complained to the union. And none of them defended me. Everyone seemed to believe that I should have translated the letter. So I had no choice but to resign. I didn't think I could continue to work for such people.'

'Of course not,' he agreed, bowing his head over the file and vowing that he would see to it that Paola and Signorina Elettra never met.

'Will that be all, sir?' she asked, smiling down at him, hoping, perhaps, that he understood now.

'Yes, thank you, signorina.'

'I'll bring up the fax when it comes in from New York.'

'Thank you, signorina.' She smiled and left the office. How had Patta found her?

There was no question about it: Semenzato and La Capra had spoken to each other at least five times in the last year; eight, if the calls Semenzato had made to hotels in various foreign countries at times when La Capra was travelling there had been to La Capra. Of course, it could be argued – and Brunetti had no doubt that a good defence lawyer would do so – that there was nothing at all unusual in the fact that these men knew each other. Both were interested in works of art. La Capra could have, quite legitimately, consulted Semenzato on any one of a number of questions: provenance, authenticity, price. He looked down at the papers and tried to work out a pattern between the phone calls and transfers of money into and out of the men's accounts, but nothing emerged.

The phone rang. He picked it up and said his name. 'I tried to call you earlier.' He recognized Flavia's voice instantly, noted again how low-pitched it was, how different from her singing voice. But that surprise was as nothing compared to what he felt at hearing her address him in the familiar 'tu'.

'I was seeing someone. What is it?'

'Brett. She refuses to come to Milan with me.'

'Does she give a reason?'

'She says something about not feeling well enough to travel, but it's just stubbornness. And fear. She doesn't want to admit she's afraid of these people, but she is.'

'What about you?' he asked, using 'tu' and discovering how right it sounded. 'Are you leaving?'

'I've got no choice,' Flavia said but then corrected herself. 'No, I do have a choice. I could stay if I wanted to, but I don't. My children are coming home, and I've got to meet them. And I've got to be at La Scala on Tuesday for a piano rehearsal. I've cancelled once, but now I've said I'll sing.'

He wondered how all of this was going to be connected to him, and Flavia quickly told him. 'Do you think you could talk to her? Try to reason with her?'

'Flavia,' he began, intensely conscious of the fact that this was the first time he had called her by her first name, 'if you can't convince her to go, I doubt that anything I could say would change her mind.' Then, before she could protest, he added, 'No, I'm not trying to get out of doing it. I just don't think it would work.'

'What about protection?'

287

'Yes. I can have a man put in the apartment with her.' Almost without thinking, he corrected that, 'Or a woman.'

Her response was immediate. And angry. 'Just because we choose not to go to bed with men doesn't mean we're afraid of being in the same room with one.'

He was silent for so long that she finally asked, 'Well, why don't you say something?'

'I'm waiting for you to apologize for being stupid.'

This time, it was Flavia who said nothing. Finally, to his considerable relief, her voice softened and she said, 'All right, and for being rash, as well. I suppose I've got used to being able to push people around. And maybe I'm still looking for trouble about me and Brett.'

Apologies over, Flavia returned to the issue at hand. 'I don't know if she can be convinced to let someone stay in the apartment with her.'

'Flavia, I have no other way to protect her.' Suddenly, he heard a loud noise down the phone, something that sounded like heavy machinery. 'What's that?'

'A boat.'

'Where are you?'

'On the Riva degli Schiavoni.' She explained, 'I didn't want to call you from the house, so I went for a walk.' Her voice changed. 'I'm not far from

288

the Questura. Are you allowed to accept visitors during the day?'

'Of course,' he laughed. 'I'm one of the bosses.'

'Would it be all right if I came over and saw you? I hate talking on the phone.'

'Of course. Come when you want. Come now. I've got to wait for a phone call, but there's no sense in your walking around in the rain all afternoon. Besides,' he added, smiling to himself, 'it's warm here.'

'All right. Do I ask for you?'

'Yes, tell the officer at the door that you have an appointment, and he'll bring you up to my office.'

'Thanks. I'll be there soon.' She hung up without waiting for his goodbye.

As soon as he replaced the phone, it rang again, and he answered it to find Carrara.

'Guido, your Signor La Capra was in the computer.'

'Yes?'

'It was the Chinese ceramics that made it easy to find him.'

'Why?'

'Two things. There was a celadon bowl that disappeared from a private collection in London about three years ago. The man they finally sent down for it said that he had been paid by an Italian to get that specific piece.'

'La Capra?'

'He didn't know. But the person who turned him in said that La Capra's name was used by one of the middle men who arranged the deal.'

' "Arranged the deal"?' Brunetti asked. 'Just like that, set up the robbery of a single piece?'

'Yes. It's getting more and more common,' Carrara answered.

'And the second?' Brunetti asked.

'Well, this one is only rumoured. In fact, we have it listed in with the "unconfirmed".'

'What is it?'

'About two years ago, a dealer in Chinese art in Paris, a certain Philippe Bernadotte, was killed in a mugging while he was out walking his dog one night. His wallet was taken, and his keys. The keys were used to get into his house, but, strangely enough, nothing was stolen. But his papers had been gone through, and it looked like a number of them had been removed.'

'And La Capra?'

'The man's partner could remember only that, a few days before he was killed, Monsieur Bernadotte had referred to a serious argument with a client who had accused him of selling a piece he knew was false.'

'Was the client Signor La Capra?'

'The partner didn't know. All he remembered was that Monsieur Bernadotte repeatedly referred to the client as "the goat", but at the time his partner thought it was a joke.'

'Were Monsieur Bernadotte and his partner capable of selling a piece they knew to be false?' Brunetti asked.

'The partner, not. But it appears that Bernadotte had been involved in a number of sales, and purchases, that were open to question.'

'By the art theft police?'

'Yes. The Paris office had a growing file on him.'

'But nothing was taken from his home after he was killed?'

'It would seem not, but whoever killed him also had the time to remove whatever they wanted from his files and from his inventory lists.'

'So it's possible that Signor La Capra was the goat that he mentioned to his partner?'

'So it would seem,' agreed Carrara.

'Anything else?'

'No, but we'd appreciate learning anything else you have to tell about him.'

'I'll have my secretary send you what we've got, and I'll let you know anything we find out about him and Semenzato.'

'Thanks, Guido.' And Carrara was gone.

What was it Count Almaviva sang? *E mi farà il destino ritrovar questo paggio in ogni loco!* Just so, it seemed to be Brunetti's destiny to find La Capra everywhere he looked. Somehow, though, Cherubino seemed significantly more innocent than did Signor La Capra. Brunetti had learned more than enough to convince him that La Capra was involved with Semenzato, possibly in his death. But all of it was entirely circumstantial; none of it would have the least value in a court of law.

He heard a knock at his door and called, '*Avanti*.' A uniformed policeman opened the door, stood back and allowed Flavia Petrelli to enter. As she passed in front of the policeman, Brunetti saw the flash of the officer's hand moving in a smart salute before he closed the door. Brunetti had not the least doubt about whom the gesture was intended to honour.

She wore a dark brown raincoat lined with fur. The chill of the early evening had brought colour to her face, which, again, was bare of make-up. She came quickly across the room and took his outstretched hand. 'So this is where you work?' she asked.

He came around his desk and took the coat which the heat in the room rendered unnecessary. While she looked about her, he put the coat on a hanger on the back of his door. He saw that the outside of the coat was wet, glanced back at her, and saw that her hair was wet as well. 'Don't you have an umbrella?' he asked.

Unconsciously, she put her hand up to her hair and pulled it away, surprised to find it wet. 'No, it wasn't raining when I left the house.'

'When was that?' he asked, coming back across the room towards her.

'After lunch. After two, I suppose.' Her answer was vague, suggesting that she really couldn't remember.

He pulled a second chair up beside the one that faced his desk and waited for her to sit before sitting opposite her. Even though he had seen her only a few hours ago, Brunetti was struck by the change in her appearance. This morning, she had seemed calm and relaxed, ready to join with him in an Italianate attempt to convince Brett to consider her own safety. But now she seemed stiff and on edge, and the tension showed in the lines around her mouth that, he was sure, hadn't been there this morning.

'How's Brett?' he asked.

She sighed and swept the fingers of one hand to the side in a dismissive gesture. 'At times, it's like talking to one of my children. She agrees with everything I say, admits that everything I say is right, and then decides to do precisely what she wants.'

'Which, in this case, is what?' Brunetti asked.

'To stay here and not go to Milan with me.'

'When are you leaving?'

'Tomorrow. There's an evening flight that gets in at nine. That gives me time to go and open up the apartment and then go back to the airport to meet the children in the morning.'

'Does she say why she doesn't want to go?'

Flavia shrugged, as if what Brett said and what

293

was true were two separate things. 'She says she won't be frightened away from her own house, that she won't run away and hide with me.'

'Isn't that her real reason?'

'Who knows what her real reason is?' she asked with something like anger. 'It's enough for Brett to want to do something or not to want to do it. She doesn't need reasons or excuses. She does just what she wants.' It was not lost on Brunetti that only another person with the same strength of will could find the quality so outrageous.

Though he was tempted to ask Flavia why she had come to see him, Brunetti asked, instead, 'Is there any way you could convince her to go with you?'

'You obviously don't know her very well,' Flavia said dryly, but then she smiled. 'No, I don't think there is. It'd probably be easier if someone told her not to go; then she'd be forced to do it, I suppose.' She shook her head and repeated, 'Just like my children.'

'Would you like me to talk to her?' Brunetti asked.

'Do you think it would do any good?'

It was his turn to shrug. 'I don't know. I'm not very successful with my own children.'

She looked up, surprised. 'I didn't know you had children.'

'It's a natural enough thing for a man my age, isn't it?'

'Yes, I suppose it is,' she answered, and considered her next remark before speaking. 'It's just that I know you as a policeman, almost as if you weren't a real person.' Before he could say it, she added, 'Yes, I know, and you know me as a singer.'

'Well, I don't really, do I?' he asked.

'What do you mean? We met when I was singing.'

'Yes, but the performance was over. And, since then, I've only heard you sing on discs. And I'm afraid it's not the same.'

She gave him a long look, glanced down at her lap, and then back at him. 'If I gave you tickets to the La Scala performance, would you come?'

'Yes, I would. Gladly.'

Her smile was open. 'And who would you bring?'

'My wife,' he said simply.

'Ah,' she said, just as simply. How rich a single syllable could be. The smile disappeared for a moment, and when it returned, it was just as friendly, but a bit less warm.

He repeated his question. 'Would you like me to try to talk to her?'

'Yes. She trusts you a great deal, so she might listen to you. Someone's got to convince her to leave Venice. I can't.'

Unsettled by the urgency in her voice, he said, 'I don't think there's really any great danger in her remaining here. Her apartment is safe, and she has enough sense not to let anyone into it. So there's very little risk for her.'

'Yes,' Flavia agreed with a slowness that showed how unconvinced she was of this. As if she had suddenly come back from a long distance and found herself here, she looked around the room and asked, pulling the neck of her sweater away from her throat, 'Do you have to stay here much longer?'

'No, I'm free now, if you'd like to go. I'll come back with you and see if she'll listen to me.'

She rose to her feet and went to the window, where she stood, looking towards the covered façade of San Lorenzo and then down at the canal that ran in front of the building. 'It's beautiful, but I don't know how you stand it.' Did she mean marriage, he wondered. 'I can stand it for a week, but then I begin to feel trapped.' Fidelity? She turned and faced him. 'But even with all the disadvantages, it still is the most beautiful city in the world, isn't it?'

'Yes,' he answered simply and held her coat out for her.

Brunetti took two umbrellas from the cabinet against the wall and handed one of them to Flavia as they left the office. At the front door to the Questura, both guards, who usually contented themselves with giving Brunetti no more than a laconic *'Buona notte'*, pulled themselves to stiff attention and saluted crisply. Outside, the rain pounded down, and the water had begun to rise over the edges of the canal and flood the pavement. He had stopped to pull on his boots, but Flavia wore a pair of low-heeled leather shoes, already soaked from the rain.

He linked his arm in hers and turned to the left. Occasional gusts of wind pushed the rain into their faces, then switched around and drove it against the backs of their legs. They met very few people, and all of them wore boots and oilskins, obviously Venetians who were out of their homes only because they had to be. Without conscious thought, he avoided those streets where he knew the water would already have risen and took them towards Barberia delle Tolle, which ran towards the high ground near the hospital. One bridge short of it, they came to a low-lying stretch of pavement where the slick grey water stood ankle deep. He paused, wondering how to get Flavia across it, but she let go of his arm and walked on, completely ignoring the cold water he could hear squishing up out of her shoes.

Wind and rain blasted across the open space of Campo SS. Giovanni e Paolo. At one corner, a nun stood under the wildly flapping awning in front of a bar, her eviscerated umbrella clutched helplessly in front of her. The Campo itself seemed to have shrunk, its far side eaten up by the growing waters that had turned the canal into a narrow lake that spread steadily outwards from its banks.

297

Walking quickly, all but running, they hurried across the Campo, splashing their way towards the bridge that would take them down towards Calle della Testa and Brett's apartment. From the top of the bridge, they could see that the water in front of them was calf deep, but neither of them paused. When they reached the water at the bottom of the bridge, Brunetti switched his umbrella to his left hand and took Flavia's arm with his right. And not a moment too soon, for she stumbled and fell forward, kept from spilling into the water only by the force of his arm as he pulled her towards him.

'*Porco Giuda*,' she exclaimed, pulling herself upright beside him. 'My shoe. It's come off.' They both stood and looked down into the dark water, hunting for some sign of the missing shoe, but neither of them could make it out. Tentatively, she moved her toe from side to side in front of her, feeling around for the shoe. Nothing. The rain pounded down.

'Here,' Brunetti said, closing his umbrella and handing it to her. Quickly, he leaned forward and lifted her from the ground, taking her so by surprise that she wrapped her arms around him, hitting him in the back of the head with the handle of his closed umbrella. He stumbled forward, one arm around her shoulders and one under her knees, regained his balance and walked ahead. He made the two turns and got them to the door of the building before he set her down.

His hair was soaked; rain poured under his collar and down his body. At one point while carrying her, he had stumbled and felt the cold water surging over the top of his boot and down into his shoe. But he had carried her to the doorstep, where he set her down and brushed his hair back from his forehead.

Quickly, she opened the door to the building and splashed into the entrance, where the water was just as high as it was outside. She walked across it and up to the second step, which was dry. Hearing Brunetti splash through the water behind her, she moved up two steps and turned towards him. 'Thank you.'

She kicked off her other shoe and left it where it lay, then started up the stairs, he following close behind. At the second landing, they heard the music that flowed down the stairs. At the top, in front of the metal door, she selected a key, placed it in the lock, and turned it. The door didn't move.

She pulled out the key, chose another and turned the lock at the top of the door, then went back and opened the first lock. 'That's strange,' she said, turning to him. 'It's double locked.' It seemed sensible enough to him that Brett would dead-bolt the door from the inside.

'Brett,' Flavia called out as she pushed open the door. The music called out to meet them, but not Brett. 'It's me,' Flavia called. 'Guido's with me.' No one answered.

Barefoot, dripping water across the floor as she walked, Flavia went to the living room, then into the rear of the apartment to check both bedrooms. When she came back, she had grown paler. Behind her, violins soared, trumpets pealed, and universal harmony was restored. 'She's not here, Guido. She's gone.'

Chapter Twenty-One

AFTER FLAVIA slammed her way out of the apartment that afternoon, Brett sat and stared down at the pages of notes that covered the surface of her desk. She gazed down on charts that listed the burning temperatures of different types of wood, the sizes of the kilns unearthed in western China, the isotopes found in the glazes on tomb pottery from the same area, and an ecological reconstruction of the flora of that same area two thousand years ago. If she interpreted and combined the data one way, she got one result about the way the ceramics were fired, but if she arranged the variables in a different fashion, then her thesis was disproved, it was all nonsense, and she should have stayed in China, where she belonged.

That word led her to wonder if she would ever belong there again, if Flavia and Brunetti could somehow manage to fix all of this – she could think of no better term – so that she could continue to work. She pushed the papers back in disgust. There was no sense in finishing the article, not if the writer was soon to be discredited as having been an instrumental part of a major art fraud. She left the desk and went to stand in front of the rows of neatly organized compact discs, looking for music that would suit her current mood. Nothing vocal. Not those fat gits singing about love and loss. Love and loss. And surely not the harpsichord; the plunky sound of it would snap her nerves. All right, then, the Jupiter Symphony: if anything could prove to her that sanity, joy and love remained in the world, it was that.

She was convinced of sanity and joy and was beginning to believe again in love when the phone rang. She answered it only because she thought it might be Flavia, who had been gone more than an hour.

'*Pronto*,' she said, aware that this was the first time she had used the phone in almost a week.

'Professoressa Lynch?' a male voice enquired.

'Yes.'

'Friends of mine paid you a visit last week,' the man said, voice well modulated and calm sounds elongated by the slurred undertones of a Sicilian accent. When Brett said nothing, he added, 'I'm sure you remember.'

She still said nothing, her hand rigid on the telephone and her eyes closed with the memory of their visit.

'Professoressa, I thought you might be interested

to know that your friend,' and his voice came down ironically on the word, 'your friend Signora Petrelli, is talking to those same friends of mine. Yes, even as we speak, you and I, my friends are talking to her.'

'What do you want?' Brett asked.

'Ah, I'd forgotten how very direct you Americans are. Why, I'd like to talk to you, Professoressa.'

After a long silence, Brett asked him, 'About what?'

'Oh, about Chinese art, of course, especially about some ceramics from the Han Dynasty that I think you might like to see. But before we do that, I think we should discuss Signora Petrelli.'

'I don't want to talk to you.'

'I was afraid of that, Dottoressa. That's why I took the liberty of asking Signora Petrelli to join me.'

Brett said the only thing she could think of to say. 'She's here with me.'

The man laughed outright. 'Please, Dottoressa, I know just how bright you are, so please don't be stupid with me. If she were there, you would have hung up the phone and would be calling the police right now, not talking to me.' He allowed that to sink in and then asked, 'Aren't I right?'

'How do I know she's there with you?'

'Ah, you don't, Dottoressa. That's part of the game, you see. But you know she's not there, and you know she's been gone since fourteen minutes after two, when she left your apartment and started towards Rialto. It's a very unpleasant day to have gone for a walk. It's raining very heavily. She should be back by now. In fact, if I might be so bold as to suggest it, she should have been back long before this, isn't that right?' When Brett didn't answer him, he repeated, voice sterner, 'Isn't that right?'

'What do you want?' Brett asked tiredly.

'That's more like it. I want you to come and visit me, Dottoressa. I want you to come right now, to put on your coat and leave your apartment. Someone will be waiting for you downstairs, and he'll bring you to me. As soon as you do that, Signora Petrelli will be free to leave.'

'Where is she?'

'You can't expect me to tell you that, can you, Dottoressa?' he asked with feigned astonishment. 'Now, are you willing to do what I tell you?'

The answer was out before she thought about it. '*Sì*.'

'Very good. Very wise. I'm sure you'll be very glad you did. As will Signora Petrelli. When we finish talking, you are not to hang up the phone. I don't want you making any phone calls. Do you understand that?'

'Yes.'

'I hear music in the background. The Jupiter?'

'Yes.'

'Which version?'

'Abbado,' she answered, filled with a growing sense of unreality.

'Ah, not a good choice, not good at all,' he said quickly, making no attempt to disguise his disappointment in her taste. 'Italians just don't know how to conduct Mozart. Well, we can discuss this when you get here. Perhaps we can listen to a performance by von Karajan; I believe it's far superior to that one. Just leave the music playing for now, get your coat and go downstairs. And don't try to leave a message because someone is going to come back with your keys and look around the apartment, so you can save yourself that trouble. Do you understand?'

'*Sì*,' she answered dully.

'Then put the phone down, get your coat and leave the apartment,' he commanded, his voice coming, for the first time, close to what must be its natural tone.

'How do I know you'll let Flavia go?' Brett asked, fighting to sound calm.

This time, he laughed. 'You don't know it, do you? But I assure you, in fact I give you my word as a gentleman, that as soon as you leave your apartment with my friends, someone will make a phone call and Signora Petrelli will be free to go.' When she didn't say anything, he added, 'It's all you've got, Dottoressa.'

She set the receiver down on the table, walked into the entrance hall and took her coat from the

305

large cupboard. She came back into the room, went to her desk and grabbed up a pen. Quickly, she wrote a few words on a small piece of paper and went over to the bookcase. Glancing down at the control panel on the CD player, she punched the 'Repeat' button, then placed the piece of paper in the empty CD box, closed the box and leaned it upright against the door of the player. She took her keys from the table just inside the door and left the apartment.

When she opened the main door downstairs, two men stepped quickly into the entrance way. She recognized one of them immediately as the shorter of the two men who had beaten her and only by a conscious effort of will kept herself from shying away from him. He smiled and put out his hand. 'The keys,' he demanded. She took them from her pocket and handed them to him. He disappeared up the steps and was gone for five minutes, during which the other man kept his eyes on her and she watched the first tiny wave of water crawl its way under the door, signalling the arrival of *acqua alta*.

When he returned, his partner opened the door and they stepped out into the rising water. The rain came down heavily, but none of them had umbrellas. Quickly, one of them on either side of her, dropping carefully into single file when they passed anyone on the narrow streets, they made their way towards the Rialto and over the bridge.

On the other side, the two men tried to turn left, but the water had risen too high alongside the Grand Canal, so they had to continue down through the market, empty now of all except the most hardy. They turned left, climbed up on to the wooden boards that had been set on their metal risers, and continued down towards San Polo.

As she walked, she realized how rash she had been. She had no way of being certain the man who called her had Flavia. But how else could he have known the exact time she left the apartment and where she was going unless she had been followed? Nor could she be certain that he or they would let Flavia go in exchange for her own agreement to see him. It was only a chance. She thought of Flavia, remembered the sight of Flavia sitting beside her bed when she woke up in the hospital, remembered Flavia on stage in the first act of *Don Giovanni*, singing, '*E nasca il tuo timor dal mio periglio*,' and she remembered other things. It was a chance; she took it.

The one in front of her turned left, stepping off the boards into the water below, and down towards the Grand Canal. She recognized it, Calle Dilera, remembered that there was a dry cleaner over here that specialized in suede, and marvelled at her ability to think of something so trivial at a time like this.

In water that was now well above their ankles, they stopped in front of a large wooden door. The short one opened it with a key, and she found herself in an open courtyard, rain pounding down upon the surface of the water trapped there. The two men herded her across the courtyard, one leading and one following. They climbed a set of exterior steps, opened another door and went inside. There they were greeted by a younger man, who nodded to them, signalling to the two men that they could leave. He turned, without speaking, and led her down a corridor and up a second stairway, and then a third. At the top, he turned towards her and said, 'Give me your coat.'

He moved around behind her to take it from her. She fumbled at the buttons, thick-fingered with cold and shock, and finally managed to loosen them. He took the coat and casually dropped it on the ground then moved up against her and wrapped his arms around her, cupping her breasts with his hands. He forced his body against hers, rubbing against her rhythmically, and whispered in her ear, 'Never had a real Italian man, eh, *angelo mio*? Just wait. Just wait.'

Brett's head hung limply, and she felt her knees going weak. She struggled to stay standing, lost the struggle against tears. 'Ah, that's nice,' he said behind her. 'I like it when you cry.'

A voice spoke from inside. As suddenly as he had grabbed her, he stepped away from her and opened the door in front of them. He stepped aside and let her enter the room alone, then closed the door behind her. She stood there, soaked and beginning to shiver.

A heavy-set man in his fifties stood at the centre of a wooden-floored room filled with Plexiglas cases on velvet-covered stands that raised them to about eye level. Spot-lighting hidden in the heavy beams of the ceiling picked out the cases, some of which were empty. Several niches in the white walls were similarly lit, but all of those seemed to contain objects of one sort or another.

The man came forward, smiling. 'Dottoressa Lynch, this is indeed an honour. I never dreamed I'd have the pleasure of meeting you.' He stopped in front of her, hand still extended, and continued, 'I'd like to tell you, first, that I've read your books and found them illuminating, especially the one on ceramics.'

She made no effort to take his hand, so he lowered his but didn't move away from her. 'I'm so glad you agreed to come and see me.'

'Did I have a choice?' Brett asked.

The man smiled. 'Of course you had a choice, Dottoressa. We always have choices. It's only when they are difficult ones that we say we don't have them. But there is always a choice. You could have refused to come, and you could have called the police. But you didn't, did you?' He smiled again, eyes actually growing warm, either with

309

humour or something so sinister Brett didn't want to contemplate it.

'Where's Flavia?'

'Oh, Signora Petrelli is quite all right, I assure you. When I last had word of her, she was heading away from the Riva degli Schiavoni, walking back in the general direction of your apartment.'

'Then you don't have her?'

He laughed outright. 'Of course I don't have her, Dottoressa. I never did. There's no need to involve Signora Petrelli in this matter. Besides, I would never forgive myself if anything happened to her voice. Mind you, I don't like some of the music she sings,' he said with the tolerance of those who have more elevated tastes, 'but I have nothing but the healthiest respect for her talent.'

Brett turned abruptly and walked towards the door. She took the handle and pressed it down, but the door didn't open. She tried again, harder, but it still wouldn't move. While she was doing this, the man had moved back across the room until he stood in front of one of the lighted cases. When she turned from the door, she saw him standing there, looking at the small pieces that stood inside the case, almost unaware of her presence.

'Will you let me out of here?' she asked.

'Would you like to see my collection, Dottoressa?' he asked, as if she hadn't spoken or he hadn't heard her.

'I want to get out of here.'

Again, it was as if she hadn't spoken.

He continued to gaze at the two small figurines in the case. 'These little jade pieces are from the Shang Dynasty, wouldn't you say? Probably the An-yang period.' He turned away from the case and smiled at her. 'I realize that's well before your period of expertise, Dottoressa, about a thousand years, but I'm sure you're familiar with them.' He moved off to the next case and paused in front of it to study its contents. 'Just look at this dancer. Most of the paint is still there; rare with anything from the Western Han. There are a few little chips on the bottom of her sleeve, but if I place her with her face a bit to the side, well, you don't see them, do you?' He reached up and lifted the Plexiglas cover from the stand and set it on the floor at his feet. Carefully, he picked up the statue, which was about a third of a metre high, and carried it across the room.

He stopped in front of her and upended the statue so that Brett could see the tiny chips on the bottom of one of the long sleeves. The paint that covered the top part of her gown was still red, after all these centuries, and the black of the skirt still glistened. 'I suppose she just recently came out of a tomb. I can't think of anything else that would have preserved her so perfectly.'

He turned the statue upright and gave Brett one last look at it, then moved back across the room and replaced it carefully on the pedestal. 'What a fine idea that was, to put beautiful things, beautiful women, in with the dead.' He paused to consider this, then added, as he replaced the cover, 'I suppose it was wrong to sacrifice servants and slaves to go along with them on the voyage to the other world. But still, it's such a lovely idea, gives so much honour to the dead.' He turned towards her again. 'Don't you think so, Dottoressa Lynch?'

She wondered if this was some sort of elaborate show meant to frighten her into doing whatever he wanted her to do. Was he pretending to be so interested in these objects, or was she meant to believe he was mad and thus capable of harming her if she refused to do what he wanted? But what was that? Did he merely want her to admire his collection?

She began to look around the room, really seeing the objects in it for the first time. He was standing now by a Neolithic pot decorated with the frog motif, two small handles protruding from the lower part. It was in such perfect condition that she moved closer in order to see it more clearly. 'Lovely, isn't it?' he asked conversationally. 'If you'd step over here, Professoressa, I'll show you something I'm especially proud of.' He moved to another case inside which an elaborately carved circle of white jade lay on a panel of black velvet. 'Beautiful, isn't it?' he asked, looking down upon it. 'I think it comes from the Warring States period, wouldn't you say?'

'Yes,' she answered. 'It looks it, especially with that animal motif.'

He smiled with real delight. 'That was exactly what convinced me, Dottoressa.' He looked down at the pendant again and then up at Brett. 'You can't imagine how gratifying it is for an amateur to have his judgement confirmed by an expert.'

She was hardly an expert on artifacts that went back to the Neolithic age, but she thought it best not to protest. 'You could have had your opinion confirmed. All you'd have to do is take it to a dealer or to the Oriental department in any museum.'

'Yes, certainly,' he said absently. 'But I'd prefer not to have to do that.'

He moved away from her, down towards the other end of the room, where he stopped in front of one of the niches in the wall. From it he took a long inlaid piece of metal, intricately worked in gold and silver. 'I usually don't have much interest in metals,' he said, 'but I couldn't resist this piece when I saw it.' He held it out for her and smiled when she took it and turned it over to study both sides.

'Is it a belt hook?' she asked when she saw the pea-sized catch at one end. The rest was as long as her hand, flat and thin as a blade. A blade.

He smiled in real delight. 'Oh, very good. Yes, I'm sure that's what it is. There's one at the

Metropolitan in New York, though I think the work on this one is finer,' he said, pointing with a thick finger to an etched curve that flowed across the flat surface. Losing interest in it, he turned away from her and went back across the room. She turned to the niche and, keeping her back to him, slipped the belt hook into the pocket of her slacks.

As he leaned towards yet another case and she saw what was inside it, Brett's knees weakened with terror, and she was swept with bone-shaking cold. For inside the case sat the covered vase that had been taken from the exhibition at the Ducal Palace.

He moved around the case and positioned himself on the other side so that, glancing through the transparent sheets of Plexiglas, he could see her. 'Ah, I see that you recognize the vase, Dottoressa. Glorious, isn't it? I'd always wanted one like this, but they're impossible to find. As you point out so well in your book.'

She wrapped her arms around herself, hoping that way to retain some of the heat that was so quickly fleeing from her body. 'It's cold in here,' she said.

'Ah, yes, it is, isn't it? I've got some silk scrolls here, filed in drawers, and I don't want to risk heating the room until I can get them protected in a heat- and humidity-controlled chamber. So I'm afraid you'll have to be uncomfortable while you're here, Dottoressa. I'm sure you're accustomed to that from China, being uncomfortable.'

'And from what your men did to me,' she said quietly.

'Ah, yes, you must excuse them for that. I told them to warn you, but I'm afraid my friends tend to be overly enthusiastic in what they think are my best interests.'

She didn't know how she knew it, but she knew he was lying and that the orders he had given had been direct and explicit. 'And Dottor Semenzato, were they told to warn him, as well?'

For the first time, he looked at her in unfeigned displeasure, as if her saying this somehow subtracted from his absolute control over the situation.

'Were they?' she asked in a casual voice.

'Good heavens, Dottoressa, what sort of a man do you think I am?'

She chose not to answer that.

'Well, why not tell you?' he asked and smiled amiably. 'Dottor Semenzato was a very frightened man. I suppose that was acceptable, but then he became a very greedy man, and that is not acceptable. He was foolish enough to suggest that the difficulties you were creating be put to his financial advantage. My friends, as I suggested, do not like to see my honour compromised.' He pursed his lips and shook his head at the memory.

'Honour?' Brett asked.

La Capra did not explain. 'And then the police

315

came here to question me, so I thought it best to speak to you.'

As he spoke, Brett had a searing moment of realization: if he talked openly to her about Semenzato's death, then he knew he had nothing to fear from her. She saw a pair of straight-backed chairs pulled up against the far wall. She walked to one of them and collapsed into it. She felt so weak that she slumped forward and put her head between her knees, but the sharp pain from her still-bandaged ribs pulled her upright, gasping.

La Capra glanced at her. 'But let's not talk about Dottor Semenzato, not when we have all of these beautiful objects here with us.' He took the vase in his hands and walked over to her. He bent and held it out towards her. 'Just look at it. And look at the fluidity of line in the painting, the way the limbs flash out ahead of him. It could have been painted yesterday, couldn't it? Entirely modern in execution. Absolutely marvellous.'

She looked at the vase, only too familiar with it, and then at him.

'How did you do it?' she asked tiredly.

'Ah,' he said, straightening up and moving away from her, back to the case, where he carefully replaced the vase. 'Those are professional secrets, Dottoressa. You mustn't ask me to reveal those,' he said, though it was clear this was just what he most desired.

'Was it Matsuko?' she asked, needing to know at least this much.

'Your little Japanese friend?' he asked sarcastically. 'Dottoressa, at your age you should know better than to mix your personal life with your professional life, especially when dealing with younger people. They don't have our vision of the world, don't know how to separate things the way we do.' He paused for a moment, considering the depth of his own wisdom, and then continued, 'No, they tend to take everything so personally, see themselves, always, as the centre of the universe. And because of that they can be very, very dangerous.' He smiled then, but it wasn't a pleasant thing to see. 'Or very, very useful.'

He came back across the room and stood in front of her, looking down at her raised face. 'Of course it was she. But even then her motives weren't entirely clear. She didn't want money, was even offended when Semanzato offered it. And she really didn't want to hurt you, Dottoressa, not really, if that's any comfort to you. She just didn't stop to see it through clearly.'

'Then why did she do it?'

'Oh, in the beginning, it was just simple revenge, a classic case of the scorned lover wanting to hit back at the person who had hurt her. I don't think she even clearly understood just what we had in mind, the extent of it. I'm sure she believed we wanted just the one piece. In fact, I rather

317

suspect she hoped the substitution would be detected. That would put your judgement in question. After all, you had selected the pieces for the exhibition, and, when the pieces got back, if the substitution was noticed, it would look like you'd chosen to send a fake instead of an original. It wasn't until later that she realized the unlikelihood of a fake piece already being in the museum in Xian. But by then it was too late. The pieces had been copied – I might remark that the work was done at considerable expense – and that, of course, made it even more necessary that they all be used in place of the real ones.'

'When?'

'During the packing in the museum. It was all really very easy, far easier than we had anticipated. The little Japanese tried to object, but by then it was far too late.' He stopped talking and gazed off into the distance, remembering. 'I think it was then that I realized she would become a problem sooner or later.' He smiled. 'And how right I proved to be.'

'And so she would have to be eliminated?'

'Of course,' he said quite simply. 'I realized I'd have no choice in the matter.'

'What did she do?'

'Oh, she gave us some trouble here, and then when she got back to China, when you told her you thought some of the pieces were false, she wrote a letter to her parents asking them what to do. Of course, once she did that, I no longer had any choice: she had to be eliminated.' He cocked his head to one side, a gesture that suggested he was going to reveal something to her. 'I was, quite frankly, surprised at how easy it was. I had thought things would be more difficult to arrange in China.' He shook his head slowly from side to side, lamenting yet another example of cultural pollution.

'How do you know she wrote to them?'

'Why, I read the letter,' he explained simply, then paused, correcting himself for accuracy. 'Actually, I read a translation of the letter.'

'How did you get that?'

'Why, all of your correspondence was opened and read.' He spoke almost in reproach, as if she should have understood at least this much. 'How did you get that letter to Semenzato?' His curiosity was real.

'I gave it to someone who was going to Hong Kong.'

'Someone from the dig?'

'No, a tourist I met in Xian. He was going to Hong Kong, and I asked him to mail it. I knew it would get there much sooner that way.'

'Very clever, Dottoressa. Yes, very clever, indeed.'

A wave of cold jolted through her body. She pulled her feet, long since grown numb, up from the marble floor and hooked them over the bottom rung of the chair. The rain had soaked through her sweater, and she felt herself trapped inside her frozen clothing. She was overcome by a wave of shivering and closed her eyes again, waiting for it to pass. The dull ache that had lurked in her jaw for days had turned into a fiery, burning flame.

When she opened her eyes, the man was gone from beside her and was standing on the other side of the room, reaching out to take down another vase. 'What are you going to do to me?' she asked, fighting to keep her voice level and calm.

He walked back across the room towards her, holding the low bowl carefully in two hands. 'I think this is the most beautiful piece I have,' he said, turning it slightly so that she could better follow the simple brushed line of the design around to the other side. 'It comes from Ch'ing-hai Province, out by the end of the Great Wall. I'd venture it's about five thousand years old, wouldn't you say?'

Brett looked dully up at him and saw a portly middle-aged man holding a painted brown bowl in his hands. 'I asked you what you're going to do with me,' she repeated, interested only in that and not the bowl.

'Hm?' he asked vaguely, glancing down at her for a moment and then back at the bowl. 'With you, Dottoressa?' He took a short step to his left and placed the bowl on top of an empty pedestal. 'I'm afraid I haven't had time to think about that yet. I was so interested in having you see my collection.'

'Why?'

He stayed where he was, directly in front of her, occasionally reaching out delicately with a finger to turn the bowl a millimetre this way, then that way. 'Because I have so many beautiful things and because I can't show them to anyone,' he said with sorrow so palpable it could not be feigned. He turned to her and offered a friendly smile of explanation. 'Anyone who counts, that is. You see, if I show them to people who don't know anything about ceramics, I can't hope that they'll appreciate the beauty or the rarity of what they see.' He stopped there, hoping that she'd understand his dilemma.

She did. 'And if you show them to people who do know about Chinese art or ceramics, then they'll know where the pieces came from?'

'Oh, clever you,' he said, lifting his hands apart in real delight at her quickness. His expression darkened. 'It's difficult, dealing with people who don't understand. They see all these glorious things,' and here he swept his right hand in front of him in a gesture that encompassed everything in the room, 'as pots or bowls, but they have no idea of their beauty.'

'That doesn't stop them from getting them for you, does it?' she asked, making no attempt to disguise her sarcasm.

He took it as said and considered it equably. 'No, it doesn't. I tell them what to get, and they get it for me.'

'Do you also tell them how to get it?' Speech was beginning to cost her too much. She wanted this to end.

'That depends on who's working for me. Sometimes I have to be very explicit.'

'Did you have to be "explicit" with the men you sent to me?'

She saw him start to lie, but then he changed the subject. 'What do you think of the collection, Dottoressa?'

She had suddenly had enough. She closed her eyes and rested her head against the back of her chair. 'I asked you what you think of the collection, Dottoressa,' he repeated, voice raised minimally. Slowly, more from exhaustion than from obstinacy, Brett rolled her head from side to side, eyes closed.

Backhanded and entirely casual, intended more as warning than punishment, his blow caught her on the side of the head at the level of her eyes. His hand did little more than glance off her face, but the force of it was enough to separate anew the healing bones of her jaw, which jolted back together with a flash of pain that exploded in her brain, driving away all thought, all consciousness.

Brett slid to the floor and lay still. He looked down at her for a moment, then stepped back to the pedestal. He reached down, picked up the Plexiglas cover and placed it carefully over the low bowl, took another look at the woman lying unconscious on the floor and left the room.

Chapter Twenty-Two

BRETT WAS IN China, in the tent set up at the dig for the archaeological staff. She was asleep, but the sleeping bag was badly placed, and the ground was hard beneath her. The gas heater had gone out again, and the bitter cold of the high-plateau steppe gnawed at her body. She had refused to go to the embassy in Beijing to have the encephalitis shot, so now she was sick with it, sick with the searing headache that was the first symptom, racked with the chills that came as the brain swelled with the infection that brought death. Matsuko had warned her about it, had had her own vaccination when she was in Tokyo.

If she had another blanket, if Matsuko would bring her something for the pain in her head . . . She opened her eyes, expecting to find the canvas side of the tent. Instead, she saw grey stone under her arm, and then a wall, and then she remembered.

She closed her eyes and lay still, listening to see if he was still in the room. She raised her head and judged that the pain was bearable. Her eyes confirmed what her ears had already told her: he was gone, and she was alone in this room with his collection.

She pushed herself to her knees, then, using the chair to steady herself, got to her feet. Her head pounded, and the room swirled around her for a moment, but she stood and closed her eyes until things grew steady. Pain radiated out from beneath her ears, pushing its way into her skull.

When she opened her eyes, she saw that one wall was filled with windows covered with iron gratings. She forced herself to walk across the room to try the door, but it was locked. At first, the pain jolted with every step, but then she forced herself to relax the muscles of her jaw, and it abated minimally. She went back to the windows, pulled the chair over beneath them and very slowly climbed up on to it. Beyond the window, she saw the roof of the house on the opposite side of the *calle*. To the left, more roofs, and to the right, the Grand Canal.

Beyond the window, the rain pounded down, and she was suddenly conscious of her clothing, wet and clinging to her body. She climbed unsteadily down from the chair and looked around the room, searching for some source of heat, but there was none. She sat on the chair, wrapped her arms around her body, and tried to fight off the tremors of cold that racked her. She clutched her hands against her sides, and her hand felt something hard. The belt hook. Through the sodden cloth, she covered it, talisman-like, with her hand and pressed it tight against her body.

A block of time passed; she had no idea how long. The light coming through the windows diminished, changing from the leaden dullness of day to the penumbra of approaching night. She knew there had to be lights in the room, but she lacked the strength to try to find them. Besides, light would change nothing; only warmth would help.

At some point in all of this, she heard a key in the door, and then it opened, allowing the man who had hit her to enter. Behind him came the younger man who had led her up the steps, how long ago she couldn't remember.

'Professoressa,' the older man said, and he smiled, 'I hope we'll be able to continue our conversation now.' He turned and said something to the younger man, speaking in a dialect that she thought was Sicilian but that was so fluid and filled with elided sounds that she understood nothing. Together, they came across the room towards her, and Brett couldn't resist the impulse to get up from the chair and put it between herself and them.

The older man stopped near the case that held the low brown bowl and turned his attention to that. The younger man stopped beside him, his eyes flitting back and forth between him and Brett.

Once again, with the delicacy of the connoisseur that characterized his every motion when handling the pieces from his collection, he removed the Plexiglas cover and lifted down the low bowl. Like a priest carrying an offering towards some distant altar, he came across the room to her, carrying it in both hands. 'As I was saying before we were interrupted, I think it's from Ch'ing-hai Province, though it might well come from Kansu. You understand why I can't send it for an expert opinion.'

Brett turned up her chin and looked at him, then shifted her glance to the younger man, who had appeared, an acolyte, at his side. She looked at the bowl, saw its beauty, and looked away, uninterested.

'You can see, just here,' he said, turning the bowl fractionally, 'where the rings were sealed together. Strange, isn't it, that it should look so much like a pot that was thrown on a wheel. And the design. I've always been interested in the way primitive people used geometric shapes, almost as if they somehow foresaw the future and knew we'd get back to them.' He turned his attention, somewhat reluctantly, away from the bowl and glanced down at Brett. 'As I said, it's the most beautiful piece in my collection. Perhaps not the most precious, but it's still the one I love the most.' He chuckled under his breath, sharing a joke with a colleague. 'And what I had to do in order to get it.'

She wanted to close her eyes, her ears, and not listen to this lunacy. But she remembered the last time she had ignored him, and so looked up at him and made an inquisitive grunt, not able to risk speech for the pain that she knew it would bring.

'A collector in Florence. An old man and very obstinate. I had met him because of some common business dealings, and when he learned that I had an interest in Chinese ceramics, he took me to his home to show me his collection. Well, when I saw this piece, I fell in love with it, knew I wouldn't be happy until I had it.'

He raised the bowl a bit higher and turned it again, studying the fine tracery of black lines that ran along its side and crawled up over the edge and into the centre of the bowl. 'I asked him if he would sell it to me, but he refused, said he wasn't interested in the money. I offered him more, made him an offer that was far more than the bowl was worth, and then I doubled the offer when he refused.' He took his eyes from the bowl and looked down at her, attempting to reconstruct and thus explain his indignation. He shook his head and returned his attention to the bowl. 'He still refused. So I had no choice. He simply left me no choice. I had made him an offer that was more than generous, but he wouldn't take it. And so I had to use other methods.'

He looked down at her, clearly willing her to

ask him what he had been constrained to do. And as that verb passed through her mind, Brett suddenly realized that all of this was no script he had prepared to justify his actions; this was not a scene he was constructing in order to fool her into taking his part. He believed this. He had wanted something, it had been refused him, and so he had been constrained to take it. As simple as that. And in the same instant she saw where she was: standing in his way, impeding the freedom with which he might possess the ceramics he had gone to so much trouble and expense to take from the exhibition at the Ducal Palace. And she knew then that he was going to kill her, blot out her life as casually as he had struck out at her when she refused to answer his question. Involuntarily, she moaned, but he took it as a question and went on.

'I wanted to arrange it to look like a simple robbery, but if the bowl had been taken, he would have known that I was involved. I thought of having it removed and then burning down his villa.' He paused and sighed at the memory. 'But then I just couldn't. He had so many beautiful things there. I couldn't see them destroyed.' He lowered the bowl and showed her the inner surface. 'Just look at that circle, and the way the lines swerve around it, emphasizing the pattern. How did they *know* how to do that?' He stood upright and muttered, 'Simply miraculous. Miraculous.'

During all of this, the young man said nothing,

standing at his side and listening to every word, following every gesture with his eyes, expressionless.

The older man sighed again and then continued. 'I made it clear that it was to be done when he was alone. I didn't see any reason that his family should suffer. He was driving back from Siena one night, and . . .' He paused here, seeking how most delicately to phrase this. 'And he had an accident. Most unfortunate. He lost control of his car on the superstrada. It caught fire and burned at the side of the road. In the confusion of his death, it was some time before anyone noticed that the bowl was gone.' His voice grew softer as he passed to the philosophic mode. 'I wonder if that has anything to do with why I love this bowl so much, the fact that I had to go to so much trouble to get it?' Then, more conversationally, 'You can't imagine how glad I am finally to be able to show it to someone who can appreciate it.' With a glance at the young man, he added, 'Everyone here tries to understand, to share my enthusiasm, but they haven't devoted years of study to these things, the way I have. And the way you have, Professoressa.'

His smile grew absolutely benign. 'Would you like to hold it, Dottoressa? No one else has touched it since I, well, since I acquired it. But I'm certain you would appreciate the feel of it in your hands, the perfection of the curve on the bottom. You'll be amazed at how light it is. I'm always so sorry that I don't have the correct scientific resources. I'd like to check its composition with a spectroscope and see what it's made of; maybe that could explain why it feels so light. Perhaps you'd be willing to tell me what you think?'

He smiled again and held the bowl out towards her. She forced her stiffening body away from the wall and put out her hands to take the bowl he offered. Carefully, she took it in her two upturned palms and looked down into its centre. The black lines, painted by some graceful hand, dead now more than five millennia, swept across the bottom, swirling up apparently at random to encircle white spaces that enclosed small black circles, turning them into bulls' eyes. The bowl all but vibrated with life, with the comic spirit of the potter. She saw that the lines did not run evenly spaced, that gaps and variations proclaimed the fallible humanity of the artist who had painted it. Through involuntary tears she saw the beauty of a world she was to join. She mourned her own death and the power of this man who still stood in front of her to possess beauty as perfect as this.

'It's fabulous, isn't it?' he asked.

Brett looked up from the bowl and into his eyes. He'd snuff out her life as carelessly as he'd spit out a cherry stone. He'd do that and he'd live on, possessed of this beauty, happy in the full possession of this, his greatest joy. She took a small step back

331

from him and raised her arms in a hieratic gesture that lifted the bowl to the level of her face. Then, very slowly, with conscious deliberation, she drew her hands apart and let the bowl fall to the marble floor, where it shattered, splashing fragments up against her feet and legs.

The man lunged forward but not in time to save the bowl. When his foot landed on a fragment, shattering it into dust, he staggered backward, bumping into the younger man and grabbing at him for support. His face flushed red and then as quickly paled. He muttered something Brett didn't understand, then turned quickly to face her. He pulled one hand free and stepped towards her, but the younger man moved up behind him and wrapped one arm around his chest, pulling him back. He spoke softly but fiercely into the older man's ear, holding his arm tightly and preventing him from reaching Brett. 'Not here,' he said. 'Not with all your beautiful things.' The older man snarled out an answer she didn't hear. 'I'll take care of it,' the young one said. 'Downstairs.'

While they spoke, voices growing louder and louder, Brett plunged her right hand into her pocket and wrapped it around the narrow end of the belt hook: the other end was pointed, and the edges were thin enough to cut. As she watched them and listened to them, their voices began to billow away and float back towards her. At the same time, Brett realized that she no longer felt the cold; quite the contrary, she was hot, burning with it. Yet they talked on and on, voices urgent and fast. She told herself to stand there, to hold the blade, but it was suddenly too much effort, and she lowered herself into the chair again. Her head dropped down and she saw the shattered wreckage on the floor without remembering what it was.

After a long time, she heard the door open and slam shut, and when she looked up, only the younger man remained in the room. There was a gap in time, and then he grabbed her by the arm and pulled her to her feet. She went along with him, out of the door and down the stairs, pain exploding in her head at every step, and then down more stairs, across the open courtyard that still teemed with rain, and then to a wooden door that was set at the level of the courtyard.

Still holding her arm, though she almost laughed at how unnecessary that was, he turned the key and pulled the door open. She looked in and saw low steps leading down towards glittering darkness. From the first step, the darkness was palpable, and from its surface she saw the reflection of light on water.

The man wheeled towards her and grabbed her arm. He flung her forward, and she tripped through the doorway, feet searching automatically for the steps beneath them. On the first, her foot plunged into water, but the second was slimy with seaweed and moss, and her foot slipped out from under her. She had time to raise her arms in front of her, and then she plunged forward into the still-rising waters.

Chapter Twenty-Three

ALL FLAVIA wanted to do was stop the sound of the music that echoed grotesquely through the apartment. As she neared the bookcase, transcendent beauty rippled up through the woodwinds and the violins, but she wanted only the comfort of silence. She looked at the complicated stereo equipment, trapped helplessly in the sound that poured from it, and cursed herself for never bothering to learn how it worked. But then the music soared up to even greater beauty, all harmony was proclaimed, and the symphony ended. She turned, relieved, towards Brunetti.

Just as she started to speak, the opening chords of the symphony crashed anew into the room. She wheeled around, enraged, and slashed a hand towards the CD player, as if to stun it into silence. Because the thin plastic box that had once held the CD was propped against the front of the player, her hand caught it, knocking it to the floor, where it fell on a corner and burst open, spilling its contents at Flavia's feet. She kicked at it, missed and looked down to see where it lay, wanting to stamp the life from it and, by so doing, somehow put an end to the music that spilled joyously through the apartment. She sensed Brunetti beside her. He reached in front of her and turned the volume control to the left. The music faded away, leaving them in the explosive silence of the room. He bent down and picked up the box, then bent again to pick up the pamphlet that had fallen from inside and a small slip of paper that the pamphlet covered.

'A man called. They've got Flavia.' Nothing else was written there. No time, no explanation of her intention. Her absence from the apartment gave him all the explanation he needed.

Saying nothing, he passed the slip of paper to Flavia.

She read it and understood immediately. She crushed the paper in her hand, squeezing it into a tight scrap, but soon she opened her fingers and placed it flat on the bookshelf in front of her, silent, terrifyingly aware that this might be the last contact she would ever have with Brett.

'What time did you leave?' Brunetti asked her.

'About two. Why?'

He looked down at his watch, calculating possibilities. They would have allowed Flavia some time away from the apartment before they called, and someone would have followed her to see that she didn't suddenly turn back towards Brett's. It was almost seven, so they'd had Brett for a number of hours. At no time did it occur to Brunetti to question who had done this. La Capra's name was as clearly fixed in his mind as if it had been spoken. He wondered where she would have been taken. Murino's shop? Only if the dealer was involved in the murders, and that seemed unlikely. The obvious choice, then, was La Capra's *palazzo*. As soon as he thought it, he began to plan ways to get inside, but he realized there was no chance of a search warrant on the basis of three dates on credit card receipts and the description of a room that could just as easily serve as a cell as a private gallery. Brunetti's intuitions would count for nothing here, especially when they concerned a man of La Capra's apparent stature and, more importantly, evident wealth.

Were Brunetti to return to the *palazzo*, there was every reason to believe La Capra would refuse to see him, and there was no way to get inside without that permission. Unless . . .

Flavia grabbed his arm. 'Do you know where she is?'

'I think so.'

Hearing this, Flavia went into the hallway and returned a moment later carrying a pair of high black rubber boots. She sat on the sofa, pulled them on over her wet stockings and got to her feet. 'I'm coming with you,' she said. 'Where is she?'

'Flavia—' he began, but she cut him short.

'I said I'm coming with you.'

Brunetti knew there was no way he could stop her and decided immediately what to do. 'One phone call first. I'll explain on the way.' He grabbed the phone and dialled the number of the Questura, then asked to speak to Vianello.

When the sergeant answered, Brunetti said, 'It's me, Vianello. Is anyone around?'

In response to Vianello's affirmative noise, Brunetti continued, 'Then just listen and I'll explain. Remember you told me you worked three years in Burglary?' A deep grunt came down the line. 'I've got something I want you to do for me. A door. To a building.' The next grunt was clearly interrogative. 'It's wooden, reinforced with metal, new. I think there are two locks.' This time, he heard a snort at the insulting simplicity of this. Only two locks. Only steel reinforcement. He thought quickly, remembering the neighbourhood. He looked out of the window; it was fully dark and the rain continued as before. 'I'll meet you at Campo San Aponal. As soon as you can get there. And, Vianello,' he added, 'don't wear your uniform coat.' The only response to this was a deep laugh, and then Vianello was gone.

When Brunetti and Flavia reached the bottom of the steps, they saw that the water had risen even higher, and from beyond the door came the roar of the rain as it bucketed down.

They picked up the umbrellas and stepped out under the rain, water reaching up towards the tops of their boots. Few people were out, so they got quickly to Rialto, where the water was even deeper. Had it not been for the wooden walkways on their iron stanchions, the water would have flooded into their boots and made progress impossible. On the other side of the bridge, they descended again into the water and turned down towards San Polo, both of them now soaked and exhausted with forcing their way through the rising floods. At San Aponal, they ducked into a bar to wait for Vianello, glad to be free of the drumming insistence of the rain.

They had been enveloped in this watery world for so long that it struck neither one of them as strange that they stood, inside the bar, in water that rose above their calves, listening to the splashings of the barman as he moved back and forth behind the counter, setting down glasses and cups.

Steam covered the inside of the glass doors to the bar, so Brunetti had to reach out with his sleeve and repeatedly wipe away the mist to create a circle through which he watched for Vianello. Bent forms ploughed across the small *campo*. Many people had abandoned the pretence of carrying umbrellas, so capricious was the wind that came from left, right, below, sweeping rain from every angle.

Brunetti felt a sudden heavy pressure against him

and looked down to see the top of Flavia's head, bent heavily against his arm, forcing him to bend down to hear what she said. 'Is she going to be all right?'

No words came to him; no easy lie sprang to his lips. He could do no more than shift his arm and wrap it around her shoulder, pulling her closer. He felt her tremble and convinced himself that it was cold, not fear. But still no words came.

Soon after this, Vianello's bearlike form appeared in the *campo* from the direction of Rialto. The wind tore his raincoat back, and Brunetti saw under it a pair of black waist-high waders. He squeezed Flavia's arm. 'He's here.'

She moved slowly away from him, closed her eyes for a moment and tried to smile.

'Are you all right?'

'Yes,' she answered and nodded as proof.

He pulled open the door of the bar, calling out to Vianello, who hurried across the *campo* towards them. Wind and rain gusted into the overheated bar, and then Vianello splashed his way in, making the place look somehow smaller for his presence. He pulled his sailor's watchcap from his head and beat it repeatedly against the back of a chair, splashing water in a wide circle around him. He tossed the sodden cap on a table and ran his fingers through his hair, splashing even more water behind him. He glanced at Brunetti, saw Flavia and asked, 'Where is it?'

'Down by the water, at the end of the Calle Dilera. It's the one that's just been restored. On the left.'

'The one with the metal gratings?' Vianello asked.

'Yes,' Brunetti answered, wondering if there was a building in the city that Vianello didn't know.

'What do you want me to do, sir, get us in?'

Brunetti felt a surge of relief at the sound of that 'us'. 'Yes. There's a courtyard, but no one's likely to be there, not in this rain.' Vianello nodded in agreement. Anyone with any sense would be inside on a day like this.

'All right. You wait here and I'll give it a try. If it's the one I think it is, there shouldn't be any problem. Won't take long. Give me about three minutes, and then you come.' He gave Flavia a quick look, grabbed his cap and stepped back into the pounding rain.

'What are you going to do?' Flavia asked.

'I'm going to get in and see if she's there,' he said, though he had no idea, in real terms, what this meant. Brett could be anywhere inside the *palazzo*, in any of the countless rooms. She didn't even have to be inside but could already be lying dead, body floating in the filthy water that had conquered the city.

'And if she's not?' Flavia asked so quickly that Brunetti was convinced she must share his vision of Brett's fate.

Instead of answering her, he said, 'I want you to stay here. Or go back to the apartment. There's nothing you can do.'

Not bothering to argue with him, she dismissed what he said with a wave and asked, 'He's had enough time by now, hasn't he?' Before he could answer, Flavia pushed past him out of the bar and into the *campo*, where she yanked her umbrella open and stood, waiting.

He left the bar and joined her, blocking her from the wind with his body. 'No. You can't come. This is police business.'

The wind swooped at them, dragging her hair across her face, covering her eyes. She raked it back with an angry hand and looked up at him, stone-faced. 'I know where it is. So I come with you now or I follow you.'

When he began to protest, she cut him off: 'This is my life, Guido.'

Brunetti turned away from her and into Calle Dilera, flushed with rage, fighting the desire to hurl her bodily into the bar and somehow keep her there. As they approached the *palazzo*, Brunetti was surprised to see that the narrow *calle* was empty. There was no sign of Vianello, and the heavy wooden door appeared to be closed. As they drew abreast of it, the door suddenly swung open from within. A large hand emerged and beckoned them inside, and then Vianello's face appeared in the dim light of the *calle*, smiling, running with rainwater.

Brunetti slipped inside, but before he could press the door closed, Flavia slipped into the courtyard after him. They stood still for a moment while their eyes adjusted to the darkness. 'Too easy,' Vianello said, pushing the door closed behind them.

Because they were so close to the Grand Canal, the water was even deeper here and had turned the courtyard into a broad lake upon which the rain continued to pound. The only light came from the windows of the *palazzo*, from the left side of which light spilled down into the courtyard, illuminating its centre but leaving the side where they stood wrapped in heavy darkness. Silently, the three of them moved out of the rain and slipped under the long balcony that covered three sides of the courtyard until they were all but invisible, even to one another.

Brunetti realized he had come here in response to purest impulse without considering what to do once he was inside. On his one and only visit to the *palazzo* he had been so quickly shepherded to the top floor that he had no clear sense of the layout of the building. He remembered passing doors that led off the exterior staircase to the rooms on each floor, but he had no idea of what lay behind those doors save for the room at the top, where he had spoken to La Capra, and the study on the floor below. It also occurred to him that he, Brunetti, an officer of the state, had just participated in the commission of a crime; what is more, he had involved in that crime not only a civilian but also a fellow officer.

'Wait here,' Brunetti whispered, putting his mouth close to Flavia's ear to speak, even though the rain would have covered the sound of his voice. It was too dark for him to see whatever gesture she might have made in response, but he sensed her move even further back into the darkness.

'Vianello,' he said, grabbing his arm and pulling him close, 'I'm going up the stairs to try to get in. If there's any trouble, get her out of here. Don't bother with anyone unless they try to stop you.' Vianello muttered his assent. Brunetti turned away from them and took a few steps towards the stairway, pushing his legs slowly through the continued resistance of the water. It wasn't until he reached the second step that his legs finally pulled free of the pressure of the water that sucked at them with every step. The sudden change made him feel curiously light-footed, as though he could float or fly up the steps with no effort whatsoever. With that liberty, however, he was suddenly freed to feel the grinding cold that spread up from the icy water trapped inside his boots, from the sodden clothing that hung heavy on his body. He bent down and pulled off the boots, started up the steps, then went back down and kicked the boots into the water.

He waited until they sank out of sight, then started up the stairs again.

At the top of the first flight, he paused on the small balcony and turned the handle of the door that led inside. It moved down under his hand, but the door was locked and didn't open. He climbed another flight but found this door locked as well.

He turned and looked over the railing and across the courtyard to where Flavia and Vianello must be standing, but he could see nothing except the pattern of shattered light as the rain continued to fall on the surface of the water beneath him.

To his surprise, the door at the top swung open under his hand, and he found himself at the beginning of a long corridor. He stepped inside, closed the door behind him and stood still for a moment, conscious only of the sound of water dripping from his coat on to the marble floor below him.

Slowly, his eyes adjusted to the light in the corridor while he waited, listening intently for any sound that might come from beyond the doors along its length.

A sudden chill shook him until he bowed his head and hunched his shoulders in an attempt to find warmth somewhere in his body. When he looked up again, La Capra was standing at an open door a few metres from him, mouth open in surprise at seeing Brunetti.

La Capra recovered first and gave an easy smile.

345

'Signor Policeman, so you've come back. What a pleasant coincidence. I've just finished putting the last few pieces into my gallery. Perhaps you'd like to have a look at them?'

Chapter Twenty-Four

BRUNETTI FOLLOWED him into the gallery and let his eyes run across the raised cases and display stands. La Capra turned as they entered and said, 'Please, let me take your coat. You must be frozen, walking around in the rain. On a night like this.' He shook his head at the very thought.

Brunetti took off his coat, conscious of its sodden weight as he handed it to La Capra. The other man, too, seemed surprised at the bulk of the coat and could think of nothing to do except drape it over the back of a chair, where it lay, water trickling to the floor in thick rivulets.

'What brings you back to see me, Dottore?' La Capra asked, but before Brunetti could answer, he said, 'Please, let me offer you something to drink. A grappa, perhaps? Or a hot rum punch. Please, I can't let you stand there, chilled, a guest in my house, and not have you take something.' Without waiting for an answer, he walked over to an intercom that hung on one wall and pushed a button. A few seconds later there was a faint click, and La

Capra spoke into the receiver. 'Would you bring up a bottle of grappa and some hot rum punch?'

He turned towards Brunetti, smiling, the perfect host. 'It'll just be a moment. Now, tell me, Dottore, while we wait. What brings you back to visit me so soon?'

'Your collection, Signor La Capra. I've been learning more and more about it. And about you.'

'Really?' La Capra asked, his smile remaining in place. 'I had no idea I was so well known in Venice.'

'In other places as well,' Brunetti answered. 'In London, for example.'

'In London?' La Capra showed polite surprise. 'How very strange. I don't believe I know anyone in London.'

'No, but perhaps you've acquired pieces there?'

'Ah, yes, that could be it, I suppose,' La Capra answered, smile still in place.

'And in Paris,' Brunetti added.

Again, La Capra's surprise was studied, as if he had been waiting for mention of Paris after Brunetti's reference to London. Before he could say anything, however, the door was pushed open and a young man came in, not the one who had let him in before. He carried a tray with bottles, glasses and a silver Thermos. He set the tray down on a low table and turned to go. Brunetti recognized him, not only from the mug shot sent up from Rome, but from his resemblance to his father.

'No, stay and have a drink with us, Salvatore,'

La Capra said. Then, to Brunetti, 'What would you like, Dottore? I see there's sugar. Would you like me to fix you a punch?'

'No, thank you. Grappa is fine.'

Jacopo Poli, delicate hand-blown bottle, nothing but the best for Signor La Capra. Brunetti drank it down in one swallow and set his glass back on the tray even before La Capra had finished pouring the boiling water into his own rum. As La Capra busied himself with pouring and stirring, Brunetti looked around the room. Many of the pieces resembled objects he had seen in Brett's apartment.

'Another, Dottore?' La Capra asked.

'No, thank you,' Brunetti said, wishing that he could stop the shivering that still tore at him.

La Capra finished mixing his drink, sipped at it, then set it down on the tray. 'Come, Dottor Brunetti. Let me show you some of my new pieces. They just arrived yesterday, and I admit I'm very excited to have them here.'

La Capra turned and moved towards the left wall of the gallery, but as he moved, Brunetti heard a grinding sound come up from where he stepped. Looking down, Brunetti saw that shards of clay lay in a small circle on that side of the room. One of the fragments had a black line running across it. Red and black, the two dominant colours of the pottery Brett had shown him and talked about.

'Where is she?' Brunetti asked, tired and cold.

349

La Capra stopped with his back to Brunetti and paused a moment before turning to face him. 'Where is who?' he asked when he turned around, smiling inquisitively.

'Dottoressa Lynch,' Brunetti answered.

La Capra kept his eyes on Brunetti, but Brunetti sensed that something passed, some message, between him and the young man.

'Dottoressa Lynch?' La Capra inquired, voice puzzled but still very polite. 'Do you mean the American scholar? The one who has written about Chinese ceramics?'

'Yes.'

'Ah, Dottor Brunetti, you have no idea how much I wish she were here. I have two pieces – they're among those that arrived yesterday – that I'm beginning to have questions about. I'm not sure that they are as old as I thought they were when I . . . ' the pause was minimal, but Brunetti was certain it was intentional, 'when I acquired them. I'd give anything to be able to ask Dottoressa Lynch's opinion about them.' He looked at the young man and then quickly back at Brunetti. 'But whatever makes you think she might be here?'

'Because there is no other place she could be,' Brunetti explained.

'I'm afraid I don't understand you, Dottore. I don't know what you're talking about.'

'I'm talking about this,' Brunetti said, stretching

out his leg and crushing one of the fragments under his foot.

La Capra winced involuntarily at the sound, but he insisted, 'I still don't understand you. If you're talking about those fragments, it's easily explained. While the pieces were being unpacked, someone was very careless with one of them.' Looking down at the fragments, he shook his head in sorrow at his loss and disbelief that anyone could have been so clumsy. 'I've given orders that the person responsible be punished.'

As soon as La Capra finished speaking, Brunetti sensed motion from behind him, but before he could turn to see what it was, La Capra stepped towards him and took him by the arm. 'But come and see the new pieces.'

Brunetti ripped his arm free and turned, but the young man was already at the door. He opened it, smiled at Brunetti, slipped out of the room, and closed the door behind him. From beyond it, Brunetti heard the unmistakable sound of a key being turned in the lock.

Chapter Twenty-Five

QUICK FOOTSTEPS disappeared down the hall. Brunetti turned to La Capra. 'It's too late, Signor La Capra,' Brunetti said, straining to keep his voice calm and reasonable. 'I know she's here. You'll just make things worse by trying to do anything to her.'

'I beg your pardon, Signor Policeman, but I don't have any idea what you're talking about,' La Capra said and smiled in polite puzzlement.

'About Dottoressa Lynch. I know she's here.'

La Capra smiled again and waved his hand in a broad, sweeping gesture that took in the room and all the objects it contained. 'I don't see why you're so insistent about this. Surely, if she were here, she'd be with us, enjoying the sight of all this beauty.' His voice grew even warmer. 'You hardly believe me capable of keeping such pleasure from her, do you?'

Brunetti's voice was equally calm. 'I think it's time to end the farce, signore.'

La Capra's laugh, rich with the sound of real

delight, broke out when Brunetti said this. 'Oh, I believe it's you who is the farceur, Signor Policeman. You are here in my home without invitation; I would guess that your entry was illegal in itself. And so you have no right to tell me what I must and must not do.' The edge on his voice sharpened perceptibly as he spoke until, when he finished, he was almost hissing with anger. Hearing himself, La Capra recollected the role he was playing, turned away from Brunetti, and took a few steps towards one of the Plexiglas cases.

'Observe, if you will, the lines on this vase,' he said. 'Lovely, simply lovely, the way it serpentines around to the back, don't you think?' He made a gossamer loop in the air with his hand, imitating the flow of the painted line across the front of the tall vase inside the case he was observing. 'I've always found it remarkable, the eye for beauty these people had. Thousands of years ago, and still they were in love with beauty.' Smiling, transforming himself from mere connoisseur to philosopher, he turned to Brunetti and asked, 'Do you think that's the secret of humanity, then, the love of beauty?'

When Brunetti made no response to this banality, La Capra let the subject drop and moved to the next case. With a small, private laugh, he said, 'Dottoressa Lynch would have liked to see this.'

Something in his voice, the tone of dirty secrets, made Brunetti glance across at the case in front of which the other man stood. Inside he saw the same gourd-like shape that he remembered from the picture Brett had shown him. Upright and striding to the left was a human-bodied fox almost identical to the one painted on the vase in the photo Brett had shown him.

Unbidden, the thought was there. If La Capra was willing to show him this vase, then it was clear he no longer had anything to fear from Brett, the one person who could identify its origin. Brunetti wheeled around and took two long strides towards the door. Just before it, he stopped, turned his body to the side, and raised his right leg. With all his force, he kicked out at the door just below the lock. The violence of the kick shocked his entire body, but the door didn't move.

Behind him, La Capra chuckled. 'Ah, you Northerners are so impetuous. I'm sorry, but it's not going to open for you, Signor Policeman, no matter how hard you kick at it. I'm afraid you're my guest until Salvatore comes back from his errand.' With complete confidence, he turned back towards the glass cases. 'This piece here is from the first millennium before Christ. Lovely, isn't it?'

Chapter Twenty-Six

WHEN HE LEFT the gallery, the young man was careful to lock the door behind him, leaving the key there in the lock. He was amused at the thought that his father would be safe with a policeman, of all people. The idea was so incongruous that he laughed outright as he walked down the corridor. His laughter died away when he opened the door at the end of the corridor and saw that, outside, it still poured. How could these people live with this weather, and with that sea of filthy black water that swelled up from the very pavements? He refused to admit it to himself, but he was afraid of that water, of what his foot might come in contact with when he walked through it or, worse, what might rub itself up against his legs or trickle down inside his boots.

But this, he believed, would be the last time he'd have to walk through it. Once this was done, once this matter was cleared up, he could go back inside and wait for the disgusting water to go back into the canals, the *laguna*, the sea, where it belonged. He felt no affinity for these frigid Adriatic waters, so different from the broad sweep of pure turquoise that spread out across the tranquil surface of the Mediterranean in front of their home in Palermo. He had no idea what had brought his father to buy a home in this filthy city. His father insisted that it was for the safety of his collection, that there was little chance of robbery here. But no one in Sicily would dare to rob the home of Carmello La Capra.

He was sure his father did it for the same reason he had the stupid collection of pots in the first place: to rise in the world and be considered a gentleman. Salvatore found this absurd. He and his father were gentlemen by virtue of their birth; they didn't need the opinion of these stupid *polentoni* to tell them that.

He glanced again across the flooded courtyard, knowing that he would have to pull on boots and plough through the water to cross it. But the thought of what he would do when he reached the other side was enough to buoy up his thoughts; he had enjoyed playing with *l'americana*, but now it was time to finish the game.

He bent down and dragged on a pair of high rubber boots, yanking hard to pull them up over his shoes. They came to his knees and gaped wide there, their tops hanging open and limp, like the petals around the centre of an anemone. He pulled the door closed behind him and stomped heavily down the outer stairs, cursing the driving rain. Pushing water in front of him with every step, he forced his way across the courtyard towards the wooden door on the other side. Even in the short time since he had locked the door on *l'americana*, the water level had risen and now covered the bottom panel. Perhaps she had been in there long enough to have drowned. Even if she had managed to pull herself up into one of the large niches cut into the walls, it would be quick work to drown her. He regretted only that he wouldn't have time to rape her. He had never raped a homosexual before; not a lesbian, at any rate, and he thought it was something he might enjoy. Well, another phone call might bring her singer friend here, and then he could have the chance. His father might object, but there was really no reason for him to know about it, was there? His father's caution had denied him the pleasure of the first visit to *l'americana*. Gabriele and Sandro had been sent instead, and they'd made a mess of it. This muddle of violence, resentment and lust occupied him as he crossed the courtyard.

Prepared for the darkness that lay all around him, he pulled a torch from his jacket pocket and flashed it across the bar that held the low door closed. He shot it back and yanked the door towards him, pulling hard against the weight of water. A high-arched space stretched out in front of him. Chairs and tables floated on the oily surface of the water, stored there during the restoration and abandoned in what had once been an inner boat dock, sunk half a metre below the level of the courtyard and protected from the canal beyond by another heavy wooden door, this one secured by a chain. It would be a minute's work, when he was finished with her, to open the door and float her out into the deeper water of the canal.

To his left, he heard the slap of water and turned the beam of the torch towards it. The eyes that gleamed back at him were too small and set too close together to be human; with a flick of its long tail, the rat turned away from the light and paddled off behind a floating box.

Lust vanished. He turned the light slowly to the right, pausing long enough to examine each of the small alcoves carved into the wall and now covered with a hand's breadth of water. He saw her at last, slumped sideways in one of the alcoves, knees pulled up in front of her, head limp on top of them. The light lingered on her, but she didn't move.

Nothing for it, then, but to cross the water to her and get it finished. He steeled himself and stepped off into the deeper water, extending his foot slowly until he was sure it rested securely on the first slimy step, and then the second. He cursed violently as he felt the water spill over the top and down inside his boot. For a moment, he wanted to rip off the offending boot, make it easier to move, but then he remembered the red eyes he had seen on the surface of the water just across the room, and he changed his mind. Tentatively, braced for what he knew was coming, he lowered the other foot into the water and felt it flood down into his shoe. He slid his right foot out in front of him, certain there were only three steps, but not willing to believe it until his feet confirmed the fact. That done, he fixed the beam of light on the form hunched in the alcove and pushed towards her through water which rose up to the middle of his thigh.

As he moved, he planned, determined to get what little pleasure he could out of this. There was nowhere he could rest the torch, so he would have to keep it upended in his pocket, hoping that it would give enough light for him to watch her face as he killed her. It didn't look as if there was any fight left in her, but he had been surprised in the past, and he hoped the same would happen this time. He didn't want too much of a struggle, not with all this water, but he felt he deserved at least a token resistance, especially if he was going to be denied the other pleasures he might have had from her.

As he splashed towards her, she raised her head and looked at him with eyes that gaped wide, blinded by the light. '*Ciao, bellezza*,' he whispered, and laughed his father's laugh.

She closed her eyes and lowered her head back on to her knees. With his right hand, he placed the torch in his jacket pocket, careful to angle it forward so that the light shone in the general direction of the woman in front of him. He could see her only vaguely, but he supposed it would be good enough.

Before he began what he had come to do, he couldn't resist the temptation to pat her lightly on the side of the jaw, touching her with the delicacy of one who taps a piece of fine crystal to hear it sing. He bent aside, momentarily distracted, to adjust the torch, which had rolled towards the back of his pocket. Because he was looking at the torch and not at his victim, he did not see her clenched fist as it arched out from beside her. Nor did he see the antique iron belt hook that protruded from her fist. He was aware of it only as its dull point dug into his throat, just where the angle of the jaw meets the neck. He felt the force of the blow and pulled back from the pain. He staggered to the right and looked back at her in time to see a thick red stream spray out. When he realized it was his blood, he screamed, but by then it was too late. The light was extinguished as he fell beneath the surface of the water.

Chapter Twenty-Seven

THE SOUND of the key turning in the lock caused both Brunetti and La Capra to turn towards the door, which opened to reveal Vianello, soaked and dripping. 'Who are you?' demanded La Capra. 'What are you doing here?'

Vianello ignored him and spoke to Brunetti. 'I think you'd better come with me, sir.'

Brunetti moved instantly, passing in front of Vianello and out of the door without bothering to speak. Only at the end of the corridor, before they stepped out into the rain that continued to pour down, did Brunetti ask, 'Is it *l'americana*?'

'Yes, sir.'

'Is she all right?'

'She's with her friend, sir, but I don't know how she is. She's been in the water a long time.' Without waiting to hear more, Brunetti strode out and ran quickly down the steps.

He found them just beyond the end of the stairs, hunched together under Vianello's overcoat. At that instant, someone in the house must have switched on the lights, for suddenly the entire courtyard was filled with blinding light, so bright that the two women were turned into a dark *Pietà* placed on the low ledge that ran along the inner wall of the courtyard.

Flavia knelt in the water, one arm wrapped around Brett, propping her body against the wall with the weight of her own. Brunetti bent down over the two women, not daring to touch them, and called Flavia's name. She looked up at him, terror palpable in her glance, forcing him to look at the other woman. Brett's hair was matted with blood; blood streaked across her face and down the front of her clothing.

'*Madre di Dio*,' he whispered.

Vianello splashed up beside him.

'Call the Questura, Vianello,' he ordered. 'Not from here. Get outside and do it. Have them send a boat, with as many men as they can find. And an ambulance. Now. Do it now.'

Vianello was splashing towards the heavy wooden door even before Brunetti finished speaking. When he pulled open the door, a low wave rippled across the courtyard and came to lap against Brunetti's legs.

From above him, Brunetti heard La Capra's voice. 'What's happening down there? What's going on?' Brunetti turned away from the two women, who remained motionless, arms wrapped around each other, and looked towards the top of the stairs. The other man stood there, surrounded by a radiant nimbus of light that poured from the open door behind him, a malign Christ poised at the threshold of some evil tomb.

'What are you doing down there?' he demanded again, voice more insistent and a pitch higher. He walked out into the rain and stared down at them, at the two huddled women and a man who was not his son. 'Salvatore?' he called out into the rain. 'Salvatore, answer me.' The rain pounded down.

La Capra wheeled around and disappeared into the *palazzo*. Brunetti bent down and touched Flavia's shoulder. 'Flavia, get up. We can't stay here.' She gave no sign that she had heard him. He shifted his glance to Brett, but she stared at him vacantly, seeing nothing. He placed one hand under Flavia's arm and pulled her up, bent towards Brett and did the same. He took a step towards the still-open door that led to the *calle*, one arm dragged down by Brett's shambling weight. She slipped, and he let go of Flavia to wrap both arms around Brett. Dragging her upright again, he half-carried her, forcing his legs through the chill waters towards the door, barely conscious of Flavia beside him, moving in the same direction.

'*Salvatore, figlio mio, dove sei?*' The voice broke out above them, high-pitched, keening and wild. Brunetti looked up and saw La Capra at the head of the steps, a shotgun clutched in one hand, staring down at them. With deliberate slowness, he began to walk down the steps, ignoring the sheets of rain that blew at him from every direction.

Slowed by Brett's pendulous weight, Brunetti knew he could never reach the door before La Capra got to the bottom of the stairs. 'Flavia,' he said, voice fast and urgent. 'Get out of here. I'll bring her.' Flavia looked from him to La Capra, still descending the stairs like some relentless fury, and then to Brett. And to the open door to the street, only metres away. Before she could move, three men appeared at the top of the stairs, and she recognized two of them as the men she had driven from Brett's apartment.

'*Capo*,' one of them called to the descending figure of La Capra.

He turned slowly towards them. 'Go back. This is mine.' When they remained motionless, he raised the gun in their direction, but he did it casually, not really aware of what he held in his hands. 'Go back. Stay away from this.' Fearful, trained to obey, they retreated indoors, and La Capra turned to continue down the steps.

He moved quickly now, so quickly that he was at the bottom of the steps before Flavia moved.

'He's inside,' Flavia said softly to Brunetti, gesturing with her chin to the door that hung ajar at the far side of the courtyard.

La Capra stepped into the water as if it weren't there, but he acknowledged the presence of the three people who stood in the pounding rain by keeping the barrel of his shotgun levelled at them as he walked across the courtyard. At the door to the cellar, he paused and cried out into the space that loomed beyond it, 'Salva? Salva, answer me.'

His knees disappeared into the water as he started down the first step. For an instant, he looked back towards Brunetti and the two women. But then he seemed simply to forget about them as he turned back towards the dark cavern, into which he sank as he took another step, and then another.

'Flavia, quick!' Brunetti said. He pivoted around, Brett's weight balanced against his hip, and pushed her, stumbling limply, towards Flavia. Surprised by the sudden motion, Flavia put out her arms without thinking and grasped at Brett, but she lacked the strength to support her and they both sank to their knees in the water. Leaving them, Brunetti ran across the courtyard, splashing heavily. Beyond the door, he could hear La Capra's voice as he called his son's name again and again. He grabbed the side of the door with both hands and forced its leaden weight through the water, then viciously kicked it closed, hand scrambling at the bar until he shot it home.

From behind the door, the shotgun boomed out, filling the trapped space with its echo. Pellets pattered against the wooden door, but the full blast missed the door and pitted the stone wall beside it. Again it roared out, but La Capra fired blind, and the blast crashed uselessly into the water.

Brunetti splashed back across the courtyard towards Flavia and Brett, who were on their feet now and moving slowly towards the main door that still stood open. He moved to Brett's other side and gripped her around the waist, urging her forward. As they neared the door, they heard loud splashings and equally loud shouts approaching them in the *calle* beyond. Brunetti looked up and saw Vianello push through the doorway, followed by two uniformed policemen with pistols drawn.

'Three of them are upstairs,' Brunetti told them. 'Be careful. They're probably armed. There's another one in the storeroom. He's got a shotgun.'

'Is that what we heard?' Vianello asked.

Brunetti nodded, then he looked beyond them. 'Where are the others?'

'Coming,' Vianello said. 'I called from the bar up in the *campo*. They put out a radio call. Cinquegrani and Marcolini were nearby, so they answered the call,' he explained, nodding towards the two officers, who had taken up a position under the balcony, out of the possible line of fire from the upper storeys of the *palazzo*.

'Do we go and get them?' Vianello asked, looking up towards the door at the top of the steps.

'No,' Brunetti said, seeing no sense in it. 'We wait for the others to get here.' As if summoned by his words, a two-pitched siren wailed in the distance and grew louder as it approached. Behind it, he heard another, wailing its way up the Grand Canal from the direction of the hospital.

'Flavia,' he said, turning towards her. 'Go with Vianello. He'll take you down to the ambulance.' Then, to the sergeant: 'Get them down there and come back. Send the men up here.' Vianello splashed to his side and, with the ease of great strength, bent and lifted Brett into his arms. With Flavia following, he carried her from the courtyard and down the narrow *calle* towards the embankment, where two blue lights flashed intermittently through the endless rain.

There followed a lull. As Brunetti allowed himself to relax a little, his body began to pay the price, and his teeth rattled together while he shook with a dead chill. He forced himself to move through the water and joined the two officers under the protection of the balcony, at least out of the rain.

A scream of pure animal terror rang out from behind the door to the storeroom, and then La Capra began to howl his son's name again and again. After a time, the name disappeared and was replaced by a shrill wailing that flowed out from behind the door and filled the courtyard with his grief.

Brunetti winced at the sound, silently urging Vianello to hurry. He recalled the sight of Semanzato's battered skull, the sound of Brett's tortured speech, but still he shied away from the sound of the man's grief.

'Hey, you down there,' a man called from the door at the top of the stairs. 'We're coming down. We don't want any trouble.' When he turned, Brunetti saw the three men standing with their arms raised over their heads.

Vianello came in then, with four men wearing bullet-proof vests and carrying machine guns. The three men on the stairs saw them, too, and stopped to call out again. 'We don't want any trouble.' The four armed men fanned out inside the courtyard, pulled by instinct and training to take cover behind the marble columns.

Brunetti started towards the door to the storeroom but froze when he saw two of the machine guns turned towards him. 'Vianello,' he called out, now with something to be angry at, 'tell them who I am.' He realized that he must be no more than a rain-sodden man with a pistol in his hand.

'It's Commissario Brunetti,' Vianello called across the courtyard to them; the machine guns turned away from him and redirected themselves at the men frozen on the stairs.

Brunetti continued towards the door, from which the wailing still issued unabated. He moved the bolt and pulled the door back. It stuck, and he had to force its swollen bottom across the stone pavement towards him. Outlined by the bright lights flooding the courtyard, he presented a perfect target to anyone safe inside the darkened storeroom, but he didn't think of this; the wailing made that impossible.

It took a few moments for his eyes to adjust to the darkness inside, but when they did, he saw La Capra kneeling to his waist in the water, bent down in a masculine *pietà* that was a grotesque copy of the one Brunetti had just seen in the courtyard. But this image held a finality the other lacked, for here a parent keened over a dead and only son whose body he had pulled to himself from the filthy water.

Chapter Twenty-Eight

BRUNETTI OPENED the door to his office and, finding it no more than warm and the heating system silent, breathed a silent prayer of thanksgiving to Saint Leandro, even though weeks had passed since he had worked his yearly miracle. There were other signs of spring: at home that morning, he had noticed that the pansies on the balcony were battering their way through the winter-hardened earth in the vases, and Paola had said she had to replant them this weekend; the wooden table, legs injected with poison, baked in the sun beside them; that morning, he'd seen the first of the black-headed seagulls that spent a brief spring holiday on the waters of the canals each year before heading off elsewhere; and the air breathed with a sudden softness that flowed like a benediction across the islands and the waters.

He hung his coat in the cupboard and walked over to his desk, but he veered away from it and went to stand at the window. There was motion on the scaffolding that covered San Lorenzo this

370

morning; men moved up and down on the ladders and scrambled across the roof. Unlike the bursting insistence of nature, all of this man-made activity, Brunetti was sure, was no more than a false spring and would quickly end, no doubt with the renewal of the contracts.

He stood at the window for some time, until he was distracted by Signorina Elettra's cheerful 'Buon giorno.' Today she was in yellow, a soft silk dress that fell to her knees, and heels so sharp he was glad his floor was stone and not parquet. Like the flowers and the gulls and the soft breezes, she brought grace into the room with her, and he smiled with something that felt like joy.

'Buon giorno, signorina,' he said. 'You look especially lovely today. Like spring itself.'

'Ah, this rag,' she said dismissively and flipped fingers down towards the skirt of the dress that must have cost her more than a week's salary. Her smile was at odds with her words, so he didn't insist.

She handed him two files with a letter clipped to the top of them. 'This needs your signature, Dottore.'

'La Capra?' he asked.

'Yes. It's your statement about why you and Officer Vianello went into the palazzo that night.'

'Ah, yes,' he muttered while he read quickly through the two-page document, written in response to the complaint of La Capra's lawyers that Brunetti's entrance into his home two months before had been illegal. Addressed to the Praetore, it explained that, during the course of his investigation, he had become increasingly convinced that La Capra had played some role in Semenzato's murder and cited as evidence the fact that Salvatore La Capra's fingerprints had been found in Semenzato's office. Acting upon that and spurred by Dottoressa Lynch's disappearance, he had gone to the La Capra *palazzo* with Sergeant Vianello and Signora Petrelli. Upon arriving, they had found the door to the courtyard open (as mentioned in the statements given by both Sergeant Vianello and Signora Petrelli) and had entered when they heard what sounded like the screams of a woman.

His report carried a full description of events pursuant to their arrival (again, confirmed by the statements of Sergeant Vianello and Signora Petrelli); he offered this explanation to the Praetore to set his mind at rest that their entrance into the property of Signor La Capra had been well within the limits of the law, as it is, beyond question, the right, indeed, the duty, of even a private citizen to answer a call for help, especially if easy and legal access is available to do so. There followed a respectful closing. He took the pen Signorina Elettra held out to him and signed the letter.

'Thank you, signorina. Is there anything else?'

'Yes, Dottore. Signora Petrelli called and confirmed your meeting with her.'

More proof of spring. More grace.

'Thank you, signorina,' he said, taking the files and returning the letter to her. She smiled and was gone.

The first file was from Carrara's office in Rome and contained a complete list of the articles in La Capra's collection that the art fraud police had been able to identify. The list of provenance read like a tourist's, or policeman's, guide to the plundered troves of the ancient world: Herculaneum, Volterra, Paestum, Corinth. The Orient and Middle East were well represented: Xian, Angkor Wat, the Kuwait Museum. Some of the pieces appeared to have been acquired legitimately, but they were in the minority. More than a few pieces had been declared to be fakes. Good ones, but still fakes. Documents sequestered in La Capra's home proved that many of the illegal pieces had been acquired from Murino, whose shop was closed to allow the art police to make a complete inventory of the pieces there and in the warehouse he kept in Mestre. He denied all knowledge of illegally acquired pieces and insisted that they must have been brought in by his former partner, Dottor Semenzato. Had it not been for the fact that he had been arrested while accepting delivery of four boxes of alabaster ashtrays made in Hong Kong and of the four statues contained with them, he might have been believed. As it was, he was under arrest, and his lawyer had the responsibility of producing the invoices and dockets that would implicate Semenzato.

La Capra, in Palermo, where he had taken his son's body for burial, seemed to have lost all interest in his collection. He had ignored all orders to produce further documents that could prove either purchase or ownership. The police, therefore, had confiscated all pieces known or believed to be stolen and were continuing to search for the source of those few which had still not been identified. Brunetti was pleased to note that Carrara had seen to it that the pieces taken from the Chinese show at the Ducal Palace were not listed in the inventory of objects found in La Capra's house. Only three people – Brunetti, Flavia and Brett – knew where they were.

The second file contained the mounting papers on the case against La Capra, his late son, and the men arrested with him. Both of the men who had beaten Dottoressa Lynch had been in the *palazzo* that night and were arrested along with La Capra and another man. The first two admitted the beating but claimed that they had gone there to rob her apartment. They insisted they knew nothing about the murder of Dottor Semenzato.

La Capra, for his part, maintained that he had no idea that the two men, whom he identified as his driver and his bodyguard, had attempted to rob the apartment of Dottoressa Lynch, a woman for whom he had the highest professional regard. At the beginning, he also asserted that he neither knew nor had dealings of any sort with Dottor Semenzato. But as information flowed in from those places where he and Semenzato had met, as various dealers and antiquarians signed statements linking the two men together in a host of business dealings, La Capra's story ebbed away as did the waters of *acqua alta* with the turning of the tide or a favourable change in the wind. And with the change of this particular tide came the memory that he had, in the past, perhaps bought a piece or two from Dottor Semenzato.

He had been ordered to return to Venice or risk being carried back by the police, but he had placed himself under doctor's care and had been committed to a private clinic, suffering from 'nervous collapse resulting from personal grief'. He remained there, physically and, in a country where only the bond between parent and child remained sacred, legally untouchable.

Brunetti pushed the files away from him and stared at the empty surface of his desk, imagining the forces that had already been brought into play in this. La Capra was a man not without influence. And he now had a dead son, a young man of violent temper. Hadn't the two thugs, the day after they'd spoken to their lawyer, recalled hearing Salvatore once say that Dottor Semenzato had treated his father without respect? Something about a statue that he had bought for his father that turned out to be false – something like that. And, yes, they thought they could remember hearing him say he would make the Dottore sorry he had ever recommended false artifacts for his father or for him to buy for his father.

Brunetti had no doubt that, as time passed, the two thugs would remember more and more, and all of it would point to poor Salvatore, bent on nothing else but the mistaken defence of his father's honour and his own. And they'd probably recall the many occasions when Signor La Capra had tried to persuade his son that Dottor Semenzato was an honest man, that he had always acted in good faith when he endorsed pieces that were then sold by Murino, his partner. Perhaps the judges, if the case ever got that far, would have to listen to a tale of Salvatore's desire to give his father nothing but pleasure, devoted son that he was. And Salvatore, not at all a sophisticated boy, but good, good at heart, would have tried to procure these presents for his beloved father in the only way he could think of, by seeking the advice of Dottor Semenzato. And given his devotion to his father, his intense desire to please him, it was but a short step to imagine his rage when he discovered that Dottor Semenzato had attempted to take advantage of both his innocence and his generosity by selling him a copy instead of an original piece. From there, it was but no distance at all to the injustice of adding to a father's grief, a father who had to bear in one blow the death of his beloved only son and the sad knowledge of the lengths to which that son was capable of going in his attempts both to give his father pleasure and to defend their family honour.

Yes, it would hold, and the association between La Capra and Semenzato would, instead of working as evidence of his guilt, be used as the opposite, as an explanation of the underlying good faith between the two men, a trust destroyed by the dishonesty of Semenzato and the impulsiveness of Salvatore, alas, now beyond the power of the law. Brunetti had no doubt that the final legal decision would be that Salvatore had killed Semenzato. Well, he might have; no one would ever know. Either he or La Capra had done it, or had it done, and both of them had paid in their own way. Were he a man more given to sentimentality, Brunetti would judge La Capra to have paid the greater price, but he was not, so it seemed to him that Salvatore had paid the greater price for Semenzato's death.

Brunetti pushed himself up, away from the desk and from the files that led to this conclusion. He had seen La Capra with his son, had pulled him from the slimy waters and helped the screaming man float his son's body to the foot of the three low steps. And there, it had taken him and Vianello and two of the other officers to separate them, to pull La Capra away from his futile attempt to close with his own fingers the bloodless hole in the side of his son's neck.

Brunetti had never believed that a life could be paid for with another life, so he again dismissed the idea that La Capra had paid for Semenzato's death. All grief was separate and discrete, relating only to one loss. But he found it difficult to feel any personal rancour for the man he had last seen howling in the arms of a policeman whose only concern was to keep him from seeing his son's body as it was carried away on a stretcher, face covered by Vianello's rain-soaked coat.

He pushed these memories away. It was all beyond him now, taken into the hands of another agency of the law, and he could no longer affect the outcome in any way. He'd had enough of death and violence, enough of pilfered beauty and the lust for the perfect. He longed for springtime and its many imperfections.

An hour later, he left the Questura and walked towards San Marco. Everywhere, he saw the same things he'd been seeing for days, but today he chose to call them signs of spring. Even the omnipresent pastel tourists lifted his heart. Via XXII Marzo pulled his steps down towards the Accademia Bridge. On the other side of it, he saw the season's first long line of tourists waiting to enter the museum, but he had seen enough of art for a while. The water drew him now and the thought of sitting in the young sun with Flavia, having a coffee, talking of this and that, seeing the way her face went so quickly from ease to joy and back again. He was to meet her at Il Cucciolo at eleven, and he already delighted in the thought of the sound of the waters stirring under the wooden deck, of the desultory motion of the waiters, not yet thawed from their winter lethargy, and of the large valiant umbrellas which insisted on creating shade, long before there was any need of it. He took even greater delight in the thought of the sound of her voice.

Ahead of him he saw the waters of the Giudecca Canal and, beyond them, the happy façades of the buildings on the other side. From the left, a tanker steamed into view, riding high and empty in the water, and even its streaked grey hull seemed bright and beautiful in this light. A dog scampered past, kicked up its hind legs, then circled back upon itself, bent on capturing its tail.

At the water's edge, he turned left and walked towards the open deck of the bar, searching for her. Four couples, a lone man, another, a woman and two children, a table with six or seven young girls whose giggles were audible even as he approached. But no Flavia. Perhaps she was late. Perhaps he hadn't recognized her. He began again at the first near table and studied everyone again, in the same order. And saw her, sitting with the two children, a tall boy and a young girl still plump with the fat of childhood.

His smile disappeared, and a different one took its place. Using this one, he approached their table and took her extended hand.

She smiled up at him. 'Oh, Guido, how wonderful to see you. What a glorious day.' She turned to the boy and said, 'Paolino, this is Dottor Brunetti.' The young boy stood, almost as tall as Brunetti, took his hand and shook it.

'*Buon giorno, Dottore.* I'd like to thank you for helping my mother.' It sounded as if he had practised the line, and he delivered it formally, as from one trying to be a man to one who already was. He had his mother's dark eyes, but his face was longer and narrower.

'Me too, *Mamma*,' the girl piped up, and, when Flavia was slow to respond, stood and held her hand out to Brunetti. 'I'm Vittoria, but my friends call me Vivi.'

Taking her hand, Brunetti said, 'Then I'd like to call you Vivi.'

She was young enough to smile, old enough to look away before she blushed.

He pulled out a chair and sat, then angled the chair to get his face into the sun. They talked generally for a few minutes, the children asking him questions about being a policeman, whether he carried a gun, and when he said he did, where it was. When he told them, Vivi asked if he had ever shot anyone and seemed disappointed when he said that he had not. It didn't take the children long to realize that being a policeman in Venice was a great deal different from being a cop on *Miami Vice*, and after that revelation, they seemed to lose interest both in his career and in him.

The waiter came and Brunetti ordered a Campari soda; Flavia asked for another coffee, then changed it to a Campari. The children grew audibly restless, until Flavia suggested that they walk up along the embankment to Nico's and get themselves *gelato*, an idea that was met with general relief.

When they were gone, Vivi hurrying to keep up with Paolo's longer steps, he said, 'They're very nice children.' Flavia said nothing, so he added, 'I didn't know you'd brought them to Venice with you.'

'Yes, it's seldom that I get a chance to spend a weekend with them, but I'm not scheduled to sing the matinee this Saturday, so we decided to come here. I'm singing in Munich now,' she added.

'I know. I read about you in the papers.'

She gazed out over the water, across the canal to the church of the Redentore. 'I've never been here in the early spring before.'

'Where are you staying?'

She pulled her eyes back from the church and looked at him. 'At Brett's.'

'Oh. Did she come back with you?' he asked. He had last seen Brett in the hospital, but she had stayed there only overnight, then she and Flavia had left for Milan two days later. He'd had no word of either of them until the day before, when Flavia had called and asked him to meet her for a drink.

'No, she's in Zurich, giving a lecture.'

'When will she come back?' he asked politely.

'She'll be in Rome next week. I finish in Munich next Thursday night.'

'And then what?'

'And then London, but only for a concert, and then China,' she said, voice carrying her reproach that he had forgotten. 'I'm invited to give master classes at the Beijing Conservatory. Don't you remember?'

'Then you're going to go through with it? You're going to take the pieces back?' he asked, surprised that she would do it.

She made no attempt to disguise her own delight. 'Of course we are. That is, I am.'

'But how can you do that? How many pieces are there? Three? Four?'

'Four. I'm carrying seven pieces of luggage, and I've arranged it that the Minister of Culture will meet me at the airport. I doubt that they're going to look for antiques being smuggled *into* the country.'

'What if they find them?' he asked.

She gave a purely theatrical wave of the hand. 'Well, I can always say that I was bringing them to donate to the people of China, that I was going to present them after I'd taught the classes, as a token of my gratitude for their having invited me.'

She'd do it, too, and he was certain she'd get away with it. He laughed at the thought. 'Well, good luck to you.'

'Thank you,' she said, certain that she'd need no luck there.

They sat in silence for a while, Brett a third party, invisible but present. Boats puttered past; the waiter brought their drinks, and they were glad of the diversion.

'And after China?' he finally asked.

'Lots of travelling until the end of summer. That's another reason I wanted to spend the week-end with the children. I've got to go to Paris, then Vienna; and then back to London.' When he said nothing she tried to lighten the mood by saying, 'I get to die in Paris and Vienna, Lucia and Violetta.'

'And in London?' he asked.

'Mozart. Fiordiligi. And then my first attempt at Handel.'

'Will Brett go with you?' he asked and sipped at his drink.

She looked over to the church again, the church of the Redeemer. 'She's going to stay in China for at least a few months,' was all the answer Flavia gave.

He sipped again and looked out over the water, suddenly conscious of the dance of light on its rippled surface. Three tiny sparrows came and landed at his feet, hopping about in search of food. Slowly, he reached forward and took a fragment of the brioche that still lay on a plate in front of Flavia and tossed it to them. Greedily, they pounced on it and tore it into pieces, then each flew off to a safer place to eat.

'Her career?' he asked.

Flavia nodded, then shrugged. 'I'm afraid she takes it far more seriously than . . .' she began, but then she trailed off.

'Than you take yours?' he asked, not ready to believe it.

'In a way, I suppose that's true.' Seeing that he was about to protest, she placed her hand on his arm and explained. 'Think of it this way, Guido. Anyone at all can come and listen to me and shout his head off, and he doesn't have to know anything about either music or singing. He just has to like my costume, or the story, or perhaps he just shouts "*brava*" because everyone else does.' She saw that he didn't believe this and insisted, 'It's true. Believe me. My dressing room is filled with them after every performance, people who tell me how beautiful my singing was, even if I sang like a dog that night.' He watched the memory of this play across her face, and then he knew she was speaking the truth.

'But think about what Brett does. Very few people know anything about her work except the people who really know what she's doing; they're all experts, so they understand the importance of her work. I suppose the difference is that she can be judged only by her peers, her equals, so the standards are much higher, and praise really means something. I can be applauded by any fool who chooses to cheer.'

'But what you do is beautiful.'

She laughed outright. 'Don't let Brett hear you say that.'

'Why? Doesn't she think it is?'

Still laughing, she explained, 'No, Guido, you misunderstand. She thinks what she does is beautiful, too, and she thinks the things she works with are as beautiful as the music I sing.'

He remembered then that there had been something unclear in Brett's statement and he had wanted to ask her about it. But there had been no time: she'd been in the hospital and then had left Venice immediately after signing a formal statement. 'There's something I don't understand,' he began and then laughed outright when he realized how very true that was.

Her smile was tentative, questioning. 'What?'

385

'It's about Brett's statement,' he explained. Flavia's face relaxed. 'She wrote that La Capra had shown her a bowl, a Chinese bowl. I forget what century it was supposed to be from.'

'The third millennium before Christ,' Flavia explained.

'She told you about it?'

'Of course she did.'

'Then maybe you can help me.' She nodded and he continued. 'In her statement, she said that she broke it, that she let it fall to the floor, knowing it would break.'

Flavia nodded. 'Yes, I talked to her. That's what she said. That's what happened.'

'That's what I don't understand,' Brunetti said.

'What?'

'If she loves these things so much, if she's so devoted to them, to saving them, then the bowl had to have been a false one, didn't it, another of those fakes that La Capra bought, thinking that they were real?'

Flavia said nothing and turned her head away to stare off towards the abandoned mill that stood at the end of the Giudecca.

'Well?' Brunetti insisted.

She turned and faced him, sun shining down on her from the left and chiselling her profile against the buildings across the canal. 'Well what?' she asked.

'It had to be a fake, didn't it, for her to destroy it?'

For a long time, he thought she was going to ignore him or refuse to answer him. The sparrows came back and, this time, Flavia tore the remaining heel of brioche into tiny fragments and tossed it down to them. They both watched as the small birds swallowed the golden crumbs and looked up towards Flavia for more. At the same time, they glanced up from the peeping birds, and their eyes met. After a long moment, she glanced away from him and off down the embankment, where she saw her children coming back towards them, ice cream cones in their hands.

'Well?' Brunetti asked, needing an answer.

They both heard Vivi's hoots of laughter ring out over the water.

Flavia leaned forward and put her hand on his arm again. 'Guido,' she began, smiling. 'It doesn't matter, does it?'